Fruiting Bodies

Fruiting Bodies

STORIES

Kathryn Harlan

W. W. NORTON & COMPANY
Independent Publishers Since 1923

Fruiting Bodies is a work of fiction. Names, characters, places, and incidents are the products of the author's imagination or are used fictitiously. Any resemblance to actual events, locales, or persons, living or dead, is entirely coincidental.

Edna St. Vincent Millay, excerpt from "Love is not all: it is not meat nor drink" from *Collected Poems*. Copyright 1931, © 1958 by Edna St. Vincent Millay and Norma Millay Ellis. Reprinted with the permission of The Permissions Company, LLC, on behalf of Holly Peppe, Literary Executor, The Edna St. Vincent Millay Society, www.millay.org.

For information about permission to reproduce selections from this book, write to Permissions, W. W. Norton & Company, Inc., 500 Fifth Avenue, New York, NY 10110

For information about special discounts for bulk purchases, please contact W. W. Norton Special Sales at specialsales@wwnorton.com or 800-233-4830

Manufacturing by Lakeside Book Company
Book design by Patrice Sheridan
Production manager: Julia Druskin

ISBN 978-1-324-02122-3

W. W. Norton & Company, Inc.
500 Fifth Avenue, New York, N.Y. 10110
www.wwnorton.com

W. W. Norton & Company Ltd.
15 Carlisle Street, London W1D 3BS

1 2 3 4 5 6 7 8 9 0

For Kit

Without you, this book could not have been written
Nor could I have become the person who wrote it.

Contents

Fruiting Bodies

Algal Bloom

That summer, Vienna ran up the driveway to our cabin and the first thing she said to me was, "The water is full of poison."

When I went, "What?" she stepped back, and scraped her eyes over me instead of answering, a clear appraisal.

"You got a little taller," she said.

She was much taller. The year since we'd seen each other last had stretched her out to a cornstalk leanness. Her blond hair was newly short, gathered up in a stubby paintbrush at the back of her skull. The difference between twelve and thirteen rested on her with a sunlit gravity and I remember that made me nervous. Vienna had the kind of sleek runner's body that I would never have. "What about the water?"

"There's an algal bloom in the lake." She bent down to pull a bur off her sock. "And my grandpa said it spits out poison. So"— she flicked the bur into the dirt—"we can't go swimming."

"I missed you," I said, and then worried that she would not also have missed me. "Have you seen it? The lake?"

She nodded as she straightened up, and I saw, already coiling in her, that restless interest in the forbidden. "Yeah. It's really beautiful."

I was a few months from thirteen, and Vienna was my best friend in a very localized way. Our families owned neighboring cabins on the mountain, both of us benefiting from the generosity of grandparents, both of us vanishing from our regular lives for a few weeks out of the year. We spent our summers in the Sierra combing up and down thickly wooded hillsides, poking at spiders that lived under the shutters, and burning little curls of our hair at campfires. I lived wild, or as wild as one could be with a warm living room to return to. I let my hair tangle in clots on my shoulders, avoided showers until my grandmother said, "Julie, you stink," and pushed me in the direction of the bathroom, patting my butt like that of a well-loved dog. I swam in the lake in my dirty clothes and lay out on the granite to dry, sticky-hot, scratching up the lichen with my fingernails. My body was animal to me then. I still thought of it as something made to do what I wanted, belonging to me only.

The rest of the year, I had other people, other concerns, other versions of myself. At school, my best friend was a tyrannical girl with the glorious Viking name of Ingrid. I was occupied with science class and a business I wanted to start, building birdhouses. I had decided I should become interested in boys. When I returned to these things, my time in the Sierra would fall away, and Vienna with it. But she was always there the next summer, and so was the part of me that loved her.

*   *   *

Later that evening, my grandmother sat us down to talk about the lake. We'd been lounging on the porch steps, watching the sun go down over the treetops and twisting up cobwebs on the ends of sticks. Vienna was trying to teach me a song. One of those joke songs about sex or overblown violence that are eternally, inescapably popular among middle schoolers. I can't remember what it was now, but I remember the bawdiness, and how proud of herself Vienna looked. She told me her aunt had yelled at her for singing that song back at her cabin, because her cousin Abigail was a tattler. She lowered her voice when my grandmother called us in for dinner, but kept humming, like she was still saying the filthy things behind her teeth.

At dinner, my grandmother folded her soft hands and told us not to go near the lake at all. She included both of us in the prohibition, wisely, because the same rules that applied to me had to be extended to Vienna, or else I would disobey and claim that it had not really been a violation, because Vienna was allowed. She wasn't able to explain to our satisfaction, told us only that it was a warm year, that the algae was overgrown, and that was dangerous. What part of it was dangerous? we wanted to know. Wasn't there always algae in the lake? It wasn't like we drank that water. In retrospect, I'm not sure my grandmother understood it herself. "Doesn't usually happen this high up," my grandfather said, paused in the process of finishing his soup, and my grandmother wrung one of her red-dyed ringlets around her finger and repeated, "Are you listening to me, girls? Are you listening to me? That water could make you very sick."

How could we be anything but fascinated? "I can do whatever I want," Vienna told me the next afternoon." Laughing, with both of us stretched on the hot flank of a granite slab. "For real, I go to bed whenever, I eat whatever. I went down to the lakeshore store this morning, and I stole a cigarette." She showed me, flicking it between her thumb and middle finger.

"Are you going to smoke it?" I was fearfully impressed.

Vienna dragged her bottom lip between her teeth. "I could if I wanted to."

Vienna's grandparents were disinclined to involve themselves in her activities. Parents were far away in the summer, their voices heard on occasional phone calls. I missed my own but didn't think of them much. My relative lawlessness in the Sierra was an anomaly for me, a vacation from my usually supervised life.

Maybe the same was true for Vienna. I don't know, because I never thought to ask her.

That was the last summer I would come up without my parents, before entertaining a teenager in the wilderness became too much for my grandparents. Trips in later years were restricted to weekends, and I lost track of Vienna. When I saw her high school graduation pictures I was shocked. Her hair long and shining, the planes of her body softened, a new solemnity and attentiveness in her expression; it all felt like it had been sprung on me too abruptly. Like she should have stayed thirteen while I grew.

In the days after her warning, my grandmother made a good effort to keep us away from the lake, but too much of the responsibility was on her. The elevation was hard on my grandfather, and he spent most of his time sleeping—snoring softly on one of the couches, sometimes with a green tank of oxygen at his feet, the plastic mask sealed against his nose and mouth. I would stop to watch the rise and fall of his chest, his exhales fogging the mask. Then I would suck in a breath as fast as I could and hold it in my lungs, trying to feel a difference between this air and other air, how it was less breathable.

My grandmother, though, was still spry, and, meticulous as she was, surprisingly at home on the docks and the back porches. She shepherded us to campfires and cookouts, drove us to lakes safe to swim in, showed us how to make pie, and pointed us toward the easiest hiking trails.

When I think about that summer, I do feel for her. I find myself trying to bend this moment just enough to see it through my grandmother's eyes. Tired from the long drive up to the cabin. Watching these girls fold themselves into the dining room chairs she had just dusted a winter's worth of insect corpses from, knowing we were in danger, but not how much, exactly, or how to convince us of it. Knowing, anyway, that we wouldn't listen.

*   *   *

On Saturday, we all went boating on one of the upper lakes. Vienna and me, our grandparents, Vienna's aunt Chelsea and cousin Abigail. Vienna found me in the parking lot by the boat rental place that morning, scrunched her nose up, and told me, "*Abby* has nightmares. *Abby* thinks a rattlesnake is going to come through the window and eat her. I'm going to sleep in your bed tonight."

"Good," I said.

We rented a pontoon boat, and brought a cooler with sodas and beer and sandwiches the grandmothers made. The back of the boat was flat, a platform raised a little above the seats at the front, and Vienna claimed this part for us to sunbathe on. She took off her shirt, lay down in her swimsuit and shorts, the pale landscape of her back glittering like the light off the water. We weren't old enough to really care about tanning, but we were old enough to pretend we did. The flooring of the boat prickled against my stomach.

"Did you put on sunscreen?" my grandmother asked, and I nodded, though I hadn't. Vienna yawned and rolled over onto her back. Her swimsuit, like mine, was old, a magenta one-piece that faded to white in the middle and pulled too tightly at the top and bottom, threatening to slip down. In my periphery, I could see the pale tops of her breasts. I turned my cheek against the canvas so I couldn't look at her.

"You're gonna get skin cancer," Abigail said.

Abigail was eleven, but so somber and so small that we both

felt she was younger. When she was around, we excluded her with the devotion of older siblings, but without any of the affection.

"Okay?" Vienna drawled, and stuck out her tongue. Abigail started to respond, but stopped, coughing into her elbow, and everyone in the boat paused to watch her. Abigail had coughed like this last year too, a dry sound that scraped up from the center of her body. As far as I'd heard, no one knew what was causing it, or what would make it stop. She wasn't sick otherwise.

"Oh, you poor thing," my grandmother said. "Still?"

Abigail smiled, curling toward the attention. "It doesn't hurt or anything."

"We're doing another allergy panel next month," Chelsea said. She slid her hand over her daughter's shoulder. "The doctor just doesn't know."

Sitting back on her palms, Abigail turned her face toward the sun.

Vienna reached into the cooler and pretended to drink an unopened can of beer, laughing when her aunt glared at her. The conversation drifted on.

"They're saying it's global warming, you know," Chelsea said. Chelsea looked young for someone's aunt. It was her hair, how long and healthy it was. She brushed it back now and bared her cheek to the sun, her pretty shoulders. "Why we're getting the bloom all the way up here. It's supposed to be too cold at this elevation."

Vienna's grandfather pushed air through his teeth. "It's just a hot year, honey," he said. "A hot year don't have to mean anything."

"But that's what a hot year does mean," Chelsea said. "A hot year means it's hot."

My grandmother laughed.

Chelsea rubbed the back of her head. "It's gotten hotter in

your lifetime," she said to her father, Vienna's grandfather. "The weather's changed so much in *your* lifetime. You've seen it."

"Colder last winter than it's ever been," Vienna's grandmother said, and her grandfather added, "Thought a ball was going to drop off."

"*Richard!*" My grandmother lifted her hands in despair. "The girls, for God's sake, do not want to hear about your privates."

"Let's not talk politics." This from my grandfather, who lay back toward the rear of the boat, his thin eyelids closed.

"All right," Chelsea huffed. "All right, then, let's not."

She was sour and quiet while our grandparents talked about the sunshine, the pies the lakeside diner had started serving, who was selling their cabins, and who might be buying them. When she spoke again, she said, "I heard the Clarks' dog died from drinking the lake water."

Vienna levered herself up on her elbows. "Really?"

"The little white Jack Russell, Bennie. I was talking to Patti Clark at the gas station. She said their boys took him down to the water and let him go swimming, and the next morning he was dead."

"Oh," my grandmother sighed. "Poor thing."

"She said," Abigail added—she had straightened too, attracted back to the conversation, like we were, by the smell of death—"that he had blisters on his mouth and he was bleeding."

"I'm sure that's an exaggeration." Chelsea's smile was bland and shallow.

"Don't be gross," Vienna told Abigail. I could see she wanted to hear more about the dog as much as I did, but if we showed any interest Abigail would never be quiet again.

My grandfather dawdled the boat into a small cove and stopped us there, while I scrambled down on deck to help him hoist the anchor over the sides. The water was dark, a vanishing blue-green. Vienna and I wriggled out of our pants, and Abigail finally ditched her cover-up.

Vienna went first, bending and arching her back, examining the water as if creating a door in it, and then diving. Her body was smooth and quick as an arrow. I hurled myself after her.

We abandoned ourselves to this safer lake for a while. Splashing, throwing our bodies here and there. We competed to see who could bring up the most interesting things from the deep bottom, fistfuls of gravel, little stones and larger stones, bits of sticks and plant matter, like we were God looking for enough material to make the world.

There was a thrill to it every time Vienna went down, when her blond hair puddled against the surface like the hair of a corpse, and then all of her disappearing into the dark, and then the long moment when I steadied myself against the metal flank of the boat, against the possibility that she would not surface again. I would have to go under, have to catch her limp body around the waist, drag her heavily up toward the light. Or I would go after her and she would be gone.

When we tired ourselves out, we joined Abigail on the hunk of granite that jutted out from the shore, which could fit all three of us, like lions sunning ourselves. Vienna crawled up to the top, curled herself around the peak. Below us, Abigail picked bits of mud and gravel off her feet, out from between her toes, the flesh of her soles like dead fish. "Do you think there are leeches in the lake?" Vienna asked her, and she paused and looked up with a timidity mostly outweighed by excitement.

"The biggest leech I ever saw was in a tank and bigger than my thumb," she informed us. "It looked like someone coughed up blood."

I leaned back, tilting my shoulders Vienna's way, laughed loud. "You're *so weird,* Abby!"

Abigail nodded primly. She pointed at a tree on the shore that was yellowing where it was not supposed to, the pallor of dead pine boughs. "That's because of a beetle. It's killing all the trees around here. That's why the fire alert is higher this year, because most of the trees are dead."

Was it really like this? The pine beetles the same year as the algal bloom the same year as Abigail's hacking cough and my grandfather barely able to breathe on the sofa? Everything around us starting to die, but only in a removed way, only in the background. There was a forest fire in August that took out half the mountain, missing our cabin by two miles. A drowning in the lake we were swimming in before we went home, a drunk tourist who tipped off his motorboat, the extra beats Vienna's grandmother took before saying names that heralded the beginning of her Alzheimer's. But I didn't know that then.

"I'm going to put beetle eggs in your mouth while you sleep." Vienna stretched out her legs. Her foot brushed against my side, her thigh right next to my cheek. I could smell the lake water on her, feel the damp heat of her skin almost in my mouth. The heat of a fire started in wet leaves. I felt suddenly panic-sick at the prospect of the dry trees, all that hollow, still-standing firewood.

"You're not," Abigail said, and I kicked her, lightly, because I could.

*   *   *

"Vienna's sleeping over," I told my grandmother as we all wandered back to our cars.

"Ask her grandparents." But Vienna's grandparents didn't care where she went, and we all knew it, so she just waved over her shoulder as she climbed into the backseat next to me. Everyone's attention was occupied by Abigail, who was having another coughing fit, bent at a right angle and hacking onto the ground. Still, Chelsea looked up, over the sound of her daughter coughing, and I watched her exchange a nod with my grandmother when Vienna got in our car.

My grandmother put on a CD of children singing hymns that came on car rides for my dubious benefit. My grandfather sat in the passenger seat with his earbuds in and his head lolling against the window, escaped into his audiobook, as the high voices ran through "Kumbaya" and a song called "Oh, You Can't Get to Heaven." I was embarrassed to have the hymns playing when Vienna was looking out the window and couldn't catch my eye roll; she might assume that saccharine enthusiasm was my choice. As soon as she looked at me, while the children on the radio proclaimed that Jesus loved them, I stuck my tongue out.

We passed our lake on the way back to the cabin, and both Vienna and I turned, as if with one body. She pressed herself to the window and I leaned out of my seat, putting my chin on her shoulder and holding the rest of myself a little apart from her. The water was a vivid green, drifting in paint-like swirls, the trees leaking, oily, off the banks and into the current. It looked like a lake in a rain forest, or a portal to another world.

"Oh my God." Vienna lowered her voice on the word *God*, because my grandmother was listening.

"Can we—"

"No," my grandmother said. "It's poison."

My grandfather looked back over the shoulder of his seat. "I'll take you girls for a walk there tomorrow, if you want. We just can't go in."

When we got back to the cabin, Vienna and I poured out of the backseat before we were even at a complete stop. We went inside to play Uno on the floor, our swimsuits dampening the carpet. My grandmother bustled between the den and the kitchen, putting jam-and-cream-cheese sandwiches in front of us, turning up Fox News on the television. They talked about global warming there too, or didn't, and moved loudly around the blanks in the conversation. It was the hottest year on record. The year before had been the hottest year on record too.

"Uno," Vienna said. I looked at the card she'd put down. It was from a different edition of the game, one with extra trick cards and props that had long since been lost.

"What am I supposed to do?" I asked. Vienna shrugged, so I drew two and kept going. When we finished Uno and our sandwiches, we switched to Guess Who, which we played impressionistically and with questions we thought were very funny. Did your person used to be a porn star? Does your person look like they ax-murdered their parents? Does your person own a vibrator? Vienna had just told me what that was, and we both blushed, saying the word and giggling helplessly. When Vienna laughed, her mouth became a new animal, this sleek rabbit-pulsed thing taking up residence on her face.

If I were to diagnose something special about that summer, other than the omnipresence of death, I would say it was the last year before language reached all the parts of me, before words started knocking softly on my head, trying to get in. When I think about it, when I think about Vienna, this is where my mind goes more often than not. To naming. The things that it has made less frightening, and the things it has obscured, and what was different, a little, when I had nothing to call it. Even accurate words you don't live in, the way you don't live in a photograph of your house.

When Vienna crawled into bed that night, her shirt riding up and her hot side pressed next to mine, she whispered, "What do you think would really happen if we swam in it?"

I considered this, that licking green slipping up our arms, accepting our waists into it. "Do you think we'd get sick?"

"If we didn't drink it, we'd probably be fine. It's probably just if little kids drink it."

Later, I would learn that harmful algal blooms produce something called cyanobacteria, which can be absorbed through the skin, or inhaled, just as easily as it can pass through the mouth. At the time this made sense, though, that there was only the one way to let something into my body, that it couldn't enter me unless I allowed it. I rolled over so that my face was in Vienna's short hair. She still smelled like the lake, that light blue-green smell, like disappearing underwater.

*   *   *

I woke up first the next morning. The room we slept in was on the second floor, a triangular chamber like the top of a church with a small stained-glass window that opened over the living room. It felt like a room for keeping princesses in. I could hear the soft sounds of my grandmother downstairs. Vienna had rolled most of the quilt around herself, the pale ridges of her knuckles curled around the dark green like tree roots. Her face was knotted up. I thought people were supposed to relax in sleep, but Vienna always looked the most worried then, like she only let serious things find her in her dreams. I padded over to the window and pushed it open with the tips of my fingers.

My grandfather was stretched on the couch again. From that height, I couldn't see him breathing, and I knew, from the rustle of my grandmother in the kitchen, from her unconcern, that he must be, but I still went down to check. He smiled at me like the crinkling of a sheet.

"What do you want for breakfast, Julie?" He offered his hand. My grandfather wasn't the most tactile man, but he liked to hold my hand, so much that I still think of him, sometimes, when someone else does. The prominent blue veins that ridged the back of his knuckles, and the gentle way his wrinkles passed over them. The firmness and faint tremor of his grip. He would hold on for a long time.

I shrugged, because I could smell that my grandmother was already making pancakes.

"Is your friend still sleeping?"

"Yeah."

"Lazy." He smiled. I knew without asking that he wasn't going to take us to the lake this morning, and so didn't ask. Maybe I could say that I realized his frailty then, but it wasn't like that. It was a long process of realizing and forgetting, and realizing again.

When Vienna got up, I asked her if one of her grandparents would take us, and she shook her head, pushing the bristles of her bedhead away from her face.

"Why not?" I asked.

She huffed. "They're busy."

"What about your aunt?"

"That bitch?"

I blanched. I liked Chelsea. How she was pretty and young-looking, kind to her annoying daughter, and, so far as I could tell, mysteriously husbandless. She was something like what I thought womanhood could be: the confidence, kindness, long hair, and narrow body. I didn't know Chelsea well, but I wanted her to like me too.

I wanted Vienna to like me more, though, so I said nothing.

Behind our cabin and down the hill, there was a place we called Settler's Fort, which was actually the long-ago, burned-out remains of someone's shed or a small cabin. There was no part of it standing except the cement that had been the foundation once, and some chunks of stone that might have been pieces of wall. But you could find bits of colored glass there, warped by the sun. Blue and white and pale green twists of it, which we'd bring home and stack on our windowsills, or carry around in our pockets. Vienna and I walked to Settler's Fort after pancakes, and Abigail caught up to us on our way down, which we supposed was unavoidable. We spread our sweaters on a fallen log, to discourage the beady carpenter ants that lived there away from our legs, and then we picked through the decaying bark with sticks, or knelt in the dirt, combing it with our fingers. Abigail gathered pieces of white glass and quartz in a little pile on the cement.

Vienna took her stolen cigarette out of her pocket again and put it between her lips. I could tell she'd been chewing on it before, from the faint waterline stain of her spit. We both looked at Abigail, waiting for her to say that Vienna would get cancer, and she sucked on her bottom lip as if trying to restrain her own predictability.

"What are you looking at?" Vienna demanded, even though Abigail wasn't looking at her.

Abigail shook her head, her body gathering toward the pavement. "Nothing."

"Do you know how to do that thing," Vienna asked me, "where you light a fire with a magnifying glass?"

"Yeah." I didn't, but I thought if the circumstances were right I could figure it out. If Vienna and I were alone in the woods, the sun baking down on our backs. If we were dependent on me, I could impress her. "You need tinfoil, though."

"Oh. Can you really kill ants like that?"

Skeptically, I considered a nearby carpenter ant. It was fat and serious-looking, almost as big as my pinkie nail. "Small ones, I think."

"Do you wanna hear a ghost story?" Abigail asked us.

"No."

"There was a boy who always killed every bug he saw, and one day he woke up to the ghosts of all the bugs, and they'd become one giant bug and they swallowed him."

"That's a kid story," I told Abigail, because it was, I remembered it. "That's in the little kids' book in the library."

"So what?" said Abigail, and I scoffed.

Vienna arched into a long stretch. She was wearing a T-shirt with part of the neck cut away, showing a pale triangle of her chest, freckles speckled across her collarbone. Sometimes I felt as if there were a cork being pressed down my throat when I saw those freckles, the soft, vulnerable pink of her. "A girl at my school died last year," she said. Vienna liked to bring stories up the mountain to me. She had told me, last year, about a girl she knew who was twelve, who'd just lost her virginity with a high school boy behind the school. I repeated that story to my dad later, weepy because I'd promised to keep it a secret. I remember he thanked me for telling him. Like there was something he could do about it.

"She had a heart problem," Vienna went on, "and she asked the coach if she could sit down during laps. He said yes." Vienna took the cigarette from her teeth, holding it between her fingers, like she would blow smoke out to make a point, if she could. "And when he came back to check on her, she was dead."

I exhaled mournfully. "Did you know her?"

Vienna shook her head. "I heard it was because she was overweight."

"Oh." I glanced down at my body, at the press of my stomach against my T-shirt. That year my friend Ingrid had told me all the girls said behind my back that I had a fat ass, that she told them not to say it, but she just wanted me to know. Vienna's body did not look like my body. Later, as an older girl, I would think how funny it was to simultaneously want someone's body and want someone's body.

"That's really sad," Abigail said.

"Are you gonna cry?" I asked her.

Vienna tipped her head toward me. "Well, why wouldn't she cry? It's sad."

I blanched, but Abigail started coughing again then, as if her rib cage were trying to push part of her body out, and Vienna's temporary alliance with her disappeared under this weakness. Vienna became what she was again, older than us and prettier and more powerful. She raised her hands to her mouth and coughed, mimicking Abigail, coughed like she was dying.

"Did you drink the lake water?" I said with a laugh between the rough sounds of their choking, watching for Vienna's eyes between her fingers. "Maybe you drank the lake water, Abby."

Abigail finished her coughing. She straightened. She drew in a long breath that I could hear rasping all the way down her throat. "Why are you so mean?" she said, and she sounded just astonished by it.

Vienna dropped her still-whole cigarette in the dirt, scraping her foot over it as if stomping out a light. "Don't be a little bitch."

Abigail stared, the pale O of her bafflement, her parted lips shivering like butterfly wings. "You can't say that."

"Bitch," Vienna said. "Bitch, whore, dyke, slut."

Horrified, I giggled into the heel of my palm. We were in middle school, and it felt good to be liked by someone who didn't like many people.

"You're both so *mean*," Abigail repeated. "You're both so horrible and so mean to me."

*   *   *

Vienna woke me up in the middle of the night by putting her hand on my stomach. Being mostly asleep has always felt to me like floating in my own body, a thin film of myself spreading across the room. When she touched me, I coalesced, coming all together under her hand, entirely conscious of her before I even opened my eyes.

Before we'd gone back to my grandparents' cabin, Chelsea had found us. She was not angry, I remember. Vienna avoided her eyes with the sleek-bodied elusiveness of a ferret. "Vienna," Chelsea said, and I felt barely there, barely included even in this scolding. "Can you even tell me why you wanted to say those things?" Vienna scraped her foot back and forth in the dirt, sucked at the inside of her cheek, kept silent.

Now, in the night, she was catlike. Her dark outline, her dark pupils. "Do you want to go see it?"

"Yes."

We crept down the stairs, pulled our sneakers on over our bare feet. We held very still as I eased the door open. Vienna had to step back in to get a flashlight. We hadn't expected how dark the night would really be.

Once we were off the porch, though, on the road, we barely needed it. Our bodies knew the way. When Vienna's feet slid in the dirt, she held on to my elbow. This alone would have been worthwhile, her careful balancing against me, the way it almost knocked me over.

I don't know why we thought we'd be able to see it in the dark. I think I'd imagined it would glow. We picked our way down to the lake, and, when we came to the shore through the trees, turned to each other as we realized. Vienna extended her hand, shone the beam of the flashlight onto a circle of green water.

The stars were so bright up there, above the light pollution, the milk and spilled sugar of the sky. The barely illuminated corners of Vienna's face. She had what I would call a cruel mouth.

"Let's go swimming," I said, and she said, "Yes," and put the flashlight down to take off her clothes. We both looked at the lake while we undressed, out over the dark water and not at each other. I was still wearing thin tank tops under my shirt, no bras yet. Vienna's bra was pink, with a little bow on it, and she turned her back to me to hang it on a tree branch. I was dizzy, in anticipation of the coldness of the water, of that green so vivid it was like one soft mouth. I left my pajama shorts in the dirt, and I started off because I didn't want to be the one to hesitate.

The water was predictably slimy around my toes, but it felt good, like wading into a field, and once it was high enough we could see the green fairly clearly. It was different than it would have been in the daytime, blacker, but it still moved around us like magic. I thought about frogs that breathed through their skin. I thought about what I could take into my body through my body.

"It's—" Vienna breathed, and then she kicked her feet off the ground, dropped onto her back, her arms spread at her sides. The algae rippled out from her. Her fingers slid accidentally—probably accidentally—against my ribs. And my throat hurt, and the curl of my fingers hurt, and I tried not to look at her naked body, focused on just her chin jutting above the water, her pale nose like the head of a fish, her cold lips.

I reached for her with both hands, touched her shoulders and nothing more, and imagined her diffusing in the water. The slow creep of green up from her fingers, up from her toes. I imagined her body dissolving into millions of cells of algae, millions of little flowers, floating there separate and together, mixing with my body, indistinguishable, until we and the lake were one thing.

*   *   *

Abigail woke us the next morning by pounding on the door. The beginning of a rash was itching under my left breast, the skin scaly when I reached under my shirt to touch it. "You have to come see," Abigail shouted. "You have to come see! Everything's dead."

She sounded so excited about it.

We followed her down to the lake. All of us. My grandfather helped my grandmother over the puddles, chivalrous with his extended hand. Vienna strode on ahead of me, shoulder blades prowling under her tank top. Was it my imagination that she could not look at me? Was she thinking of the lake water? Of what we might have taken into ourselves? Abigail's feet pounded up dust as she led us. I wonder how she ran so fast without coughing. I wonder what she got out of heralding death.

When we reached the shore, we saw that she was telling the truth.

In the night, dead fish had floated to the surface of the lake. There must have been hundreds of them, all drifting near the shoreline. Their bodies lying together, intimately, flank to flank, open eye against open eye. The waves brought them toward us in a scum of silver corpses.

"See?" demanded Abigail, rocking up on the balls of her feet, straining flower-like toward the lake until my grandfather reached for her shoulder with a firm hand, and pulled her back before she could get any closer. His mouth pinched at the corners, turning down a little. I wanted, embarrassingly badly, to ask him how scared I should be.

Vienna would not look at me. Even when I touched her shoulder, even when I scraped my foot against the back of her ankle. I willed her to turn to me, to laugh, even to give me a fearful look so that at least we could be afraid together. She swallowed and swallowed again, her throat hitching. I was suddenly frantic that she couldn't breathe. Her mouth hung open a little, showing just the tip of her tongue. "Vienna," I said, but when I reached for her shoulder again, she shrugged my hand off, and walked a couple yards down the inlet beach, keeping her eyes on the lake all the while. I felt something opening inside me, all my nestled organs shuffling apart to create an empty space. Maybe I was about to throw up, or pass out. Maybe we would both have to go to the hospital, hours down the mountain. Maybe Vienna would tell her grandparents what we'd done. In retrospect, perhaps she worried that I'd tell mine.

We watched the fish wash in, hesitating like driftwood in the shallows, inching farther and farther up the beach. Each wave slid flesh against flesh, bringing them together and apart in little sighs, only to spit a couple soft, silvery bodies onto the sand, and drag the rest back without them.

"Look at that," my grandmother said, and I nodded. It looked like nothing I had words for, like the end of the world.

Hunting the Viper-King

At the mathematical heart of Dorothy's father's RV, at its golden ratio curl, there is a tarot card pinned to the corkboard. The High Priestess; she has been there longer than Dorothy can remember. Worn at her edges, drawn in lines of gold and white and blue, crowned by a crescent moon. She tips her head to listen to the snake coiling up her white throat, whispering in her ear. Dorothy has always loved her, the wisdom writ into her lines, her beneficent gaze on the RV's interior, the art nouveau spill of her hair down her shoulders.

The acquisition of the High Priestess was Dorothy's first and last bedtime story. She thinks she will be able to call it up, in all the curves and contours of her father's telling, for the rest of her life.

"Right after you were born," Dad says, sweaty palm on Dorothy's quilt, when she is three, five, twelve, flat on her back and searching out patterns in the RV's beaten metal ceiling, "I was in this bullshit cubicle job, going nowhere. But I had a little girl to take care of. And I couldn't just clear out unless I wanted to starve her. And I didn't ever wanna do that.

"My boss was the stupidest man I ever met, though. And what was I supposed to do except tell him, one day, 'Mister, you are the stupidest man I ever met'? So there I was, then, walking home with my things, my plant and my picture of you, in my little fuck-off cardboard box, and I see this house with this sign in the window."

And Dorothy asks, "What did it look like?" on cue.

Dad smiles at her. "Hand-painted, just like Our Lady." The tarot card, Our Lady: of the house, the hunt, and hope. "Blue and white and gold. Looked just like a fortune-teller's sign oughta look and it said 'Lives Told.'"

"And what'd you get told?"

"Wait just a minute, kiddo," he says, even though she's supposed to ask. He'll let the pause just hang there if she doesn't. "I'm getting there. So I walk in, Dot, and I see this beautiful girl. Hair long as Our Lady's and eyes as dark as anything. And she looks *right* at me, then she tells everyone else to get out of the room."

It's always been hard for Dorothy to imagine this part. The woman, ethereal and strange, with her sudden arrow focus on Dorothy's father, who is stringy-muscled and untidy, who looks perpetually uncertain and just on the right edge of mean. More and more lately Dorothy's been thinking, *Like a dog.* Like a hungry stray.

But the rest of the story pivots on this moment of prophetic recognition. And so it *must* have happened. Dorothy's father says it did.

"She tells me to sit down. I'm still thinking this must be some kind of scam. But she tells me to sit down, and she takes my hand and she says, 'It's you.' Then she hands me the deck like it hardly matters at all, like she knows what card I'm going to pull. And, of course, it's Our Lady. Our Lady. Do you know what she said then, Dot?"

"What?"

"She said, 'You're going to find the King.'"

"King of what, Dad?"

"Well, that's just what I asked. And she said, 'King of the Vipers, mister. You'll find the King of the Vipers, who is older than the land we stand on and has lived a dozen lives. When you find him, you must simmer the fat from his body and eat it, and then you will know everything.'"

Who else's life's purpose, Dad likes to say, reaches out to take them by the hand?

Their corkboard is plastered with false starts: tabloid clippings from Maine to Mexico, printed blog posts, the photograph of the escaped pet python in Florida and the snake trails Dad and Dorothy drove all the way to Utah to see that, in person, were obviously just from a real big rattler. "Larger than that," Dad told the farmer's wife, whom he'd refrained from calling a *dumb bitch* until they were driving away. "Bigger than you, lady. Bigger than me."

The Viper-King hails from Scandinavia. At least, Dad's pretty sure. They found a story about it in a Scandinavian myth book, in a college library in California. Dad was scared to steal the whole book, so he'd taken his shaving razor out of his pack and they'd worked apart the safety stuff with the little screwdriver from Dorothy's glasses repair kit. Dorothy knelt on the dusty linoleum floor and dragged the razor over the pages. They're a little ragged at the edges, but she didn't do a bad job.

The myth was brief, less than two pages, about a farmer who happened upon the Viper-King in his field and did battle with it. In the end, the farmer was killed by his servant, for the privilege of the Viper's fat. Those myths had a concise lack of morality to them that Dorothy found interesting, that she liked. Nothing happened for any reason.

Anyone who eats the fat of a Viper-King gains its wisdom. Its

wisdom is a whole world of wisdom, is the inside and back and
underside of everything. But it works only for the first person who
eats it, only for one.

*   *   *

Fate, in the fourteenth year of Dorothy's life, has finally extended
its hand to her father again. The singularity of the quest does not
bother him, Dorothy knows. It would bother him if he were *not*
singular, not chosen.

Fate has extended her hand and fate has led them to a rip-off
print and copy shop in Chicago, Illinois, so that Dad can print out
his latest lead and honor it with a spot on the corkboard.

The only parking spot big enough for the RV is half a mile
away. Dorothy's flip-flops are starting to break, a hole wearing in
the plastic bottom of the left one, so she can feel the hot roughness
of the pavement under the ball of her foot with every step. She'll
be glad to see this pair go. Dad picked them up last summer, when
they bought their latest round of new clothes with the last bit of
his pay from a construction job. The straps are cheap plastic and
give her blisters. When she feels them wearing open she pauses to
pry her shoes off her feet, looping the straps over her fingers. She
drags them along the chain-link fence by the path, listening to the
clank-clank, until Dad twists around and snaps, "*Shoes.*"

Dorothy balances the left one on her finger. "It's going."

"Damn." Dad takes the flip-flop out of her hand, and bends it,
stretches the weakening purple plastic until it turns white. "Put
'em back on for now."

"They *hurt.*"

"I'll buy you new ones soon."

The print shop is lit and tiled in gray. Dad cradles their laptop
against his chest while they wait in line, and Dorothy watches sweat
puddle between the shoulder blades of the man in front of them.

At every counter they pass, Dad tips the screen back to study Fate's open palm in his AOL inbox. A photograph of a mosaicked fragment of shed snakeskin, laid for scale over the spectral arm of a woman. At the picture's edges, where the skin doesn't swallow everything, there are slivers of vivid color: yellowish dirt, the warm brown crease of the woman's elbow. The measurement from that crease to the tips of her fingers is the *width* of the skin. The length extends beyond the photo. And it is a *fragment,* tattered at its ghostly edges.

"Look at that, Dot," Dad says. He takes Dorothy's hand and guides her finger to the screen, like the plastic is magic, and if Dorothy smears her fingerprints over the photo some of its realness will rub onto her hands.

Fate's emissary calls herself Elaine, from Kansas. It is her arm giving the skin scale. Her email is blunt. Dad calls it "no-bullshit."

"Found this in my cornfield. Thought with your website you might like to see it." And then her address, on a line by itself, like a baited hook.

Dad's "website" is just a blog on a free hosting service, which he updates periodically for an audience of, so far as Dorothy can tell, mostly no one. Dad's email address is posted there, though, and every so often someone will use it. Dorothy's already had to explain Photoshop to him once, following a mishap in Georgia that ended with him threatening a gangly teenager with his gun. When they were back in the trailer, Dorothy sat him down in front of the laptop. "See," she said, "he just cut a picture of the barn, and he made it smaller than the rattlesnake. It isn't hard." Dad dug his nails into his hands until he bled. He couldn't understand it, he just couldn't understand it, why any person would lie like that, for sport and nothing else.

Dorothy wanders off while he's printing. It's too hot outside, but that's all right. Kansas'll be even hotter.

Dad's another ten minutes. He comes through the door clutch-ing the already creased photograph to his chest like he's got the most infinitely precious thing in the whole world. When he grins, Dad shows the two missing teeth at the back of his mouth. It's taught Dorothy to be wary of smiling. She takes the picture from him, watches her sweat smear over the ghost of Dad's quest. "It looks pretty real," she says, "I guess."

Dad laughs with his head tipped back. He looks like he's howling. "I guess it does, Dotty Dot. I *guess* it does."

Dorothy watches an ant carry a dead ant over a crack in the sidewalk. "Yeah," she says. What else is she supposed to say?

*   *   *

Dad announces, "Ten hours to Kansas," when they're back in the RV, and Dorothy watches him cross to the corkboard and carefully fasten the photograph there, under the gaze of their Lady. He's beaming like a revival preacher on Judgment Day. "Wanna come up front with me?"

Dorothy shakes her head. "I gotta do math."

All Dorothy's homework comes from the homeschooling site that's the first result on Google, except her math, which is from one of those programs for gifted kids. Dad went to a lot of trouble to get her into that class, after Dorothy started complaining of how bored she was with the online curriculum she'd been fol-lowing since she was eight, which itself came about when Dad decided she needed something more than what he was teaching her. Dorothy does her best to be grateful. She's always had a touch for math, what one of her new lessons calls "number sense," and what Dorothy thinks of as having a good idea of the shape of things. That's really all it is, knowing how stuff comes together, knowing where the hard edges are.

Dorothy thinks a lot about probability, about the fact that there must be several other young people in her situation. Figuring out how many was a project she performed in fits and starts whenever they had internet and Dad wasn't monopolizing the computer.

She started with the number of men in America, 49 percent of the population, 160,194,191 men. Then the percentage of men with children: 47 percent, and that brought her down to 75,291,270.

It wasn't necessary that the men be unmarried. Dorothy's own father is perpetually single, her mother a gray, sparking patch on the surface of her life, like a video game glitch. But Dorothy doesn't define herself by her motherlessness. A sibling, however, would have altered the shape of her world. The percentage of only children is 23, and that brings her to 17,316,992.

Dorothy did her math with a pad of paper. Calculators are for cheaters.

It got trickier once she had the only children. Then Dorothy had to figure out how many people lived in RVs full-time. The only number she could find was 260,000, and it was old. But she wasn't giving up, so she figured out what percentage 260K was of the whole population. 0.08 percent. If Dorothy assumed that living in an RV had no effect on how many children you had, even though it probably did, that was 13,854 dads with one kid, living in RVs.

The last category was hardest. Dad would have Dorothy's scalp if she so much as thought of him as a "conspiracy theorist." And he isn't, really. But Dad's quest was a necessary part of the equation. The best she could manage was how many people believed in Bigfoot (13.5%). Dad doesn't, but Dorothy has to make do. That brings her total number to 1,870.29.

One thousand eight hundred and seventy kids. Upon starting the exercise, Dorothy assumed the answer would be something like twenty. She could make paper dolls of them. A severed arm, maybe, for the .3 left over.

Making one paper doll a day, Dorothy could make 1,870 in barely more than five years. She might have met one of those kids by then. She wishes she could calculate the probability of that, as she watches the city of Chicago fall away outside the RV's window and become the fields of corn that will flow right on into Kansas, but it's beyond her.

Dorothy wonders if it's even possible to calculate the odds of finding the Viper-King on this journey. What sort of numbers would she need? How many people send prank emails? How often "evidence" of mythical monsters is debunked? The size of the snake? How much of the world has gone unmapped, uncharted, long enough for something massive, omniscient, and strange to lie hidden there? The odds of finding such a thing, if it has not already been found, seem infinitesimal. Vanishing.

Who wrote about the Viper-King in the first place, anyway? And how did he know about the fat? Did he take moments out of his omniscience to record the legend for others? Was there more than one of these creatures? Did they *breed*? Or was it really like kingship, a mantle passed down, that no one got rightly until the previous owner was dead? Did a regular viper occasionally get a hell of a shock?

Dorothy supposes if you were omniscient, writing down what you knew would be as good as doing anything else.

*   *   *

They get to the farm at two p.m. the next day with the RV hot enough to melt around them. Elaine flags them down at the edge of her field, her driveway too narrow for the RV. She is unmistakable, tall and tawny, with a lot of curly hair knotted up in a handkerchief, sweat glittering on her face and bare arms. She whistles through her teeth at them, like a birdcall.

"You Billy McPherson?"

Dad looks like a black hat in a modern western, his jeans dragged low on his hips by the shotgun he's shoved through his belt. Looks like he's coming to steal cattle. "Yeah? You Elaine?"

"That I am," and she wheels her arm in the air again, and jerks her head toward a house, dusty and small in the distance. "Come on and see it, then. I tell you, man. Some-fucking-thing."

She falls into step with Dorothy while Dad forges ahead like it's his house in his field. She's pretty, up close. She smiles a lot, right away, a lot of little separate smiles like she's laughing at something, and she only asks Dorothy's name fifty paces after Dorothy hasn't offered it.

Dad shouts back over his shoulder, "That's my Dot."

"Dot?"

Dorothy shrugs. She doesn't feel like talking, is sore from sitting too long and now walking too far. Her flip-flops are opening old cuts on her feet. She bets soon there'll be scars. "Dorothy."

Elaine laughs at the sky, a soft, buoyant laugh, and tips toward Dorothy to slap a friendly hand on her shoulder. "Welcome to Kansas, honey."

*   *   *

The skin is real.

It sits, the resident phenomenon, on Elaine's kitchen table. The sunlight flutters against it, casts diamonds of light and shadow on the walls. "Don't touch it!" Dad snaps, and Dorothy realizes that she had been about to. Standing by the table, she is nearly shorter than the skin. She could wriggle inside, make it her own. It is big enough to shut Dorothy away from the rest of the world.

Dad does touch it. Of course, he cannot do anything else. It caves, ever so slightly, beneath two of his fingers, and bends the light. Dorothy imagines her stomach dropping out of her and rolling across the floor, picking up dust.

Evidence is not an end. The path still curves out before Doro-thy. They will not—Dad *could* not—be content to take the skin to a museum, or to a university, have it sampled, examined, and dis-played, have a team of scientists take up their search. No, *Dad* has to find the Viper. It is his destiny, corked up in the RV, to find it.

Yet, the skin means there is an end. Dorothy breathes in and imagines flecks of it dropping off, swirling in the breeze from the air-conditioning, being pulled into her lungs. Coating the inside of her, along with dust and particles of Elaine's skin. God knows how much of her father Dorothy has inhaled over the years. And the skin means that they will not be shut up in the RV together, forever and always, until the end of the world.

"Guess you'll want to overnight," Elaine says, into the silence.

"We can sleep in the RV." Dad picks his own moments to exhibit manners.

"Don't bother. I don't mind. Got a couch and a spare room." She looks at Dorothy. "I bet you'd like a real shower, wouldn't you? Why don't I make everyone coffee?"

They all sit together in the living room. Dad nods magnani-mously when Elaine looks for permission to pour Dorothy a cup of coffee, and Dorothy sips at it while Dad tells Elaine about the Viper-King. He tells her about the myth, and the fortune-teller, and Their Lady Pinned on the Corkboard.

He talks like a roadside preacher who's caught someone by the wrist and knows he only has a minute or so to get his spiel out; all quick *and*s, and *anyway*s, and *so*s, and earnest *you see*, *don't you*s.

Elaine goes into the kitchen again, while he's rambling, and comes back with three peaches and a pack of cigarettes. She puts one of the peaches in front of each of them, and takes a lighter from the drawer of the coffee table. Dad doesn't smoke. He doesn't like people to smoke around Dorothy. Dorothy involves herself in watching Elaine light up, hoping he won't say anything. Elaine's fingers are calloused and deft, her dry lips purpling.

She tips the pack in Dad's direction, offering, and he stops, mid-sentence, mid-explanation, and says, "Why not? Haven't done this in a while."

Dorothy puts her coffee cup down on the table, for the sound it makes, the break in the moment when they're both taking a breath and Dad is looking at Elaine while smoke pours out of her mouth, and then eats her peach. She wonders while she sucks the pit if it should surprise her more that the Viper-King is real. It's really real, its skin is in the other room.

She cannot forget the moment when it occurred to her that Dad might be wrong. She was eight, cross-legged on the RV's rough blue carpet, her hands in her lap. Dorothy spent a lot of days in RV parks clicking through channels. She'd landed on a television preacher, who was different than the ones she'd seen before, because he was combed neatly and his voice was soft. He was quoting Revelations in that soft voice. "Worthy is the Lamb that was slain to receive power, and riches, and wisdom, and strength, and honor, and glory, and blessing." He spoke like Dad. Dorothy has always read credibility foremost in the voice.

When Dad came in, he watched the television for a handful of minutes, swaying on his feet. "Come and see. And there went out another horse that was red: and power was given to him that sat thereon to take peace from the earth, and that they should kill one another."

Dad said, almost with affection, "Loon," and then turned the TV off. He crossed from there to the corkboard, letting his hand fall just slightly above Our Lady of the Giant Snake.

That, Dorothy guesses, was about that.

Still, the Viper-King seems to her like continental drift, like

global warming, like the slow, inexorable crawl of time. For Dorothy, not believing in it is being an atheist in a time when the gods
descended from the heavens with their hands out.

*   *   *

In the early hours of the morning, Dorothy sits on the RV's first
step, watching the dusty road slide slowly under her dangling feet.
The sun, just up, but already too hot in the sky, is an open hand
across the tops of her knees. Her neck's prickling under the gust of
the air conditioner. Dorothy doesn't think anything can smell hot
like farmland, manure and dry stalks and the oppressive stink of
your own sweat. Her jean shorts have edged up too high, and her
butt is plastered to the floor, itching.

They're winding along the roads that run around the farms.
Elaine sits inside, on their slatted table, swaying back and forth
with her nose pressed to the crack where the window is leveraged
open. Her shoulder blades glitter over the lip of her top, sharp
enough that her skin is almost translucent around them.

Dorothy feels brittle at the edges, like her fingers might snap
off if she tries to bend them. She is still sandy-eyed, and aching
from sleeping on the exposed springs of Elaine's guest bed.

They stop at every field and walk a grid across the ground,
search for trails or scraps of snakeskin. Dorothy scuffs her flip-
flops. The sun has bleached the possibility from the world.

What was real in Elaine's house, with that immense fragment
of skin glowing and glancing beneath her kitchen lamps, is not
real in the flat, bracketed realm of a cornfield. Dorothy has always
believed in the Viper-King the way that other people believe in
ghosts, or angels, or God; she might, in a properly combative
mood, tell a stranger how real it was, but she'd be damn surprised, all the same, to find it on a Kansas farm. She is thinking
of doing her math homework tonight, itching and covered in dirt.

She is wondering about dinner, the almost-expired tomato soup that she's going to cook over the hot plate.

Then Dad's shotgun cracks the sky open.

When the Viper-King bursts up from the corn, Dorothy drops to her knees, an instinctive reaction, duck-and-cover. She presses her hands against the back of her head, forces her face down into the dirt. She is thinking, in a blind panic: *Don't make me look. I don't want to see.*

Above her, the King of the Vipers hisses and spits. Dad's gun hammers apart the air.

The corn curves protectively over Dorothy's head. She wonders if she could hide this way forever, on her stomach against the dust, her body a hillock in the field.

What are you afraid of? the corn demands of her.

Didn't she already see the snake break the horizon? Hasn't she already met the dazzling, black eyes of her father's grail? Seen that it's real, that it breathes, that every cramped and sweating second of her life has been spent on this moment? And seen that the argument could be made that it was a worthwhile exchange? Dorothy rolls onto her back, and sees the silhouette that the Viper-King cuts in the sky.

Dorothy has never dreamed the colors of the Viper-King. The inside of its mouth is pink, bodily, more fearsome than if it had been red. Animals in fairy tales have red maws, like shed blood. Wolves that eat up children, and dragons that rise from caverns, these things are red all the way down. They hardly have organs, or stomachs, or throats. Real animals have these things, have intestines and kidneys and fat. Real animals have mouths of infected pink.

When the Viper moves, its body, like a coiled muscle, shimmers the colors of desert sand.

Its eyes remind Dorothy of photos of a solar eclipse, the way that the sun flares out dangerously around the hole the moon eats in the sky. Dorothy could put her hands into the center of those eyes. They flit over the corn, over Dorothy's father and the long arm of his shotgun. There is intelligence in those eyes, and an almost lordly wisdom. If they had approached it more politely, Dorothy thinks, it might have sat up and told them riddles before having them for lunch.

When the King of the Vipers falls, the very earth shakes.

Dorothy runs toward it. The strap of her left shoe breaks, and she leaves it behind her in the field. The Viper's body is like a felled redwood. Dad has the sole of his boot on its triangular head. Elaine is sitting on crushed corn, biting into the heel of her palm. Dorothy kneels by the corpse, and wonders if it will be ringed inside, like a tree, lined with the strata of centuries of life.

*   *   *

Their butcher knife has been at the bottom of a drawer for thirteen years. Dad has to plant it deep in the Viper's belly and pull it toward him with both hands, so that it looks only a slip away from slicing him up the middle, splitting him in half like Rumpelstiltskin.

He makes a cross section at the snake's stomach, and Dorothy and Elaine wear unwieldy rubber gloves to help pull back the flaps of skin. Dorothy hikes the top of her shirt up over her nose.

They don't need much fat, but the process of cutting it is arduous. The wet back-and-forth of the knife and the mythic stink. Dorothy brings out their folding breakfast-in-bed tray so that Dad has somewhere to plunk the meat. Then, between the three of them, they carry the cut back to the RV, resting it on their shoulders like pallbearers.

They try to set the little table down gently, once they're inside, but it slips in their hands anyway and blood spills onto the carpet. That might not ever come out. Dorothy sits, cross-legged, on the table, while Dad saws the fat away from the rest, bit by bit. The fat goes into a pan, the discarded pieces of meat drop into their mop bucket. The whole room stinks like raw insides.

Dorothy is charged with monitoring the melting fat on their hot plate, while Dad and Elaine go out into the cornfield to decide what to do with the Viper's body. She can hear them debating, as she watches the top of the pan mist over, whether to drag it back to Elaine's farm whole or cut it into chunks. Dad keeps laughing, a barking sound that rasps against the metal doorframe.

They did it.

Dorothy gets up and closes the door. She puts a hand on the wall, and then crosses two steps to put a hand on the opposite wall. The very tips of her fingers shake. In summer, the trailer heats up. It's like living in a microwave.

They'll never get the smell of fat and blood out of the RV. They've never gotten any of the other smells out of it. It still stinks like old scrambled eggs, like cooking chili, like the jalapeños Dorothy puts in her grilled cheese. It smells like combined sweat, and the strawberry milk she drank when she was six.

How would it be, to live in a ten-by-twenty-five-foot trailer, with a man who knew everything?

Dorothy opens the window just a crack. She hears Elaine offer to take off to the neighbors and ask for their tractor. Dad is straddling the King's stomach, his legs spread just above its slit belly. Dorothy has to wonder exactly how old their Viper is, how much it had seen and felt, and how long it had buried itself beneath cool earth or glittered under a peaceful sun, how long it went undisturbed before they took an interest in disturbing it.

Dorothy hasn't had anything to eat. Her shoulders ache. Her

hands are still shaking. She takes a piece of sourdough bread, one of the last two in the pack that haven't gone moldy yet, and puts it in the toaster.

Dad took her to the Grand Canyon once, and they went out on the skywalk. Dorothy was nine years old, scared and determined not to be. But something shifted when they got to the platform's edge and she could lean against the railing and see the ground fall away red beneath her. She realized that if she put her foot on that railing she could hoist herself right over the glass guard wall. Her stomach absolutely *ached* with the knowledge that she was a metal rail and a bent knee away from being dead, and Dorothy identified in herself for the first time that instinct for the worst-case scenario, which claims that a ledge, once found, must be leapt from.

Once, she looked it up. It's called the high-place phenomenon. It means, supposedly, having increased sensitivity to danger, not wanting to die.

When her toast pops out of the toaster, she jumps.

There are still chunks of fat floating in the pan, the rest going toward a faintly golden liquid. It shivers when Dorothy touches the bread to it. The crust comes away glittering, and Dorothy does not allow herself to look at it long before she puts it in her mouth.

She pulls her hand back very quickly, and the rest of the bread flies across the trailer. It's hot. She sticks her head under the sink like a dog and gulps water.

Dorothy stands.

Perhaps she spat all the fat out, perhaps she did not swallow anything, and her life is still intact and narrow.

She presses her nose against the wide, boxy window that looks out over the road, over the farm opposite, brackets a view of the horizon.

Dorothy sees that one of the cows in the next field is pregnant.

She sees the fetus curled inside it, its pink, alien body translucent and veined with dark blood, the flat moonstone of its underdeveloped eye. She sees the knotted hair network of the corn roots beneath the ground, and the deep, wide tunnel that the Viper's body cut far beneath them. She sees, and shies away from, the long, cool mass of its life, its hundreds of years of slow knowledge, its enormity of consciousness and simplicity of thought, knowing without interest, without analysis. The world spreads out in front of Dorothy, flat and shimmering and somehow small.

She knows that Elaine and Dad sat up all night, after she fell asleep, that they drank coffee and beer, that Dad took a cigarette from her even though he doesn't smoke because he liked the sinewy lines of her arms, and thought about asking her to dinner and how he didn't have any place to ask her. And she knows that Elaine would have said no, though she would have said it nicely, and that Dad didn't ask anyway, because when he told Elaine that just one person could taste the fat, she shrugged one of her sharp shoulders and said, "I guess I know a thing or two more than I ever needed to anyway." Dad liked her less after that, he liked her a lot less.

And Dorothy knows why that is, because she looked so certain while she said it, the light glancing off the hard edges of her eyes. Dad has never known what to do with people who are anything but discontented in the boundaries of their lives. She knows that Elaine would have said no because she's discovered she likes to be alone more than she likes to be not alone, and that she discovered that after she caught her husband with his brother's wife in her shower, but she got the farm out of it so she could mind more than she does.

She sees that her 1,870 is actually only 73, and that she had been within ten miles of one of them, once, when she was eleven. His name is Stuart, but he is in Canada now, with his dad, looking for Bigfoot. Only 73, and now 0, because this last experience is hers alone.

She knows who her mother is, that her name is Amy Dorsett and that she got pregnant when she was seventeen and her boyfriend Bill, nearly twenty-one, offered her $7,000, every cent he had plus more than a little he stole from the parents, to have the baby, because he wanted it—he wanted it *so badly*. Dorothy knows that her father sat beside her mother in the hospital while she was being born and squeezed both his shaking hands between his knees and cried, because he was afraid his daughter would not be born alive, and that when she was he looked at her little red crinkled nose and paid every cent of the seven thousand and left town the next day in case Amy changed her mind, even though Dorothy knows that Amy never did, because he wanted her so badly.

And Dorothy tries to reconcile that wanting with the two hundred square feet of the past fourteen years of her life and knows that it is at once perfectly unified and irreconcilable. She knows that seven months to the day later her father got an offer to bring something else into the world, and that sitting at a card table while a woman looked straight down the barrel of his eyes and selected him for greatness was one of those happinesses from which a person never recovers.

She knows that the fortune-teller was named Tanya, that she has since gone into real estate, and that at the time that she pulled Their Lady of the Corkboard out of her deck she was nineteen, a college dropout with a baby girl in the back room of her apartment. She put silver dye in her hair on Saturdays and told unusual fortunes because she got bored, and because people tipped higher when she said extravagant things. If Dad had ever looked near her left elbow he would've seen the book on urban legends she was reading between appointments. She knows that Tanya did not for a moment imagine anyone would take her seriously.

Dorothy guesses she won't have to do her math lessons any-more. She remembers filling out the scholarship application for those with Dad in time to take them instead of seventh-grade math, the warmth of his breath just above her shoulder, and how proud he was when the acceptance email came. She knows that he had a beer that night, and considered a future where she went to college, and away from him, and that he had not really thought about that before.

Always, Dorothy assumed that her father was hunting the King for a reason, that there was a plan she never knew, that they might sell the first bite of fat and live well for the rest of their days, or that he wanted to use it to find her mother, that he had a ques-tion, an earnest, urgent question that drove him to the road, to the desert, to a myth's hunting and slaughter.

But there is a similarity between Dorothy and her father firmer and more defining than genetics. Dorothy sees that her father wanted the fat for the same reason that she took it, because she was able, because it was there.

Dorothy turns, and sees her father coming through the doorway.

The Changeling

My parents tried to define *miscarriage* for me with a plastic anatomy doll.

My father had bought it at a school book sale the year before, when I was in fourth grade. The doll was one of a pair of figures set back in a cardboard box, a man and woman posed in identical skeletal rigidity. Their skin was translucent, their genders identified not only by their anatomy, but by the fact that, while the man was bald, the woman had a clod of sculpted hair fused to her plastic head. Under their skin, a tangle of blue and red veins was visible. You could open their hinged bodies at the hip, and lift their insides away in layers, clear skin to veins, veins to russet muscle tissue, tissue to organs, and organs to twiggy skeleton. Their genitalia was detachable, and the woman came with a miniature, plum-colored fetus. My father squatted on the wooden floor of my bedroom. With a tremendous earnestness, he opened the woman, and commenced to take her fetus in and out.

"Aunt Vera might still have a baby," my father said, and clicked the fetus into place in the woman's body. "A miscarriage is when a woman is going to have a baby"—his fingernail tapped on the plastic stomach—"but then something goes wrong in her body, and what was going to become a baby—"

"A fetus," my mother supplied. She was dragging our air mattress into my room, her back arched with the effort, it having mostly unrolled onto the floor already. I already knew what a fetus was, because I had seen a cow's at the Museum of Natural History that year, suspended in amber liquid.

"The fetus comes out of the woman, and then she isn't going to have a baby anymore." My father reached back into the figurine. "Do you understand, Judith?" I held my hand out for the fetus, expectant. It was the size and color of a grape Jolly Rancher, and looked like a movie alien, curly and insectoid. I closed my fingers over it, and then opened them again.

"Aunt Vera might still have a baby." My father returned the fetus to my aunt's macabre stand-in. "But only if the doctors take good care of her, and she gets a lot of rest."

"Which is why"—my mother plugged the air mattress pump in, and it roared to sudden life, a beast, outraged, in the silence of my attic room—"Cousin Ruth is coming to stay with us."

*   *   *

My aunt Vera loved to call her pregnancy a miracle, and it did seem miraculous to me, if also disquieting. She was the first pregnant woman I'd ever known before she was pregnant, and closely enough to be present for the transformation. I'd known as long as I could remember that Aunt Vera was not capable of having children. This fact did not carry for me any of the connotations it did for the adults in my life. Her marriage, her divorce, the fertility treatments she tried first with her husband and then on her own all happened before I was born. I knew it because Ruth was adopted, and it had been necessary to explain to me, when I was small and she arrived, where my new cousin came from. This incapability of Aunt Vera's body was what had produced her, Ruth emerging from negative space, and so it seemed as natural and impenetrable to me as my cousin's presence in my life.

Aunt Vera and Ruth lived two blocks away from us. I could have sleepwalked to their door, if I sleepwalked. I spent a quarter of my nights on the floor of Ruth's living room, the two of us sleeping on our backs on Aunt Vera's sheepskin rug. Aunt Vera, who worked from home, drove us both to the same after-school activities, took us, occasionally, off-campus for lunch, cheered, the year before, at both our soccer games. Ruth and I were both only children, and Aunt Vera and my father were so close. Our sisterhood was inevitable.

Aunt Vera had gotten pregnant just before the start of that summer, when I was eleven and Ruth was ten. The pregnancy was announced to all of us at once, my father, my mother, Ruth, and me all gathered in Aunt Vera's living room. I loved Aunt Vera's living room more than I had ever loved any part of my house, because it was made of flinty gray stone, on both the walls and floor, and had a fireplace like a yawning mouth. Aunt Vera poured champagne into tall, thin glasses for my parents, and apple cider for Ruth, me, and herself. "Can't drink," she said. "It wouldn't be good for the baby." She beamed like a pillar of quartz.

Aunt Vera would be forty next year. She'd wanted to try just once more, she said, before her odds got even worse. She used the word *miracle* in those early months of her pregnancy with such persistence that it began to drip into everyone else's vocabulary. "Miracle baby," my father and mother both called the child, and my mother said, "I hope she doesn't name it that." "It's a miracle," Ruth and I said, when we passed spelling tests, when we found our lost toys, when we located a creek deep enough to swim in. Miracles were abundant.

Ruth spent more time at our house than before, and she had

always spent a lot of time there. Aunt Vera's pregnancy must have been difficult from the beginning, because we often heard that she was sick, that she was too tired for us to play at her house, or to drive Ruth to Junior Biologists Camp. Our air bed got regular use.

"I think it's admirable," my father said, as he shut the car door on Ruth and me in the backseat, ready for him to drive us to camp. Ruth was a Junior Ornithologist that year; I was a Junior Entomologist. "That she's doing it on her own."

"I think it would be admirable," my mother answered, probably not knowing that the other door was still open and we could hear, "if she *was* doing it on her own."

My aunt Vera's artificial insemination was explained to me in the same concrete and semi-scientific terms as Ruth's adoption had been, and miscarriages later would be. I was not told at the time that my father had helped pay for it, though he had given Aunt Vera the money with the intention of paying off her student loans.

My aunt's condition baffled and frightened me, not because of its origin but because of its details. She was a small woman, and dieted extravagantly during her pregnancy, reciting, whenever food was offered to her, how little weight she had gained while creating life. "Barely more than the baby weighs!" And so the protuberance from her abdomen dwarfed her. Her morning sickness was unrelenting, and was the first time I had seen an adult throw up. She carried herself delicately, with a hand on her lower back and another groping for things to balance her, as if she were in constant pain. Looking at her, I thought inevitably of parasites.

*   *   *

My father went to get Ruth, while my mother and I stretched my spare linens across the air bed. I kept getting in the way, bouncing on my knees on the rubbery mattress until the sheet corners tugged free. I wondered what Ruth might be feeling about the endangerment of her sibling in potentia, and what the appropriate way to act around her was, and I was thinking about a kind of wasp that laid its eggs in caterpillars. Parasitoid wasps, which instead of stingers have a needle-sharp ovipositor and deposit their larvae beneath the host's skin. I'd learned about them in the spring, when my mother brought a monarch cocoon inside for me and it sat, inert, in a little plastic terrarium on my dresser, slowly darkening with black splotches as the wasp ate away inside it. After learning what the splotches meant, my mother shook the cocoon out onto the cement of our driveway and crushed it with her foot. I had wanted to keep it; just long enough to see the wasp come wriggling out.

Ruth brought her mother's carpetbag with her, instead of just her bluebird backpack. The bag smelled like Aunt Vera's fortune-teller perfume, singed and musky. My father hefted it onto the floor, and then stood in the doorway, and it made me feel very grown up to catch the look that passed between him and my mother, as if we, all three of us, were assessing the direness of the situation.

My mother stepped around the air mattress to hug Ruth. "Are you hungry, honey?"

"No."

Ruth did not look very worried to me, but she paused in my doorway like she was not sure whether she could enter, like we had not played war with my dolls last night on the blue tie rug, and shaved one of her stuffed animals the weekend before. "You can come in," I said.

"Are you sure you wouldn't like me to make you a sandwich?" my father asked her.

"I'm sure." When Ruth sat down on my bed, she crossed her

legs primly at the knee, holding them out from her body like she wanted to touch as little of the room as possible.

"I have to get to work." My mother leaned against the doorframe. I reached under Ruth to get my toy box from beneath the bed. "Will you three be okay?"

My father nodded her off amicably. "Sure. How about some water, Ruth? Ice cream?"

I had pulled a toy out of the box, and now I held it up in front of Ruth's face. "This," I said, when she looked at me, "is what I think fairies look like."

"What?"

It was a small rubber model of an orchid mantis, from a set of plastic bugs my mother had gotten me at the science museum. The orchid mantis was my favorite, extraordinarily delicate, with a waxy pink body fading to white at its pointed limbs, and eyes like opal beads set against its skull. "This is what fairies look like."

"Ruth?" my father repeated.

Ruth ignored him, studying me. "You haven't seen a fairy."

"Be good," my father said, and shut the door behind him.

I thought it made sense that fairies would be small things, that crept on spindled legs sometimes instead of flying—that they would have narrow, fragile bodies, and be beautiful in a way that was neither human nor comforting, sharp at all their angles, and equipped with mandibles to sever the heads of their mates. Nothing magical is safe, nothing safe is magical. I knew that from reading fairy tales. I sat down on the air mattress in front of Ruth, and gave her the orchid mantis. "They look like that, so when they sit on plants everybody only thinks they're bugs. Nobody bothers bugs. Their houses are under rosebushes. They climb down the roots, and they make tunnels." I knew that fairies lived underground. It made perfect sense to substitute green hills for the little

hillocks of dirt that rise around the trunks of bushes. The ground
can hold anything. "If you see a mantis on the ground, you should
always put it back on the bush."

Ruth considered this, putting her head at an angle. "What
about the scientists?"

This had occurred to me, and so I was proud of Ruth for
thinking to ask it. "Sometimes they let entomologists look at them,
because they like to have pictures of themselves drawn, and they
like to be given food. But if they don't like it, and someone bothers
them, they kill them."

"Really?"

I took the mantis back from Ruth, and I set it on the flat back
of my hand, the sheen of its body on my own skin. "They climb on
people's faces while they sleep, and they put a spell on their nose
and their mouth, so they die."

*   *   *

"I don't want to go to sleep," Ruth said that night. We lay curled
around each other on the air mattress, so that her head was under
my chin, her shoulders pressed tightly into my chest. I was thinking about the anatomy doll, about someone coming to my aunt
Vera's bed in the middle of the night and opening her body like
a treasure chest, petting their finger over the red-purple lining
of her organs, shifting them about, so they could reach in and
wrench out her fetus.

"We don't have to sleep."

"I didn't see Mom when it happened," Ruth said. Sometimes
I felt that Ruth and I could read each other's minds. We'd spent
afternoons trying, sitting in the bean bag chairs in the library,
thinking of questions and trying to answer each other. "But I went
into her room, and there was some blood on her bed."

I tried to imagine, without asking Ruth, the size of the bloodstain. For science, that year, I had been shown a two-liter soda bottle and told that most people have about three times that much blood in their bodies. One of those soda bottles, maybe, tipped over the bed, flowing deep into the sheets and down the sides of the mattress. "Is she gonna be okay?" I asked.

Ruth was diffident. "I think so. She really wants the baby."

A point had been made to both Ruth and me as children about how wanted we were. My mother had her own story about fertility treatments, marking off days on her calendar, calculating with my father how long they could afford to do this, the budgets still on the dining room table the morning she discovered she was pregnant with me. Aunt Vera's want of a child was well and widely known, that she had tried hormonal treatments, essential oils, crystals, and prayer, before and while she waited for her adoption application to be approved. There were photos in our family album, taken by my father, of a short, round woman, limbs all slim and pointed like a pixie's, the social worker passing Ruth into Aunt Vera's arms, Ruth a small bundle, a slice of her shining head and a soft fuzz of hair, poised perfectly in between the moment of transfer, when she ceased to be one person, part of one family, and became another.

"Isn't it interesting," my mother said once—it was amazing the things that I could hear through the wall of my room, how much thicker my parents thought that barrier was than it was— "how she seemed to start really *needing* a child only after you told her we were trying?"

"Do you think that's something you can copy?" my father asked impatiently. "Being a parent, do you think you invented that, Patricia, do you think that's something you can copy?"

I had not stopped thinking about this, this suggestion that Ruth could be in some way a replication of me. We were not the same. Ruth frightened easily, and didn't like to talk to people she didn't know. Ruth's hair was shorter and darker, she liked to wear dresses and was good at math. Ruth was missing her back left tooth and her bottom front one, and most of my adult teeth were already in. When I looked into her mouth with a flashlight, I'd found a new tooth, a little ridge of white bone stabbing out of her gum. I put my finger on it to see if it would hurt her. I told her, "If your mouth was a cave, this would be the door." It made a lot of sense to me, though, if Ruth had been brought here to our town, and grown into herself, only because I was first.

"Do you know if it's a girl?"

"No. She wants to be surprised." The bones in Ruth's back shifted under my hand as she folded more tightly into herself. Behind her, the green glow from my night-light looked like the headlights of an alien ship. When I thought about being abducted by aliens, I imagined them realigning my bones, or pulling out my teeth and dropping them into a set of small and separate jars, all the individual secrets of my body.

"Do you want it to be a girl?"

When Ruth shrugged, her shoulders slid against my skin. All my life, long after this, this was what I liked best about holding someone else, feeling their bones, the simultaneous firmness and fragility of them, like holding a mouse in your palm.

"I don't even want it," Ruth said. "I didn't even want it."

"You'll get to be a big sister."

Ruth hissed through her teeth.

My mother used to tell people that she did not need to have another child, because she had gotten it right the first time. She had stopped saying this since Aunt Vera got pregnant, of course, but it made me wonder the same thing Ruth must've, what part of her her mother was dissatisfied with.

"Do you ever think about being kidnapped?" Ruth asked.

"Sure." We had a Stranger Danger assembly in school every

year, where a police officer came and talked to us about what we should do if a stranger tried to take us. Last year, they told us about a girl our age who had been stolen and kept in a basement for five years. The police officer rolled tape across the floor of the gymnasium. "This," he said, standing in a square the size of an airplane bathroom or a coffin, "was the size of the room Nicole was kept in. Think about that." The gasp from one of our teachers made me feel that we were being shown something illicit. The photo of the girl up on the projector looked like something from the television, her pursed, serious face, her blond hair in strings around her cheeks. Abduction was a horror story for children our age that also carried a tentative thrill. It was such an extreme thing to have happen to you. "What would you do?"

"I heard about this girl"—Ruth rolled her head to stare up at the ceiling; I looked at the side of her nose—"who got kidnapped right out of the hospital when she was a baby, and this woman who was a stranger raised her like her daughter. And she never even knew until she was grown up."

I drove my elbow, quick and sharp, up under her ribs. "Ow." Ruth stilled. I roughhoused a lot with other kids at school, but that didn't really work with Ruth. She didn't fight back when you hurt her, just went limp, boneless like a scruffed cat.

I buried my face in the back of her neck. "What's that got to do with anything?"

*　*　*

We still had to go to school the next morning. I thought we might not have to. The year before, when Ruth broke her arm, I'd been allowed to take two days off to spend with her. We'd stayed at Aunt Vera's house, eating her peanut-butter-and-jelly sandwiches, better than my mother's because she made them with soft white bread and a little butter and honey.

Ruth seemed newly awkward while we were changing into our school clothes. As if the change in her mother were contagious, she was heavier and more clumsy, turning her back to me and crossing her arms tightly over her chest for longer than it would have taken her to just put on a shirt, hunching all her body so close together she shrank.

Over breakfast, oatmeal with raisins and apples but, by my mother's ruling, no sugar, my father told us that Aunt Vera and the baby were going to be okay. They would have to stay in the hospital a little while longer, until the baby was born, to make extra sure that she was safe, and Ruth would stay with us until then.

"How long?" Ruth asked.

"As long," my mother said, putting the sugar bowl down in front of Ruth gently, conspiratorially, "as it takes."

Ruth and I were in different grades, the fourth and fifth, respectively, so I only saw her during recesses. Our schoolyard was large, composed mostly of a field, with a border of trees blocking us off from the residential streets on two sides, and, at the back, a swath of undeveloped land where some thick, raggedy oaks grew on the slope of a brown hill. I was sure that hill was haunted. The tree nearest our fence had the remains of some structure nailed up in it, a few mossy boards and a fraying bit of cloth, an abandoned tree house or something more sinister. In the third grade, I had heard a story about a girl who ran away from home, and was mauled and eaten by a mountain lion. I had decided that it had to be in this place that it had happened; there was the tree house the girl had built herself, there was the ground where she was eaten.

Most breaks Ruth and I spent walking along the chain-link fence that bordered that hill, looking for manifestations of this haunting. We disturbed the piles of leaves and mud that accumulated at the base of the fence, speculated about what the holes dug under it could mean, traps made for us to fall into or corpses burrowing up from under the earth.

"Are we gonna see your mom after school?" I asked her.

Ruth shrugged. "Your dad said probably. He said if she's feeling up to it."

I had been to a hospital once before in my life, when Ruth broke her arm, and then I'd only been allowed to sit in the pale waiting room for a couple of hours, to investigate one of the sparse vending machines, before my mother came to take me home while my father waited with Aunt Vera. I was interested by the idea of going back. "Did she call you or anything?"

"No." Ruth looked soft, with her curls resting fuzzily against her ears. I wanted to pet her. I turned over a clump of leaves with my shoe. There was something mounded up under there, something moving darkly, and I realized after an indrawn breath that I had disturbed an anthill. They swarmed up my leg in a slurry of black chitin. "Look," I said to Ruth, but she'd already gasped and jumped back, out of range.

"They don't bite," I said, though they did, a little. I could feel the small attempts of their pincers at the places between my jeans and the high end of my sock.

"Oh my God." Ruth covered her mouth with her hands. "Get them off you. Judith, get them *off* you."

Her voice was pitching up so high that I worried one of the supervising teachers would come. "Shut up," I told her. "Quit it."

I got down on my knees in the leaves. "Look," I repeated. The ants that were not scrambling up my leg were swarming now, their legs scuttling like breathing. With their delicate mandibles, they lifted little white sacs, dots like the teeth of very small animals. "Look." They were rushing their loads into tunnels, under the earth. "They're burying their babies."

I interfered with a stick, causing a small riot amid the swirl of their bodies. The eggs were too small for me to touch, but I lifted one delicately with the stick, trying to get it into the sunlight. I wanted to see the shape of a miniature ant inside it. And then it moved, and startled me, squirming at the end of my stick, horrible because of its suddenness. It fell backward off the stick, wriggling in a miniature, awkward motion, and landed a little ways away from the nest. The bell rang then, but I watched a moment, wondering if one of the sister-ants would notice and reclaim it.

*   *   *

"Did you know there's a kind of butterfly," I told Ruth, our sweating knees slicked together in the backseat of my dad's car—he was driving us to the hospital—"that makes ants raise its young?"

"How does it do that?" My father craned his neck to look back at us through the rearview mirror. His radio blared cheerful, innocuous country music.

"The larva of the Alcon blue butterfly smells like an ant baby to an ant, so the ants take them back into the nest and raise them. And the ants feed them more than even their own babies."

"What happens"—Ruth had turned her face away from the window; her mouth was cinched up small—"to the baby ants?"

"They starve to death," I told her, "or the butterflies eat them."

The hospital seemed extraordinary at the time, a catacomb of brightly lit tunnels. It smelled of cool hand sanitizer, and, going in, we were given masks that lay flat against our chins and the bridges of our noses, cutting us off from the air.

"Do you think someone's dying here right now?" I asked Ruth, thinking of a room down a tunnel, and down another tunnel, and around a corner, a fluorescent identical hallway, a soul escaping.

"Maybe," she said, her wide, staring eyes. "Maybe someone just did."

"Stop that, Judith," my father said. "Stop that, girls."

"They're like changelings," I told Ruth in the elevator, "the butterflies."

"What's a changeling?"

We came into Aunt Vera's room then, which we entered by pulling back a curtain. Aunt Vera was contained like a dead bird in a cardboard box, set in four small white walls. On one side of her bed was a window, which looked out over the hospital parking lot. It was winter, and the sun was already setting, spreading a low orange glimmer over the parked cars.

Aunt Vera lay in the center of the room on a raised bed, with blankets bundled so close around her I wondered if she could even move her arms. Aunt Vera did not look like Ruth at all. Aunt Vera, before she was pregnant, was a collection of bones held together by her skin. Her face was narrow, with pale blue eyes and long blond hair she treated with mayonnaise and cracked eggs. She looked like a lady in a fairy story, and might as well have been laid on an altar or a bed of roses. Her stomach rose out of her body like a tumor.

My father went to her and they hugged, he shifting her awkwardly so he could hold her, and he kissed her on the forehead.

"Ruth," Aunt Vera said, and she opened her arms.

Ruth stayed back by the door. Her body strained as if someone were holding her there.

"Come here, Ruth."

In Aunt Vera's arms, Ruth looked too big. The roundness of her body, her bones bulging ungainly beneath her skin.

"How's the baby?" my father asked.

Aunt Vera pressed Ruth down into a chair by the bed, and rested her hand in Ruth's curls. "He's going to be okay." Her face was resplendent. "They told me," she said, resting her pinked-up cheek on the pillow—even chalky-sick she was beautiful; I was always comparing Aunt Vera to my own mother, how young and not like a mother Aunt Vera looked—"that it's a boy. They didn't know I was waiting. They said, 'Your son is just fine, Vera.' I would have had them not tell me, but I'm so glad they did. I'm having a boy."

"You're having a boy." My father was holding Aunt Vera's free hand, his fingers closed around hers like curling bark. It had never struck me before how alike my father and my aunt looked. Their same goose-down hair, and the same laughingness about their eyes. "What are you going to name him?"

"After Dad, I think. Nick."

I was named after my grandmother, my mother's mother, Judith. There were tears welling in my father's eyes, and I looked over at Ruth, my face hot. Aunt Vera had wound one of Ruth's curls all the way around her finger, so that I could see the raised peaks of her scalp being pulled with it.

"Oh, Vera," my father said. "I'm so glad he's okay. I'm glad you are."

Aunt Vera laughed, and stretched her head back on the pillow, her neck a sleek arch, pulled taut with tendons. "It was something. It didn't hurt at all, actually. I woke up because of the wet spot. I *honestly* thought I pissed myself, and I was like: *Okay, this is a new level of pregnancy. I've lost bladder control. It's fine.*" She held up her hand, as if in the moment, comforting her shaken self, "It's fine. It's my miracle, it's fine. And then I go to take my panties off and there is blood—not just on the bed but like *gushing* out over my fingers. I thought I miscarried. I called 911, they thought I lost the baby, the girl on the phone I mean. I was crying."

"Ow," Ruth said.

"Oh no, sweetheart, it didn't actually hurt. It looked like it would hurt—"

"*No.*" Ruth raised a clawed hand to her head, held it against the place where Aunt Vera had tangled her fingers in her hair. "*Ow.*"

"Oh." She held her hand delicately, turning it loose from Ruth's hair. "Did I hurt you, Ruth?"

Ruth lifted one shoulder. "A little."

"Sorry, baby." Aunt Vera petted her hand, her long, manicured nails resting briefly on Ruth's knuckles. "They're going to tell me tonight," she said, again to my father, "whether they think I'm going to need to do a C-section." My father nodded, in time with the bob of Aunt Vera's head. "I wanted it to be natural." Aunt Vera sighed. "I really want it to be natural. But obviously, whatever the baby needs."

* * *

"Changelings," I told Ruth, in the car on the way back, "are babies that the fairies give you. They aren't really babies, though."

"What are they?"

"Sometimes they're the babies of fairies." My father was singing along to his country music in the front seat. "Or they're bad fairies that just look like babies. Sometimes they're not even anything at all, the fairies just weave them out of sticks, they make them out of grass and mud, and they switch out the real babies for them. They steal real babies, and they leave behind the changelings. And just like with the ants and the butterflies, you can tell a changeling is a changeling because it eats and eats until there's nothing left for anybody else. "

"Your mom's gonna be fine, Ruth," my father said. "Stop telling her scary stories, Judith. Your mom is gonna be fine, and your baby brother is going to be darling."

"What's a C-section?" Ruth asked him. She'd opened her hands on the seat next to me, peeling her fingers apart as if it were painful, and I saw that there was a series of small crescent cuts on her palm, places where she had, again and again, clenched her fists so tight she bled.

"It's when they have to take the baby out with surgery," my father said. "But it's very safe, for your mom and the baby."

Ruth had a look like she was carved out of stone. I had caught enough of medical dramas over my mother's shoulder to have a basic, visual concept of surgery, to understand that it was the reduction of your body to its nonhuman parts, the opening of you to reveal things that oozed and squirmed. It was so like the picture I had had already, the opening of my aunt Vera like an anatomy doll. When I asked my mother, whom I trusted to tell the truth, she only said, "No worse than labor."

That night Ruth sat on my blue tie rug, with my room closed up around us like a pair of clasping hands. I was eleven years old and had never seen anyone look so sad. I remember that it made me angry, with Aunt Vera and with the baby, who had made her so sad already, existing in the hypothetical, and also with Ruth, because in the bow of her neck and her small balled fist, it seemed to me that she was feeling something I was not capable of understanding or sharing, like she'd gone beyond a wall into a different room, an area of adulthood where I wasn't welcome.

Ruth pressed her knuckles against her teeth, like she was about to bite. "Why does she even want a baby so bad?"

And I said, "It's not even a real baby. It can't be."

"A changeling," Ruth said.

I was anticipating argument. "Wasps put their babies in the babies of butterflies, they kill the caterpillars and make them wasps inside the cocoon. Those are changelings. It's not even any different."

When Ruth looked up at me with huge eyes, like the stunned eyes of a deer, I got down off the bed and sat on the rug behind her. I pulled her body against my stomach, hair and her squirming bones. I dug my chin into her shoulder until it must've hurt, and held her around her ribs until she turned to me and pushed her wet face against my throat. I told her about butterflies raised in the nests of ants, about wasps that paralyzed spiders to incubate their eggs in, and wasps that filled the bodies of caterpillars with their squirming larvae until they burst out through the skin. I stroked her hair and told her about tricksy fairies weaving babies together from sticks and vines. The world was full of frightful things, but I knew about them and so I could help her. People in fairy tales dealt with changelings; I could hold Ruth close and explain to her that so could we. Her back was bowed and trembling. I pictured knobby hands plunged into my aunt's body, plucking out my real cousin, replacing this creature that scraped her insides and made her bleed.

*   *   *

The days following were tracked in Aunt Vera's ultrasound pictures.

My father sat Ruth down and explained that they were going to have to take the baby out of my aunt. He told her that this happened to a lot of women, all the time. He told her that the doctors would monitor the baby, so that it could stay inside my aunt Vera as long as possible, and then come out.

"They're leaving him in her?"

My father touched her shoulder. "Not for very long."

The ultrasounds were taken daily, and my aunt Vera sent copies of the pictures home with my father whenever he went to visit her. Sometimes they ended up on our fridge, sometimes facedown on the dining room table with mailed flyers for school events, sometimes set on top of Ruth's inflatable mattress. "That's gruesome," was all my mother said about it, not in earshot of my father. Some of the photographs looked like they had been drawn with white sand sprinkled over a black background, a suggestion of the baby. There were newer ones that did not look like the ultrasounds on TV. One of these was given pride of place on our fridge, a picture of the baby that showed its facial features as if they were sculpted out of mud, the flat nose, uncanny half-closed eyes, mouth small and carved, like the body of a clay vase caved inward with the press of a thumb. If Ruth and I were not already convinced that this was not a real child, that it was sculpted from dense earth and dead foliage, maybe this would have decided us.

On Saturday, my mother let us walk to the library. We took home, between us, all the books on fairies, even the thick collections of folklore intended for adults. I had read many of them already, but it seemed, still, essential to have them on hand.

The road from the library to my house ran along a hill. When you were close to the top there were, on one side of the street, the big homes of our wealthier classmates, houses with windowed faces and sprawling backyards, rough gravel driveways and solar-panel-topped garages. The ground on the other side arched into grass, the dry, blond kind that was never really dead or alive. This had been Ruth's and my favorite place for a while. It sloped down, farther on, into the haunted hill that bordered our school-yard, and felt, thus, loaded with power. That hill was just hard enough to climb to make us desperate for it. Some of the trees grew practically sideways out of the slope, and once we got high enough we could lean ourselves in the Vs between their branches and trunks, our knees bunched up to our chests, our hair sticking on the bark.

We left our packs by the road that day, wanting to be free of the strain of them. I loved to go up the hill on all fours, my back bowed like a werewolf and my knees going to pieces in the dirt. "Right here," I told Ruth, at the base of one of the biggest oak trees, and she scrambled up first. She crawled out over a branch low on her stomach, her shirt riding up so that she was dragging her belly over the bark.

I stayed closer to the trunk, leaning my back against it. "You should've let me go first," I told Ruth. "You're heavier than me."

Ruth shrugged, sitting up with her legs splayed open, like she was riding a horse.

"We should've brought the books up."

Ruth looked down at our backpacks, already brown with the dust a passing car had kicked up. "Yeah. Don't you know it anyway?"

Because of this confidence, I was willing to forgive her. "Sure."

The slope of the hill was steep and close beside us, so that I could reach back, sitting against the trunk, and brush the sharp ends of the low bushes with my fingers. It was easy to feel powerful here, above the street and close to the earth, and over the hill behind us that field where the girl had been mauled by the mountain lion. I imagined her ghost pink and translucent like a gummy bear, with indecent bloody rips in her throat and side. This was the wildest place I knew.

We had discussed, already, the signs of a changeling. Bad luck and strange, hard babies. "She wasn't even supposed to get pregnant," Ruth said. The miracle baby. That seemed to me to be the surest sign that maybe, like a character in a tale, Aunt Vera had had dealings with fairies, gotten what she wanted but not how she wanted it. What we were left to discuss, now, was what there was to be done.

"There might be more ways," I said, "when we read all the books." And Ruth nodded earnestly, making the branch sway under her. "You can use tongs, and hold the changeling in a fire." Down below, a group of older boys were passing, wearing football uniforms from the high school, kicking dirt up, and shouting at each other in the ringing, amorphous way of teenagers. I watched as they strayed close to our backpacks, glaring and wondering if they could see me.

"Or you can beat them with a switch, I read." I wasn't sure what a switch was. Something like a whip, I guessed. "Until they give up and leave, or they die."

"Hey!" one of the boys barked. "Hey!"

The branch bobbed as Ruth turned to look at them too, balancing herself with a hand splayed on the bark.

"How old are you?" he shouted. It was the boy in front, tall and big, carrying himself with the mysterious self-assurance of a high schooler. I couldn't have guessed how old *he* was. He looked, to me, twenty-five.

"Eleven!" I shouted back. His foot was close to my backpack, and I was mostly worried about this. If he kicked it over, there would be dirt on the library books, and he might well kick it over by accident, but I knew enough of the boys in my own grade that it seemed more dangerous to alert him to it, make it a weakness.

"Not you!" the boy next to him yelled, his voice ringing up the hill. "You." From where we were, and how close we were together, it was hard to be sure which of us he was shouting at, but, presumably, Ruth. "How old are you?"

"Ten!" Ruth called back to him.

"Shit!" the first boy exclaimed, turning away as if we'd disgusted him. "Shit! Ten!"

They went on then, knocking over my backpack but not seeming to mean to, and both of us watched the prickly backs of their necks, like the backs of warthogs, until they were gone. Later, it would be the same, despite the solemn effort Ruth made that summer to hide the shape of her body. Later, her age would be a less effective ward. I studied her, her eyes and the roundness of her cheeks, the places where sweat had smeared with dirt on her face, and wondered how they'd ever thought she was older than me.

"My mom has a fireplace," Ruth said, "but I don't think we have any switches."

*   *   *

The books gave us other ways, which seemed more manageable. Though my mother had seen us come through the living room, holding our dusty backpacks in front of our chests to try to manage the weight, we still hid the books in my room; in my pillowcase, behind the science kits that lined the top shelf of my closet. We read them after bedtime, both of us lying on our stomachs, on the cooling wood floor in front of my night-light, mouthing words by the glow. Ruth fell asleep, her cheek pressing against my shoulder, and I stroked her back, where her flesh caved inward toward her spine. How could either of us need siblings, having this?

If a changeling could be tricked into revealing itself it would go away, but the ways of tricking them seemed beyond us: gathering hundreds or thousands of pieces of silverware and placing them in front of the changeling, so that it would exclaim in shock; cooking a meal in the broken half of one eggshell. A changeling might be starved out, but this was not, we agreed, something we could convince Aunt Vera to try. If a changeling is taken, though, into the woods, and set on the ground there, the books said that the fairies would come and take it back, and in its place they would leave the real baby.

"The real baby is probably dead," Ruth said, her small voice rasping across my floorboards, lying so close to me that her breath tickled my face. I nodded. The fairies, surely, had no body in which to place a half-formed fetus, though I did imagine this briefly, a dark leather sack full of fairy-water for a child to grow in, or tucked and developing under the stretched skin of someone else, sewn into a thigh like with Zeus and Dionysus or an oviposited wasp egg.

"Probably."

"But at least the changeling will be gone," she said, and I put my arms around her, happy to hold her while she grieved her brother in the hypothetical. I kissed the crown of her head, the place that all her curls seemed to twist away from, which was nearly bare like the head of a baby.

My aunt Vera was scheduled to have a C-section at thirty weeks. We went to see her once more in the hospital, where my father surrounded her with flowers he had bought in the gift shop, laying them on the tables on both sides of her bed. "Oh, don't do that," she said, laughing. "The nurse will only move them." I took one out of a bouquet and put it on her chest, between her hands. She clasped them sweetly around it, and I thought that she looked like Sleeping Beauty or the painting of Ophelia on the cover of a book my mother owned.

Aunt Vera kept reaching for Ruth from her pale bed of flowers, holding her hand out in the air whenever Ruth drifted to the other side of the room, as if to gather her closer by a transparent thread between them. She would pull Ruth into the bed with her, half out of the awkward hard chair and close against her side. She would press her nose into Ruth's hair. "There's no reason to be scared, Ruthie," she murmured. Her arms jarred a little, side to side, as she shifted as if to rock Ruth, and Ruth did not move at all. "Are you scared?"

Ruth shrugged one shoulder. She was so still, a hard curve passing all the way from her jaw down her huddled spine. Aunt Vera stroked her hair, stroked a hand over her cheek, tapped the small, jutting bone of her chin with one of her soft fingers. "Don't be scared," she said, and kissed Ruth's forehead. "There's nothing better than having a brother, Ruthie." And she smiled at my father over Ruth's shoulder, almost shyly, almost like a little girl. I dragged my foot across the floor. "There's nothing," my aunt repeated, "better than that."

Later, after Ruth had slipped back to me, to our far corner of the room, and I caught her round wrist in my hand, my father sat in the chair at Aunt Vera's bedside, and put his arms around her while she cried a little. "I just—" she said, and she sniffled into his shoulder. "I just really wanted this to go differently. I really wanted to *have* a baby this time, you know. I really wanted everything to be natural."

My mother made a noise in her throat, low and displeased like the sound I thought a mountain lion might make. "Ruth," she said, "Judith. Why don't I take you girls down to the gift shop?" When the door was closed, she squatted down in front of Ruth and put a heavy palm on her shoulder. "Don't even listen to your mother right now."

Ruth turned her cheek away, her hair falling a little into her eyes. "It's all right."

Ruth talked with Aunt Vera on the phone, the night before they did the C-section. My father gave her his phone, and he let her sit in my mother's office, in my mother's soft desk chair that spun. I sat on my rug and lined up my praying mantises, the orchid mantis sitting at the front of the line, with its delicate thorax and the lines of petals. It looked, to me, so real.

"Why did you take the baby?" I asked it. "What do you want with a baby?"

I had never thought, really, of the baby in my aunt as my cousin, just as Ruth was, except actually related to me. Perhaps we could have been even closer than Ruth and me, made of the same stuff. It made me angry, all of a sudden, that the fairies had deprived me of that.

* * *

My father woke us in the middle of the night, shifting Ruth's air mattress gently with his toe so that it moved beneath us both like open water.

"Your baby brother's arrived," he said. "Do you want to go see him?"

Very quietly, in the half-woken darkness of the room, Ruth said, "He's not my brother."

"Of course he's your brother." There was warmth in my father's voice, in the green-lit curve of his smile. "Let's go and see him."

I held Ruth's hand in the backseat of the car. The streets were black, and longer than they were in the daytime, with the lamp-posts spilling pools of gold-dark light onto the asphalt. Ruth put her chin on my shoulder, moving her lips against my ear. "Don't let it trick you," she murmured.

I nodded.

My father and Ruth went to see Aunt Vera first. "They should have a private moment," he said, folding Ruth's hand in his. "We'll see if she's still awake." And my mother and I went to find the baby.

It was a small hospital, and the NICU wasn't full. Still, my mother had to have the changeling pointed out to us by a nurse. It was lying in a tub, at the far left of the room, under two yellow glowing lamps, so that it looked like it was splayed out in the sunshine.

"Well, God," my mother whispered, "he's so small."

Its head was overlarge, and the rest of its body thin and crumpled. Its skin was tinged an orangey color, and its face crinkled up, like an old man in a lot of pain, or like it didn't know how to make a right face. I thought of laying it down under a copse of trees, of the knotted fairy hands that would take it back.

"Oh, baby Nicky," My mother said. "Well, look at you."

"Why does it look like that?" Almost soundlessly, Ruth had come to stand beside us, her face leaning so close to the glass that I saw her breath fog it up. The changeling moved its fist with an aching, jerky movement, pulling it down over its own needle ribs. "It doesn't even look like a baby."

*   *   *

The changeling stayed at the hospital for another two weeks, though we didn't see it much during that time. It was not good for it to be out of its incubator very long, and when it could be, we were mostly told that Aunt Vera needed some time alone with Nicky, that we would see her and the new baby again soon.

When we saw the changeling with Aunt Vera, she held it to her breast with a tender awe that I had never seen her apply to anything. She pulled the collar of her blue dotted hospital gown low, and fitted the little body against her chest, arranging the small red limbs so that it was hugged up around her neck, and seemed to move even tighter to her when it squirmed. She cooed to it, rocking her whole body back and forth slowly. "Hush, little baby, don't say a word. Mama's gonna buy you a mockingbird." She seemed as if swallowed.

Ruth and I used these weeks planning.

When the fourteen days were past, my father drove with Aunt Vera to bring the changeling home from the hospital. My mother waited with Ruth and me, helping package meals that she and my father had made the previous night into Tupperware. "It's hard with a new baby," she said, pressing her hand against her forehead as if to wipe away sweat. "I'm sure your mother will have plenty of help, Ruth, but it is hard."

In her car, she reached into the backseat with a bottle of green Purell. "Scrub your hands well, both of you. It could really hurt Nicholas if he gets sick. Do you understand me?"

"Yes," Ruth and I both said, and we both dropped the Purell into our hands in glops. I watched the lump of it shiver in my palm, like the body of an alien, and raised it to my nose for the dizzy smell before scrubbing my hands together, working it between my fingers, down my wrists.

We put together a party in Aunt Vera's living room, just the
five of us and the changeling. My father tied blue balloons to the
chairs, in addition to foil ones with cartoon babies on them, and
my mother set a fruit tart my father had made on the table and
put a candle from the grocery store in the middle of it that said
"Nick." My aunt Vera sat on the couch, holding the changeling like
they were alone.

"Isn't he beautiful?" she kept saying. Her mouth stretched all
the way to its corners. Then she would touch the changeling's soft
stomach and coo, "Aren't you a miracle?"

The changeling had to be put back, after a little while, in the
heated crib, because it was not supposed to get too cold, and while
it rested there we all sat around Aunt Vera's low coffee table and
ate little slices of tart.

Aunt Vera fell asleep before she was done, her fork slipping
down to sit on her knee. My mother, carefully, pulled it out from
between her fingers as she cleared the plates.

"Can I hold the baby?" I asked.

"Not right now," my father said. "He's sleeping."

My mother took the plates into the kitchen. Ruth had gotten
up and gone to stand over the crib, her face leaning close to the
heat lamp so it lit her up as well.

"Careful, sweetheart," my father said.

"I will be."

In the kitchen, my mother's phone rang, and there was the
sound of her professional voice, clipped and sweet. In a different
voice, she said, "Shit," and called to my father. "Will you come
finish up the dishes?"

My father glanced back at us as he headed through the open
door, as if having some idea, but still he went. We heard the door
close as my mother let herself out into the backyard.

Ruth moved very quickly, lifting the changeling so steadily

and gently that it must not even have known it was being lifted. Under its thin red lids, I could see little eyes moving. I was worried that it would scream. It looked more like a baby now than it had before.

We carried it down the hall, with the blankets wrapped around it, held tightly. We went in our sock feet, without putting our shoes on. We left the door open, so as not to risk the sound of shutting it. When we were outside, and down the block a little, we put the changeling inside Ruth's backpack, fitting it in there straight up and very snugly. She held it against her chest, wearing the backpack on her front, so that the changeling would not be jostled so much and would stay asleep as long as possible.

The asphalt was hot through my socks, though we were coming close to sunset now. Not talking, solemn and afraid of being overheard, we walked. With every car that passed us, I half turned my body toward Ruth, trying to shield her from sight. Through the open top of her backpack, I could see the thin hair on the changeling's swollen head. I wondered how it had slept so long. Its hand, clenched up against the inside of Ruth's backpack, was so small, and each of its fingers so particular it looked like the hand of a real baby.

Our parents would be out looking for us very soon, I knew, and we walked along the edge of the road, and ducked behind houses when the backyards weren't fenced. We did not walk quickly. We did not want the changeling to wake up.

In front of us, the street was sloping, rising into our brown hill, in all its tawny hauntedness. What better place was there to return the changeling to? That hill, being ours, was more magical than any proper forest.

"Do you think ghosts are real?" Ruth asked me, thinking, maybe, of the hill also. I could feel my pulse pressing against my fingertips. My head was thick and dizzy. This felt like a very brave thing we were doing, because it was so frightening. In Ruth's backpack, the changeling stirred, bringing its curled fist up against its mouth. I lowered my voice, and looked away from it.

"Sure," I murmured, imagining that mountain-lion-mauled girl watching us, imagining fairies darting their glittering carapaces through the ragged gap of her ghost throat.

"Yeah." Ruth scraped her foot against the grass at the edge of the road. I wondered what she was doing, jarring the baby like that. "Have you ever met one?"

"What?" As if I would not have told her, before anyone else.

"I have," Ruth whispered. "I have. My mother's a ghost."

"Aunt Vera's not dead." Though I knew, already, and furiously, what she meant.

"Not her. My mother. She's dead, that's why I'm here. And she's a ghost. And when I'm frightened or upset, she comes and she's with me. I can feel her. She opens doors in my house and makes things creak. She was with me when I stayed with you, she said that this was all right. She said we were doing the right thing."

"She wasn't," I muttered. "She didn't." We were climbing the hill now, our feet sliding a little in the dust. That bit of scraggly lot was the closest things to woods we had. It opened, if you followed it far enough, into a park, which even had a river running through it and true groves of trees. We didn't need to go that far, though, only to the edge of the woods. The changeling was stirring insistently against Ruth's chest now, squirming, and she squeezed it to try to make it still. "Your mother's not even dead. How would you know if she was dead?"

"She is," Ruth said. I could see, not far ahead, the oak tree that we had been sitting on last time we came here. We would have to climb just a little past that, I decided. Just to the grove past that.

"Your mother's alive," I snapped at Ruth, too loud, my voice too much of a crack in the evening-stained air. A car blew past below us, and I waited until it was gone. "Your mother's alive," I said again. "She just didn't want you. Aunt Vera wanted you."

The changeling started to scream.

It was such an inhuman sound, splitting and ringing and awful. Ruth and I both clutched our ears, and she dropped her backpack, almost, caught it against her chest before it hit the ground. The changeling wailed again. Its eyes were open and set narrow. I knew it was going to stop us.

Ruth's mouth was a thin, tight line, and when she started to cry I didn't know what to do, so I pretended she wasn't crying. I took the changeling out of her backpack, switching it back and forth in my arms, trying to get the blanket that had come loose wrapped again. "Keep going," I said, and Ruth shook herself like she needed to rebalance her head between her shoulders. She went on all fours as the hillside steepened, knocking dust and pebbles down behind her. The changeling writhed in my arms, trying to press its little limbs free of the blanket. Its face was all wrung up, squeezed tight, and the sound it made was like pain, or terror.

Ruth got a foothold against a tree stump, and held her hands out so that I could pass her the changeling, and then I climbed up past her and she passed it to me, and in this way we went.

It was harder, moving so fast, and only one of us at a time, and in the growing dark. Halfway up, Ruth's foot slipped out from under her. She went a bit down the hillside, with a little cry that seemed to scrape open the inside of her throat. She caught herself against a tree branch, the muscles trembling hard in her arms, a struck bowstring, and then scrambled back up, bleeding from her knees and the bottom of her chin, biting her lower lip with muddy tears down her face.

Nearly at the hill's top, there was a copse of trees. The changeling had stopped crying now, and when I held it, it blinked at me, sluggish and baffled. As if it did not know what was happening to it.

The trees were oak and birch, the bark peeling and ashy and the ground prickling under our feet with oak leaves. I stepped on one wrong, and jumped, and almost dropped the changeling, but it didn't scream again. It was so silent.

"Is it dead?" Ruth asked, with a voice like the point of a needle. She sounded frightened.

"No."

I handed the changeling to her, at the edge of the trees. These were woods enough. And Ruth unwrapped it from its blanket and unzipped the yellow pajamas my aunt Vera had put it in. She took off the diaper too, squinching her face, and laid the baby down on the dry oak leaves.

"What do we do now?" she said. She was still crying, new tear tracks appearing in the dust on her cheeks. The changeling squirmed on the ground, turning its head, pressing its soft face into the sharp edges of the leaves.

Below us, my father's car turned the corner, and the baby screamed again, a renewed, painful sound.

Ruth and I both watched the car stop, watched my father and Aunt Vera get out. Aunt Vera was like nothing I had ever seen, narrow and stark as the birch trees, a ghost and a carved monument to herself.

"Ruth!" my father shouted. "Judith!"

Ruth was still looking down at the baby. Its head thrown all the way back, its mouth peeled open like a rotted fruit. She took a long, raspy breath in through her mouth, and started to sob. "I wish I'd never come here." She covered her face with both hands. She did not even look at me. "I wish I'd never come here. I don't want to be here. I wish I'd never come here."

I looked at Ruth, with her cut and bleeding hands, her tears peeling the dust away from her fingertips, dirty and with leaves in her hair. She did not look like me and never had, and she was ugly when she cried, a wrinkled, hurtful ugliness. And though I pitied her later, I hated her then, seeing for the first time in her something that had always been there and that I would know about, now, forever. Watching her stand, a few minutes later, in front of Aunt Vera, numb and unresisting when Aunt Vera pulled her scrabbling down the slope by her hair and slapped her, and they both stood in the aftermath, considering each other. Watching her at the onset of middle school, hunching her covered body in front of her locker like a mushroom sprung up in a yard, overnight and unwelcome. And watching her walk herself home after school, when Aunt Vera drove past her with Nicky in the car, and Ruth turned her head to catch her own face in the passing mirror of the window, and then spat on the ground only once the car was well past. Watching her, after, from a remove, like a wasp trapped, spindled and buzzing, under a jar.

I saw her now unbelonging, her rejection of us, of me, even as hard as I had tried to make her mine. How she was lost to me beyond hope of regaining and I was not sure, anymore, why I had even wanted her.

"Dad!" I shouted, calling down the hillside, calling away from Ruth's wet face that would not even look at me. "Nicky's here! Ruth brought him up here!"

Take Only What Belongs to You

To the Library of Congress, Esther carries a slim blue book, clutching it beneath her coat. Her free hand is jammed into her fleece-lined pocket, her fingers tapping against the fabric like the skin of a drum. With every breath, she feels as if she is trying to inhale under a great weight.

Beside her, Cora hums something unrecognizable, breathing white music into the winter air. She isn't even wearing her hood, and she looks like a character in a Christmas movie, flecks of snow caught up in her dark hair.

A corner of the book's cover presses into the meat of Esther's left breast. It's a volume of short stories, bound in old cloth, with a silver tree embossed on the front. The title page reads *Housecat, Wildcat: A Collection by Anais Casey.*

Most people are familiar with Casey's more famous work. Her story "Kitchen Things," about a woman who made a set of silverware from her husband's bones, was taught in a lot of college classes alongside "The Cask of Amontillado" and "The Yellow Wallpaper." English 220: Gothic Literature. "And of his femur I made a serving spoon."

They stop at the broad white steps of the library, and Cora steals the last sip of Esther's coffee before giving her a mocha-flavored kiss. "When do you think you'll be done?"

Esther bites her lip. Cora's said she's fine entertaining herself while Esther works—*It's D.C.*, she said, *I've never been before. I won't be bored*—but Esther still doesn't feel right saying she'll probably be here until the library closes. And back the next day. "I'm not sure."

Cora gives her a fond, tolerant look, which comforts Esther even as it irritates her. "Do you want to meet for lunch?"

Relieved, Esther nods. "Come back and get me when you're hungry?"

"No problem." Cora shakes her hair out, dislodging a little tumble of glittering snow, and clasps Esther's shoulder for a second, firm and steadying. "Good luck," she says, with an earnestness that Esther cannot help but smile back at, grateful.

When Cora waves goodbye, her bony fingers stand over the wool cuff of her coat like birthday candles. Esther is occasionally astonished by the beauty of Cora's individual components. This is—arguably—Esther's first real relationship, and she's unused to this new kind of intimacy; noticing the poetry of someone's knuckles, the fracture lines of dark hair sweat-stuck to a throat.

The manuscript reading room is less lovely than the rest of the library. No marble statues, no blue-and-gold frescoes. The room reminds Esther of college: the flat ceiling LEDs, plain tables, pocked navy carpeting. At the librarian's desk, Esther turns in her bag and identifies herself as the woman who called about the Anais Casey boxes. She feels, even as she recites this legitimizing phrase, like a trespasser.

The first story in *Housecat, Wildcat* is small and sad, a silver button of tragedy called "Slack Your Rope." It's a monologue delivered by a woman whose lover is to be hanged the next day.

The narrator will not name her lover or say what he is hanging for. It seems as though, in the patter of her speech, she is being asked by some invisible interviewer and refusing. "That part is not important. I won't tell you. I don't have to." And then, on the last page, she begins to list the things she would trade so he could be allowed to live:

> I would give you the sight of my eyes, I would give you my eldest daughter, I would give you myself, I would give you my little house with the thatched roof, I would give you my son in my stomach, I would give you my shoes.

*   *   *

Anais Casey was born Anais Hamilton in 1918 and raised unglamorously in a lower-middle-class suburb of New York. Her father was a translator and traveled often. Her mother was an alcoholic of the housewife variety, and so Anais was raised primarily by an older sister, Victoria, with whom she mostly quarreled.

Esther pictures Anais as very narrow, thinks of her as someone who fails to take up space. She feels a little guilty for this imagining, does not want to understand Anais as young and thin and pale and pretty, but she pictures her with too much tenderness to do otherwise. Tenderness and beauty are inextricable for Esther, though she wishes that they weren't and that her understanding of beauty was different.

Esther cannot say exactly when she began to fall in love. It's not a process she wants to minimize by pinning it somewhere specific, to an exact line in an exact story. But, in the titular story of *Housecat, Wildcat*, a girl, Tabby, goes away to boarding school and makes a friend, Alice, who is angelic, all gold and loveliness. It reads like a chapter of *Jane Eyre* until the two girls get up one morning and, without any reason, hold hands and walk into the woods. The rest of the story, its majority, comprises descriptions of survival—building fires with callusing hands, felling an injured deer, sleeping curled like pigeons in the trunk of a tree. It's one of Casey's earliest published stories and far from her best. But it belongs to Esther and is about love.

> *I always imagined that Alice had a beautiful secret knowledge, something that she kept from me, not out of cruelty. Out of savage kindness, I think, knowing I wouldn't be able to know in the same way she did, not wanting to hurt me like that. I did not like to think that she was confused, or frightened, but I did like, a little, having a secret knowledge she couldn't yet, knowing something about what we were that I couldn't tell her. I stroked the hair at the back of her neck, like she was a great cat curled in my lap. I thought I could be the first person to ever show her kindness, to ever know her for herself and love her. "I am going to make you a house in the trees," I told her. "I am going to grow all the boughs together so you can live there like a pear. I am going to bring you chocolate and cheese and not leave you alone." I wish that I had told her our secret then, but I thought I would have her forever.*

*   *   *

Esther is seated at a table. Anais Casey has thirty-nine boxes in the Library of Congress, and the letter Esther is here for is in Box 31, Folder C, but she asks to start at the beginning. The buildup feels necessary. Esther thinks there must be some threshold of context that will make her able to approach this letter.

The librarian fetches her request. He is a thin man, scholarly, big round glasses with gold rims and a first fine layer of wrinkles on his brown hands. Esther wonders if there is something here he defines as belonging to him, certain boxes he pulls when the room is empty.

There are only a few other people in the reading room. A fair-haired woman, perhaps a graduate student, in a red wool coat poking at her pink phone instead of the daunting stack of papers next to her; a frail man holding a trembling magnifying glass over a scroll of paper; a broad woman in a floral dress who keeps lifting a hand to her cap of curls to twist the strands. In the corner a gray water fountain hums, and the room smells of dust and distant cologne. It is not at all spiritual in the way Esther expected, but she still feels choked and uncertain of her own worth.

The librarian wheels out the cart, tells her, "Boxes one through six," with soft disinterest.

Esther thanks him, watches him amble back to his desk; watches the blond girl finally lose interest in her phone and, with a delicacy that Esther would not have credited her, lift the first page on her pile; watches the old man lay down his magnifying glass as if he needs to rest from it; thinks of snow crunching under Cora's shoes as she meanders toward the nearest museum. In this way she delays opening the first box.

*   *   *

Anais has a story, "The Stoddard Woods Angel," about a newly-wed woman. Her husband isn't cruel, and he doesn't beat her. He's fine. She doesn't mind him. But she keeps seeing a woman in the woods. The woman may be a ghost, always disappearing around blind corners. The new wife unspools pages and pages thinking about her—her fingers like slivers of light, her face a bowl of still water, her incredible, inevitable strangeness. The wife wants to know her so badly.

One evening, the wife is eating dinner with her husband, dry meat loaf and greens. She stands while he is speaking to her. She watches his mouth continue to work on its hinges, and turns from it. She walks into the uncanny darkness of the woods, intending to keep walking until she meets the woman, but the woman only appears to her at a distance. She is too like the strange and pale trees, and the ashen trees too like her. The wife comes close, is within fingertips' distance of her hem, then the woman disappears, reappearing a little farther off. Again and again this happens until the wife is hopelessly lost, not wishing, exactly, to go back, but out among the strange trees and alone.

*   *   *

All three of Anais Casey's biographers agree that she wasn't a lesbian. Only two of the books even reference sexuality. Esther emailed the biographers one at a time. The third was the first to respond, and his answer was a pretty clear negative. Only one of the other two replied, the woman who wrote *Kitchen Witch: The Life & Writing of Anais Casey*. She said, "Look, anyone can lie about anything in a letter. It's impossible to know every relevant detail. We can know what she said and say what we think is likely. I think it's unlikely." It was nice of her to write back.

The books that mention Anais's sexuality both quote from one letter she wrote to a friend in 1968.

> *It's not that it's very important to me, Harold, but I do wish, actually, that you hadn't alerted me to this. It's not worth my thinking about. Except that I wonder if it's possible, anymore, to say anything and be understood. [. . .] I assure you that if I have produced something unholy, I did not mean it.*

Esther first read this when she was twenty-one, in *Kitchen Witch*. Her forehead sweaty, pressed against a train's leather seat back, nauseated from the thick rosy perfume of the woman in front of her. Her impulse was to shut the book very quickly, as if to keep something from escaping, her palms pressed against either cover. Anais's rigid eyes peered between her fingers, and Esther reopened the book tenderly, turning that face against her thigh so she couldn't see it. She felt as if the air were pinching her, flat hands on all sides of her body; she felt laughed at. There was no more of the letter offered in either book, and though Esther emailed the biographer asking for a complete scan, she never received it.

Esther would have liked to come to D.C. years ago. But there was school, internships, and a lack of funds. Now she's an administrative assistant at a local college and makes just enough money to afford this trip, provided she splits the hotel with Cora.

Esther has only been with Cora five months, but it's been a promising five months, Esther's thoughts about her sticky and glowing like honeycomb. Esther's still not sure if it was a good idea to bring Cora along; it's not exactly a romantic first vacation together, sending her girlfriend out to wander the city while she pores over a dead woman's ephemera. Still, Esther can't deny that she's glad; Cora has a coaxing, cheerful warmth about her, and it's nice to know that whatever Esther finds here, she will not be alone with it.

Esther believes she will find something, though she is not, she tells herself, looking to catch anyone in a lie. It is only that she does not trust that a biographer would catch a belying turn of phrase, a bit of subtext, a hint. Those ellipses have been undoing her for three years.

* * *

The first story Esther showed Cora was "The Stoddard Woods Angel." It was their eighth date, and Esther watched Cora read it while sitting on the arm of the love seat in her apartment, looking over Cora's shoulder in the awful, rubbery silence. The story was only six pages, and Esther tried to see if she lingered over descriptions. "The Stoddard Woods Angel" was beautiful, and that was part of why Esther had chosen it, the other part being how blatant it seemed to her. Of Anais's stories, this one felt particularly clear-headed about its own meaning, its obliqueness thin and diaphanous as silk, almost a flirtation. Esther wanted to see recognition in Cora's brow and the curl of her fingers.

"Wow," Cora said, when she was finished, and dusted her palms together like she'd just done hard work.

"Right?" Esther reopened the book to give herself something to do with her hands.

> Turning from me, she was the brightest thing against the night, imprinted on my eye as afterimage and visual defect. I thought of Apollo and Daphne, of coming, finally, upon her as her body took an untouchable rigidity. If I could have seen her soft face at the edge of the river. If she had a real, human face. If I could turn her over and make a charm of her. That would have mattered. I think it would have mattered very much.

Esther has imagined reading Anais's paragraphs as love poetry.

Cora smiled, stretched until her spine gave a ratcheting crack. "Yeah. It's pretty spooky."

Esther waited. She pressed her hand on the arm of the love seat, muscle quivering a little under her own weight. She was suddenly afraid the sofa would collapse beneath her. Esther thought of how this story had made her feel the first time she read it, vivisected and pinned open, all the softest, pinkest parts of her exposed. And then every reading after, as if Anais reached into

that gap and pressed a curious finger to Esther's heart, softly fon-
dled the sack of her lung. The sweet stab of being touched somewhere so vulnerable, the low, sharp shock of being handled so
tenderly. She didn't want to lead Cora to water, didn't want to have
to. *I mean, it's there, right?* Esther thought, and her skin tightened
with embarrassment she couldn't pinpoint the origin of. *Don't you
see it too?*

Cora's lip flicked up, a nervous flash of white teeth. She laid a
hand light against Esther's knee. "It's beautiful. I get why you like
it so much."

* * *

The first page in the box is brittle. Esther swallows a dusty breath,
does a little marveling: Anais's handwriting, her sketches, her stories outlined in her jagged print, and then her typewritten manu-
scripts. Esther can imagine her at her writing desk, the kind with
a rolltop and twenty little drawers, an antique delicately carved
with flowers and scrolls in perfect complement to her clicking at
her typewriter.

This letter is from Anais's sister. July 1937. Anais would have
been in college. Esther knows she can't read every letter. She and
Cora are in D.C. for three days, and Esther has promised to reserve
one of those days to spend together. But she can read this one.

Annie,

Have seen the grades you have sent home. I hope you are trying
to improve your French now, but otherwise very good! Mother
& Father & I are all very proud of you. Am including a post-
card Father wrote you from London. He does not have your
address yet.

I should tell you that Roger is sick. Am sorry to start the letter like this, but I think he is going to die before you return in summer, and I don't want to have to surprise you with it. I will take some pictures of him so that you will have them after he is gone, but he is not as handsome as he was when you left. Has lost most of his fur.

Am also including some recipes from mother's diet book. Dreading how you are cooking for yourself there. You are very pretty if you only take care of yourself, and I don't think you're much aware of that.

Loving you,
Victoria

It's a revelation in its mundanities. Here is evidence that Anais really lived, that she had a pet, that she sat in her dormitory and read this letter, smudged it with her fingerprints. There they are, greasy in the corners. There is no biography that can compare to this, to reading Anais and touching what she touched.

Esther looks around the room, fervid, then presses her fingertips to Anais's gray fingerprints. Anais is alone in her dormitory, hearing the faint, ghosted voices of other people talking down the hall. It's snowing outside. Her pointed shoulders are pulled up around her ears against the cold, and Esther is touching just her fingers, warming them.

*   *   *

When Esther was fourteen, she told herself this story: Anais Casey writes in a large stone apartment. The building is gray, historic, somewhere between an academic hall and a castle, ivy lying over it like the tentacles of a Gothic, grasping beast. Esther sees Anais, initially, through the window, a flash of her very black hair, the sleeve of her white dress. Maybe Esther is sitting in a tree out-side, romantic, or in the building opposite, likewise trapped. Anais comes to the window. Her face is a pale mirror, curious and inviting.

In Anais's little room, they sit together on the bed. The rest of the house is far away, like Anais lives in the hand of a thrust-out arm. A fine layer of dust has settled over the room, and it seems to Esther like no one ever comes here, and even Anais moves only enough to cause regular, quiet weather patterns in the accumulating dirt. There is maybe a faded tapestry or a wooden carving hung on one wall. It isn't an ugly room; Esther would never consign her to ugliness.

They don't talk much. What would Esther say? She only opens her book with its silver tree embossed on the cover, turns to the story that is called, like the book, "Housecat, Wildcat."

"I wrote this when I was very young," Anais says, touching the page like it's the face of someone she loves. That is how Esther touches that page.

"I understood it," Esther says. She is clumsy even in her own fantasies. She struggles with the words. "I understood what you were saying about them." The word *lesbian* feels like it would embarrass them both, but Esther tries for it. She should want to say it to Anais, say the thing Anais could not write down about herself. Esther says, "They're in love," because it feels more grate-ful than calling all of them what they are.

She stops herself short of explaining Anais's own story to her. She is already so in the habit of explaining.

Anais says, "That's right." She doesn't look particularly proud or surprised. But she lifts her hand from the page and lets it fall lightly on Esther's upper arm. She has long, fine hands with bones that jut at the knuckles, ink stains on her fingertips, nails trimmed in neat crescents. Esther lends her warmth and delicate calluses.

"I understood," Esther says in that room with her and also from very far away, listening so carefully.

Sometimes Esther kisses Anais at the end of this story, but that is not the important part.

*   *   *

When Esther showed Cora the letter in *Kitchen Witch*, Cora read it with great care. Esther appreciated this, that she leaned in so far that her forehead nearly touched the page, her back an arch where Esther could see the bumps of her spine. Esther had always envied those bumps on skinny women, that delicate evidence of bones.

They were sitting in the outdoor café at the Norton Simon Museum, ducks bobbing on the green pond next to them, and Cora wiping the grease off her fingers on a napkin patterned with a Van Gogh. She sucked on her teeth, a little hiss, and turned her face up to Esther's.

"That's why I want to go to D.C.," Esther said, tearing her own napkin. "I want to see that letter."

Cora tilted her head. "Why?" Cora was a music teacher at an elementary school, finishing her last few months student teaching before she was certified. But Esther thought she would make a good therapist for that little head tilt and that unloaded *Why?*

It made Esther struggle for an answer, or rather for the precise and cogent phrasing of an answer. "I don't think it's right," she tried, and amended, "I don't think it's telling the truth. The whole truth. I think that if I saw it myself, I could understand it better."

"All right," Cora said. She was quiet a moment, expression thoughtful enough that Esther knew not to interrupt her. And then, voice tinged with pleasure in her own self-conscious spontaneity, "We should go."

It was the first time they would travel together, and Esther had doubts about that since she wouldn't have the focus or the time for entertaining Cora. But, with school out for winter break, Cora went unworriedly and so Esther did her best not to worry about it either. She liked the idea of having Cora along for support—she got tremors in her hands when she flew alone—but beyond that, no one had ever shown interest in a subject just because *Esther* was interested. Cora's curiosity, uncomprehending as it could be, made Esther want to open herself like a neglected vacation home. Shuck the curtains wide, dash from room to room sweeping dust off the shelves and shaking out the furniture covers, calling, *Yes, yes, I'm here, welcome. Come inside and look around.*

*   *   *

When Esther was in elementary school, her best friend was Hope. It's miraculous to her now the way that childhood friendships run, because she couldn't name, for all the money she's ever had, a single thing she and Hope had in common. They had gone to the same school for only one year before Hope's parents opted for homeschooling instead, but they were friends longer. Esther was dimly aware that Hope's family was Christian fundamentalist. Her awareness of what that meant was even vaguer, except that she had a list of forbidden topics of conversation that included dinosaurs, trick-or-treating, ghosts, and politics.

Of course, the omissions mattered more as they got older. Slowly, the list became longer or more relevant or both. Esther lost touch with Hope entirely sometime in high school, but for a while before that they saw each other a couple of times a year.

Esther had a fantasy around then, when she thought that she was very wise and very worldly and Hope lived in a glass coffin. Hope would be visiting her, sitting on her pink quilted coverlet, and then she'd say that she wanted to read Esther's books. She felt as if the world were keeping a secret from her. Her face would be pale and sweet as cake frosting, and Esther would trip over herself pulling books down from the shelves, scrambling to finally, *finally* give them a common language again. She would start Hope with Anais, open the book in her lap, pressing warm shoulder to warm shoulder on the bed until their bones slid together.

Or, after reading several stories, Hope would confess, haltingly, like she barely knew the words for it. She would say, "I think there's something wrong with me," and then just sit there, trying to chip language out of the silence. Esther would listen to her like a doctor, waiting for Hope to hook and dredge out all her feelings. And then she'd say, "It's okay. It's actually okay." She'd put her arms around Hope, and she'd kiss her just to show her that it was.

*   *   *

Cora gets Esther for lunch at eleven. Esther feels like she has barely been in the library. It's horribly strange to lift her head and see Cora silhouetted in the winter light, the acute angles of her elbows and the windy mane of her hair. She feels as if she has been snapped back to reality from the stretch of a long rubber band. Esther pulls her hands painfully away from the life-warm paper and follows Cora out into the daylight.

"Did you find it?"

Esther turns her shoulder toward Cora as they walk and wishes she had enough hair to hide her face. "I'm working up to it."

Cora considers her. "Working up to it?"

Something less lovely Esther is beginning to notice about Cora: how she can accuse without accusing. She's one of the least confrontational people Esther's ever met, and Esther doesn't know how to feel about that, but it lays an additional weight on her gentle questions. "It's all her letters and things," Esther says. "I mean, I want to see everything. I know we don't have time for me to see everything, but I'm not going to skip right to the end."

When Esther tried to explain Anais to Cora properly, it was

something she was angry to find she didn't really have words for, could only come at sideways by telling stories about herself. The credit she gives Cora is that she listened even without understanding, but Esther does wish now that she had understood.

Cora's arm closes around her shoulders, and Esther realizes she is steering her away from the road, which, yes, she'd been about to step into.

"It makes sense to go in order," Esther protests, leaning her cheek into Cora's thready coat. "But everything by the end of tomorrow. I promise."

Cora lets it go so easily that it makes Esther's stomach hurt. Cora chatters amicably about her morning, some monuments and an exhibit on Japanese photography. She takes her phone out and swipes through photographs, a child blowing a bubble so big that it distorts her, a model splayed in a field before a bridge, her robe falling away from an exposed breast. She is so stark, so confrontationally beautiful, that Esther looks away with a hard swallow bobbing in her throat.

Once they are in a coffee shop, the cold safely behind glass walls, Esther cannot keep herself from talking about Anais. She reels off what she has seen today. The letters, recipes, postcards, photographs. Photographs of Anais have always made Esther feel strange because she doesn't look anything like how Esther pictures her. The Anais Casey on the book jackets is a broad, prematurely aged woman with wiry, thinning hair and a small, wicked mouth like the beak of a jackdaw. She is clearly not comfortable smiling at the camera. And she is a good deal heavier than the woman Esther imagines, which is the part Esther feels guiltiest about. She too is always skinnier in her own fantasies.

Esther focuses on the letters, which have been wonderful. She has learned the kind of pen Anais made notes with, a black Sheaffer Admiral #5, that the first room she rented had a wasp nest, that as a toddler she was scolded for biting people. All this reality an embarrassment of riches. Cora is patient as Esther details letters from Victoria, from her parents, her school friends, her professors, her husband.

That is when Cora interrupts. "She was married?"

Esther thought she'd mentioned this. She shrugs, defensive. "What else was she supposed to do?"

*   *   *

Anais Hamilton met Leonard Casey in 1942. He was drafted in 1943. There isn't information about Anais's earlier relationships, and though they wrote to each other while he was away, they weren't engaged until his return. This is something Esther holds on to, all that "cat's away" time unaccounted for.

Casey was an arts reporter, not really anyone who would be known anymore. He does not have his own collection in the Library of Congress, and probably today his articles are read only by people researching his wife. Esther mostly skimmed over them in the biographies. She had always assumed that Leonard Casey was something that happened to Anais, something she had to accept, like a bad review, a social obligation.

On his letters to his future wife, Leonard Casey made sketches. He drew uneven cartoons of other soldiers, a jagged mountain range at the end of a paragraph, a miniature starburst of an anise seed near the top, labeled, so that his charm wouldn't be overshadowed by his poor artistry. And he was charming, easy, and amusing. Esther dreads having a grander picture of him, something like the war letters she's seen in documentaries, the acute earnestness of someone facing death. But Leonard Casey had not confronted his mortality by the time Esther had to break for lunch. Anais's responses are not included. Esther wonders what Leonard did with them. Unfortunately, he seems like the kind of man who would have treasured them in his breast pocket.

Anais and Leonard had a daughter, Gertrude, in 1948. Anais wrote and occasionally taught elementary school. She published two novels and four collections of short stories. She died in 1972, from complications during kidney surgery. Leonard died in '89.

Maybe because Esther is so young, she cannot conjure these last years of Anais. She tries to, not wanting to abandon her to them; she pinches crinkles into her skin, lets out her waist, and clouds her eyes, but seeing this Anais, Esther feels an aching pity and cannot hold the picture long.

The letter Esther returns to is one of Leonard's, his disordered, birdish script.

Anise,

I wish you'd send me a picture of yourself instead of poetry. Rather, I wish you'd send me a picture of yourself in addition to the poetry because I don't want you to think that I don't appreciate the poetry. You're awfully clever, but cleverness, not meaning you any offense, has got a limited aesthetic value, and I'm starting to forget your pretty face. As I recall it now, you've got a pimple in the center of your forehead and eyes like an old woman and three witch warts on your chin. Is this correct? Please do let me know.

My bunkmate—Georgie—was so drunk last week he pissed in my shoes, so be grateful you aren't here to look after me. I'd tell you a good story about that, but that's about all the story there is. See if you can do me one.

Have to sleep soon and want to get this out to you rather than wasting time thinking of more to say.

Love,
Leonard

Of course he would expect her to wash piss out of his shoes.

Esther skips along after that. She omits the letters from Victoria, which are dull and mostly the same: "Hope you are well." "I am not well and here is why." "I worry that you aren't dieting." Leonard's letters are better reading than the rest, excluding Anais's, but there are very few of her own letters in her papers. There's less sweetness further in, more fondness, amusement, a little creeping resentment, but he loved her, or he seems to have loved her.

It's not a problem for Esther that he loved her. For Esther's understanding of her, at least. It is not proof that she loved him, nor is it proof that she couldn't have loved him and also loved women. Anais could have loved her husband and still have meant to write so delicately and powerfully about what she did. Esther is not sure why she dislikes reading his letters so much.

It's a hard jolt, like a train shuddering to a stop, to come upon Gertrude Casey's birth announcement and a photo of the baby. She is red and damp, a liver cradled in her mother's arms, and the fact that the woman staring at the camera and not exactly smiling is Anais is so strange. She too is red, exertion red, her eyes glazed, sweat collecting under her nose, but she looks, for some value of the word, happy.

That baby is still alive. Esther puts the photograph aside very quickly.

*　*　*

By the time Cora returns in the evening, Esther's moved through the publication of *Housecat, Wildcat* and Anais's second book, *The Woman Responsible*. There are birthday cards for Gertrude, and the long letters and shopping lists of a marriage. Esther feels like someone has sucked her blood. The grad student in her red coat is still folded over her papers, and Esther suddenly wants to see her face. She thinks she'd have a very beautiful Pre-Raphaelite face.

After the coat check, Cora puts her arm around Esther and kisses the top of her head. They don't talk much until they are back in their hotel room with the heater on high and loud.

"So you found it?"

Esther, stripping off her coat, wonders if she looks that bad. She shakes her head. "Where did you go after lunch?"

"The National Portrait Gallery and the Freer." Cora sits on the edge of the bed. The hotel gave them two queen beds without asking. Cora wanted to say something, but Esther didn't.

"I just got to her daughter."

Cora picks up the TV guide and flips through it, fingers and pages flickering. Esther can't tell if she is actually indifferent or acting casual, but then, why wouldn't Cora be indifferent to this information? "How many kids did she have?"

"Just two. Only one's still alive." Esther had learned this from an interview with Gertrude she read in the *New Yorker*.

All the women in our neighborhood absolutely hated her. When we first moved in, she put one of them in a story. She changed the name of course, but she put one of them in a story, and it was one of her funny ones. For years, she would only let us read the funny ones. She was actually quite conservative about what we read—no sex, I mean, not much violence. We had it out about that.

The teachers liked her, though. Ben and I never came without our homework finished or our hair brushed or our shoes tied, and we knew to say "please," "ma'am," and "thank you." What I'm getting to is one of her stories, when Ben was a freshman I think, was going around and causing a commotion because—well, it was that one with the meat grinder. Yes,

*all the boys especially remember that one. And Ben's English
teacher thought it would be right to have a word with her about
it, say this sort of thing couldn't be going around school. She
thought that was the funniest thing. "It isn't my fault," she said.
"You ought to take trash like that away from them."*

That was not how Esther imagined Anais as a mother.

Cora hums. She sets the TV guide down and turns to consider
Esther directly, the tilt of her head slightly avian. "You know that
you don't have to read it, right?" she says, after an extended pause.

"I want to."

"I just—" Cora threads her fingers together over her stomach, fidgeting. Esther feels shitty for making her nervous. "Does it
really matter what she—whether she was gay or not, or whatever
she thought about queer people? *You're* still gay; those books still
meant a lot to you. Is reading some homophobic shit she wrote
going to do anything other than make you feel worse?"

Esther blanches, though she knows Cora is trying to be kind,
is partly embarrassed by that kindness. "I know that. That's not
why this matters to me." She sighs, rubs at her forehead, hands
still cold enough from their snowy walk here that her own touch
feels alien. "I wish I knew how to explain it." Though some child-
ish part does not think she should have to, is bitterly disappointed
that just handing over Anais's words was not explanation enough.

"That's okay. I'm not, like—I get that it's important to you."
Cora shakes her head, not in denial but as if she is trying to loosen
the right language from its crannies in her mind. "That's enough
for me. I just—I'm wondering if the best outcome here might be
not knowing?"

Esther tries to give Cora credit by considering this, but she
is already positive of her answer. "No." She goes over to the bed
and puts her chin on Cora's shoulder, tries to reassure them both

with a little body heat. "I don't ever want to not know something about her."

The only way to really love someone is to know them. Even more so, Esther thinks, that is what love can be broken down to. That is what intimacy is. With enough love you could conjure someone perfectly in a room they are not in.

* * *

Later, in bed and not asleep next to Cora, whose breathing against Esther's collarbone still sounds awake, Esther says, "It's just weird that she has a kid who's still alive."

Cora sighs and kisses the skin under Esther's earlobe.

"I mean"—Esther rolls over onto her back, staying in Cora's arms—"it's weird to me that there's this person still out there who knew her so well . . . who saw her every day of her life, for this huge part of her life." Gertrude probably never misremembers what her mother looks like.

"Yeah." Cora noses at the part of Esther's scalp where she's shaved close. "I love how your hair feels here."

"Thanks. You should read Julia Kristeva."

Cora snorts. "It's almost one."

"She's a literary theorist. She wrote this essay about abjection."

"What about abjection?"

When Esther lies in bed next to Cora, she feels too big, like she has swollen to take up more room than she's owed. She imagines that her flesh gives too softly under Cora's sharp weight, like the skin of a rotting fruit. She doesn't like the sound of Cora tolerating her, though maybe she shouldn't mind this time, because she doesn't remember enough of the Queer Theory course she read Kristeva in to answer many follow-up questions. Just this one concept, which stuck in her mind. "It's the idea that sometimes, when we reject someone or something—violently, that is—it's because we see ourselves in it."

"Oh." Cora is quiet for a minute. She runs her fingers up and down Esther's arm. When Esther looks over at her, her eyelids are dragging.

"You know, there was this friend she wrote to. For decades, I mean, since college. Her name was Emilia."

"Emilia," Cora repeats, trying to show she's listening. It occurs to Esther, blearily, that at least by description Cora looks a lot like how she's always imagined Anais. Slender, dark-haired, a little clever laughter in her smile. Does that mean anything? Esther wonders. Does it mean anything that she only just noticed?

But it's late, and Esther rolls onto her back, looks up at the bumps and slashes in the sloppy white paint on the hotel ceiling, and continues, "Her biographers mention her writing letters to Emilia, but there's only one in her papers. They only know they wrote for so long because Anais refers to Emilia in letters to other people." This is something else Esther has been hoping to find, a significant letter. She hasn't, only a note sent by Emilia in college in admiration of a story of Anais's published in a school periodical. It is very cheerful, dull, and ordinary.

Cora's breath is hot and her voice is sleepy against Esther's neck. "Do you think Emilia has them?"

It's probably Gertrude, Esther thinks. Esther decides that it is Gertrude. It makes her jaw lock so tight it hurts.

*   *   *

There is a story Esther tells herself, one she is still telling herself, where she meets Anais a little older.

Anais is conducting a book signing, and Esther is, for Anais, just one in a number of people. Esther sits down at her table—she gives her a broad, wooden library table, not one of those cheap folding ones. Anais's smile curls delicately at its corners, and her gray hair is thick and lovely. Anais does not mind taking the time to listen, and so Esther thanks her with great grace. She says something that sounds more perfect and original than anything anyone has ever said about a book they love, and Anais knows exactly what she means.

Cora has a movie coming-out story. Counselor at a summer music camp, just broken up with her boyfriend, teaching a bunch of sixth-graders to play the oboe, and falling for the flute teacher. One of the senior counselors caught them making out in a shed that smelled like rosin and brass instruments. Cora told Esther that story on their first date. Of course she did; it's a first-date story.

Esther envies Cora's unwavering moment of recognition, how kissing a girl was such clear evidence, how everything being dealt with from there began from that point of certainty.

Esther believes, a little, that Cora got this story because she looks like she could be cast in one of those movies. It is easier to tell a story about a beautiful woman. Of course, Esther had crushes, had Hope and her Algebra II tutor, whom she liked to imagine giving things to: pretty notebooks, packaged pastries from the corner store, a necklace. She had an entire adolescence of baffled, stomach-aching love. She would have preferred the sharp and clear-cut moment instead of the silence and then the language unspooling uselessly into it. Long phone calls with her mother during college in which Esther layered explanation over explanation until she had to hang up or risk faltering, asking for reassurance: *I mean, it's there, right? You see it too?*

When she was fourteen, fifteen, sixteen, the truest stories Esther could tell about herself were Anais's. The women were not only queer but also like Esther and grander and lovelier and more beautiful than Esther. Anais Casey, in her gray stone apartment, seated at her rolltop desk and writing across time.

*   *   *

Esther leaves Cora sleeping, a warm, graceful curve under the quilt. She walks to the library and asks the librarian if he can search the senders of the letters in Anais's papers. She asks him to search for letters from an Emilia Obel, please, and he taps the name into his computer in the jagged rhythm of a movie typist. His tweed is brown today. He pulls only one folder, pages through it with slick, careful fingers, and hands Esther the letter she has already read.

The page crinkles in her grip. "Thank you," she says, and smooths the paper back down into the file. "Could I have Box Thirty-One, please?"

He shrugs. "Should I take this back?"

"Yes, please."

Esther tells herself the beginning of "Housecat, Wildcat" until there is no more shaking in her hands.

On the morning before I went away to boarding school, my mother made eggs for breakfast and let me take one to tell my fortune. I poured the egg white into hot water and picked out shapes in the cooking tendrils: a star, a leopard, the lifting anchor of a ship. Something very beautiful was going to happen to me. My suitcase stood by the door, full of dark blue socks and oxford shirts, waiting. But I did not want to go to Rowland Girls' School. I wanted to crawl under the porch stairs, lie down, forget language, let my teeth fall out, and become a soft, sleeping animal.

Esther finds the letter, uncut and unbracketed.

Harold,

Thank you for the letter. It came at the most brutally unkind of times. Gertrude has caught the flu, and Ben has got it from her. L has exiled himself to the far corners of the house so his Work may not be interfered with.

Do not think I overlooked the review you sent. I wish you wouldn't. Am beginning to think that the people who write for newspapers do not read books at all. I am including L in this because I know that he does not. There is nothing else to say about it.

It's not that it's very important to me, Harold, but I do wish, actually, that you hadn't alerted me to this. It's not worth my thinking about. Except that I wonder if it's possible, anymore, to say anything and be understood. I write a story about a woman, and I am all at once a pervert. I find myself wondering, you know, if it is worth writing at all. If it is impossible to be understood, if it is only possible to be corrupted, and to be so vulgarly corrupted, is it worth writing at all?

And I do wonder if Mr. Clement intended to say anything about me, and if he is not the only one. Who do these reviewers imagine I am, I wonder? Do they imagine that I do not have a husband and children, like anyone? Does Mr. Clement imagine that his words do not have consequences for me?

Perhaps I have never, not in a word, been understood at all.

All this to say: I assure you that if I have produced something unholy, I did not mean it.

Yours, wearily,

Anais

*   *   *

There's a story at the end of *Housecat, Wildcat* titled "Friendly Strangers," about a young woman who is disowned. Not by, or only by, her parents, though it begins with them. She comes home from college for a holiday. No one picks her up at the train station, but she is able to find a taxi, and when she gets to her house, her keys turn the lock on the door. The people inside, though, assure her that they cannot be her parents. She knows that they must be. She is in all their photographs; that face is her very own face. But they tell her, "No, you are not ours. We don't know where you came from, but you are not ours." And the thing is, they are very different from the people she remembers; she becomes convinced that they must not belong to her. She turns from them and attempts to go to the house of an old family friend, to her grandparents, to an aunt. They, each of them, turn her away. "We don't know where you came from," they say, "but you are not ours." And she cannot disagree because they are not hers either. They are not the people she was sure she knew.

She boards the first train back to school, but when she reaches her dormitory, she is greeted by one of her housemates, who shakes her head and says, "I don't know you. You aren't one of ours."

The girl finds that she is not able to recognize anyone, and when she goes to the housing office, confused and only wanting somewhere to stay for the night, she cannot give her name when they ask for it. She doesn't know it, it isn't hers, and she has nothing that belongs to her.

Esther goes back to the hotel, forgetting her jacket at the coat check. Cora is still lying in bed, watching a morning show with glazed half interest. She sits up a little, and here's something nice: she doesn't ask any questions when she sees Esther's expression, just holds her arms out and lets Esther climb into them.

"Okay," Esther says after a while, snuffling a little even though she hasn't been crying.

"Okay?" Cora says. "So you read it?"

"It's just what they said it would be. A little more, I guess."

Esther buries her face in Cora's shoulder, her warm skin and the cheap cotton strap of her tank top. She breathes. Cora's hand strokes up her back, hovers at the crest of Esther's spine, a warm ghost of a touch, and then settles on the back of her skull. Cora cups her gently as an egg, and Esther nearly cries from it.

"I wish . . ." Cora's voice startles Esther, and she hesitates a moment, so Esther knocks her forehead against the soft skin of Cora's neck, not sure whether she is reassuring or seeking reassurance. Regardless, Cora is warm there. "I'm sorry. I wish I understood enough to help."

Esther wishes she did too. Esther wishes she had better language for what she was feeling, or any language at all. She wishes she didn't feel so close to some wretched, adolescent cliché—*nobody understands me.* When Esther was an adolescent, though, Anais had seemed to understand her, in a way so complete and novel that Esther had felt a window open between their two lives. The hubris of this, in retrospect, is humiliating. Still, Esther takes a wavering breath and presses her mouth to the hot, thin skin just below Cora's jaw, where she can feel Cora's pulse beating against her lips. Still she says, "It's all right, that's all right," and then "I'm glad you're here." After a moment, Cora begins to stroke her hair.

*   *   *

Cora suggests they go to the Smithsonian that afternoon, but Esther returns to the library. She doesn't explain herself, though Cora also doesn't try to make her. She pulls Box 31 again, Folder C. She lifts that letter. Isn't it strange that she wants to read it again? But Esther wants to make herself know it.

There is another letter under it in the folder, and Esther lifts it only because the handwriting is unfamiliar.

The tag on it designates the sender as Obel, Emily. And Esther scoffs, a sound that catches roughly in her throat. She looks at the librarian with his curly head bent over his keyboard. She could laugh at him. *You ass*, she thinks, *you filed it wrong.*

A

I have been thinking of you very often since we last spoke. I am sorry that it took me so long to write, and there is more that I would like to say to you than I think I can say. I hope that Trudy and Ben are well, and that Leonard is well also, and that you are the very best of all of them.

I have been thinking of your last story without stop since I read it. Between you and it, that is a lot of my mind you have occupied. I think the last story was like an egg. That is not a metaphor I'm going to explain to you. I am trying my hand at them now too, and if you can tell me how it was like an egg and you are right, then maybe I will tell you more of what I thought of it.

I also want you to know that you were very beautiful the last time I saw you. The silver in your hair is more becoming than you think it is, but more than that, I don't think you know how well you have made yourself from yourself. I think you would be much happier if you knew how clearly I am able to see you. Sometimes I feel it is just me who really knows you.

With love,

E

So, there is that.

Esther reads this letter three times, and she doesn't know what it makes her feel, only that it opens a hole in her lung with bright rims like burning paper. She thinks of Gertrude, who might have the rest of these letters. Or an address at which Emilia can be contacted. She tries to imagine a letter she could write that Anais would ever want her daughter to read.

If Esther saw Anais Casey walking down the street—walking down the street, holding hands with her daughter—she would not know her. There is a fair, dark-haired woman who wrote books directly to Esther, and there is Anais Casey. There is Anais Casey, who may have loved her husband, who may have loved this woman, who may have loved neither of them or both. But who said that she did not want this definition Esther has, for years, draped over her. If she is to be believed, if her writing is to be believed.

Esther listened to a recording of Anais reading one of her own stories once, just one scratchy recording. She had to turn it off because she did not recognize the voice and hated it.

She pictures Emilia Obel with reddish-brown hair and a quick smile and then as a thin, worrying housewife with a pen between her fingers. A disembodied hand, almost, but capable of love.

This is how Esther feels, disembodied. Without body, without a place within herself to return to.

Cora was in part correct and the biographers who responded to Esther's emails were correct. Both of them. That the best outcome is not knowing because that is the only outcome; there is only not to know.

Ester cannot know Anais—she is not hers.

On her way out, she stops at the coat check. She's handed her gray down coat in a rustling bundle, her shoulder bag. She points over the clerk's shoulder to where *Housecat, Wildcat* rests in a cubbyhole, its silver tree catching a little of the LED light. "That book back there too. That's mine."

Fiddler, Fool Pair

The game has been running under-the-hill since before London was new and it may well continue under-the-hill long after London is gone. Even the boxy arrival of the modern calendar has failed to persuade its custodians; they do not keep to a human schedule. Like trees and cliff faces, the game under-the-hill answers to a more biological kind of time. Only and always, it plays when the moon is new.

Naomi leaves the library at five, in the height of midsummer, shoulder bag heavy against her side. When the moon is new, Naomi has a routine. She walks from the library to Victoria Station and stops to buy two snack bars and two bottles of water, then boards the Metropolitan line toward Chesham. When a seat opens, she pulls a thick notebook from her bag to lay across her knees. Naomi's handwriting is small and precise; her ex-girlfriend said once that each word looked like a city for unhappy people, but Naomi likes her script. She likes her notebook, with its flashes of canary-yellow highlighter and the inky smudges of her fingerprints at its corners. All its little cities are full of gold.

When she disembarks, Naomi secures her research in her bag,

touches the pages of the notebook once, twice as she slips through the small evening crowd in the station. On her walk to the River Chess, she lapses in and out of half-memorized old rhyme, counts her steps by seven, *one for sorrow, two for mirth.* By the time Naomi comes within sight of the hill, the sky has turned a suffocating purple, almost dark.

Nearly three years ago, when she made this journey the first time, Naomi was planning to write her graduate thesis on gambling in fairy tales. It's a popular motif; dice games with death, wagers on one's soul. Folktales rarely locate themselves specifically, rarely name landmarks, and so it was curiosity that first made Naomi hike out to the old, tumbling hill by the Chess; curiosity or the interior propulsion of a narrative. Fairy tales have laws, Naomi knows, which is why she loves them. She finds a deep aesthetic satisfaction in that defining and organizing of things, which is maybe why her childhood heroes were zoologists and mapmakers, astronomers and botanists, researchers who created meaning out of raw presence.

It might have been luck or it might've been the law and logic of the fairy tale, that that first time Naomi walked past the hill, someone else was going into it. The infinitesimal odds transfix her either way, that visible hinge where her life pivoted on coincidence. Naomi standing with her bare ankles in the Chess, her shoes discarded on the bank, watching a woman come to the base of the hillside and pause, holding herself still as a praying mantis on a leaf, and then plunge smoothly into the earth. The place where her body entered the ground is a little greener than the rest. Foxglove grows graciously out of it.

There's no getting used to that passage under-the-hill. Naomi would call herself a steady person, comfortable with a measured amount of danger. Still, when she walks into the green earth, she shuts her eyes, holds her breath, her pulse races in her wrists. The only truly bad moment is when the dirt is all around her, damp and hot and always heavier than she's prepared for. She comes out on the other side choking and has to balance herself with her palm shoved against the soft wall.

Inside, the hill caverns open around her. Its ceiling is shot through with oak roots like veins in the roof of a mouth, little golden lanterns hung all over them and dripping their convivial light onto the floor. At the center of the room is a sturdy table, like one might find in any number of pubs, and a small party gathering at it like one could not find anywhere else.

Here is the House: in this case, represented by one individual. Naomi calls her Magpie, with good reason. Her body is narrow and avian, barbed at every angle. She wears a gown of oily black feathers that may not be a gown at all, and the long arch of her face calls to mind a plague doctor's mask. Most folklore agrees that true names hold power among the fair folk. Naomi has never heard them used here, only gestures and titles, Sir and Lady; perhaps this is why, or perhaps they have no names at all. For the sake of caution, when she is under-the-hill, Naomi calls herself Fiddler.

Their dealer is already seated. Naomi calls him Menagerie; a fair man in two, but not three, senses of the word, with smooth limbs like rolled-out wax. The folk have captured the idea of a human appearance, Naomi thinks: four limbs, a head, fingered hands, and two eyes. She cannot yet tell if their unique interpretations are accidental or stylistic.

The London Den plays a game called Midsummer Switch. It's played with a sixty-three-card deck in three suits: White, Black, and Blood. The cards assemble into hands first by familiar poker rules, pairs and triplicates, and then symbolically, according to their nature. There's a thrill, tingling sweetly at the back of Naomi's tongue, in gathering these archetypes into the loose shapes of stories—Treason, a lower-ranking hand, consists of a Duke, Knight, Horseman, and Cupbearer, but the hand is invalidated by the presence of a Queen. The best possible hand is the Full Court, a Queen High, Consort, Prince, and four of the seven remaining court cards, one of which is the Fiddler, who cradles a bone instrument tenderly against his cheek, like he's listening for the music inside. The stakes are too high to enjoy this game, but Naomi can't always help it. She likes to imagine that she is the first person ever to write down the rules.

The third party in the room is, ostensibly, human, perhaps in her early fifties. Her gray hair is cropped close to her skull and she wears a sharp black pantsuit. Naomi has seen her here before, and every time the woman looks like she has just come from a board meeting. Her hands, resting on the table, are a creation of delicate metal, silver jointed fingers and gears whirring gently in her knuckles. In her notes, Naomi calls this woman Oracle, after yet another of the cards.

Menagerie shuffles the deck with a snap loud enough to turn Naomi's head and then greets her impassively, "Fiddler."

"Sir."

His eyes flicker and slit. Naomi may have been incorrect about the manner of address. She may have made a mistake. Her pulse jumps and she presses her tongue to the dry roof of her mouth.

It's impossible not to make mistakes beneath the hill, where there are laws for everything; esoteric, unspoken, and compulsory. What was Naomi wrong about—gender, her relative station, should she have bowed, curtsied, remained silent? If mistakes can't be avoided, what matters is tracking them precisely, not making the big mistakes or the wrong ones. It would be easier if Naomi could write things down while she was here. There are silver trays by the table filled with candied violets and rose cakes, pheasant on a bed of curling fern, a bowl of softly luminescent fruit. Naomi thinks of Christina Rossetti. *Who knows upon what soil they've fed their hungry thirsty roots?* The wrong mistake would be to eat these.

"With what have you come to play?" There's something dead in the motion of Menagerie's pale lips, almost like Claymation.

Every time, he greets her with that question, as he greets every player that comes through the hillside. The folk are deliberate in a way Naomi finds appealing; formulaic in the same way the stories about them are formulaic. Observing them, Naomi is touched by the same thrill that she imagines she might feel looking into the belly of an astonishingly well-constructed watch, the clockwork components numerous and intricate, but each one solid, and, with enough patience, comprehensible.

From her bag, Naomi fishes out the knife she won last time she came here. She'll be glad to be rid of it. Though it's supposedly enchanted, none of the tests she thought up for it have managed to reveal how exactly. And she doesn't like taking it on the tube. Menagerie accepts her offering with a clockwork incline of his head. "Seat thyself and fare thee well."

Naomi is a good gambler for all the usual reasons. She bets small and nothing she is unwilling to lose. She plays close and folds early. Naomi is also a good gambler because she isn't invested in winning. She has won things down here; her favorite prize was a copy of Sophocles's lost play *Clytemnestra*, perfectly preserved in the original Greek. Besides that, a small assortment of magical artifacts, and other, stranger prizes, mostly useless to her. In the third game every night, the House offers a favor, a fairy-tale-style wish, its possibilities nigh limitless, but this is not what Naomi plays for either.

For three years, the notebook in her bag has been swelling with observations on a secret people. Someday, she'll have a treatise of publishable quality. Someday, she will have enough information for coworkers, research assistants, headlines, the dependable imprint of her name on a book cover. Naomi has not shown this notebook to anyone else yet. She keeps no copies. Her project is, for the moment, too infant and dangerous, though she couldn't say whether she worries more about being followed or plagiarized. She is far from the first person to discover this place, but in this age of documentation, of hard evidence, chemical tests, neat rows of footnotes at the bottom of the page, Naomi is determined to be the first person to document it.

People would argue—people will argue—that it is selfish of her to keep this to herself. Not to tell someone with more credentials, find some research agency to take the little snow globe of the hill from her hands and crack it open. Naomi is willing to admit that she might be selfish. Self-involved, at least; she spends more time within herself than some seem to, and has never worked well with others. It's not as simple as that, though. This place is not built for traditional methods, for the rough edges of cooperation and bureaucracy. This is not first contact, the fair folk are well aware of humanity; if they wanted to be better known, they would be already. And they are dangerous.

The last two players enter together. They come, like Naomi did, through the hillside.

She knows one of them, though she doesn't know his name any longer. The place where she did is a scar in her mind, smooth and pale. The place where she wrote it down in her notebook is the same. This is how she knows that he came under-the-hill with his real name, did not take Naomi's pseudonymous caution, because he could not have bet and lost a name that wasn't his. For her purposes, Naomi identifies him as Cupbearer, one of the cards, and it evokes, for her, the image of Ganymede in the talons of the eagle. Not inappropriate.

When Naomi first encountered this boy, he was beautiful in

a romantic—it would be accurate, if ironic, to say *elfin*—sense. When she was green to the game, she thought he might be one of the folk. He looked how she pictured Tam Lin: long golden hair, rose-pink cheeks, that androgynous beauty common to the fay. He was missing, then, two fingers down to the knuckle on his right hand, music, and a few of his teeth. He was dressed very well.

There is still something arresting about Cupbearer's appearance, the way the appearance of a hairless cat is arresting. His mouth and nose are blank cuts in his face and he breathes with a faint, rasping whistle. Draped over the back of Menagerie's seat is a shawl woven of fine golden hair. Even the *eyelashes*. Naomi has to give him credit for the creativity of betting those. The socket of his remaining eye is gummy and pink, the pupil utterly colorless.

Cupbearer has lost other things since Naomi has known him: Reading, writing, his voice and tongue on separate occasions. Every poem he ever learned, dancing. Pleasure in food and pleasure in sex. Smell. Fear, color, sleep. And, once, a pair of expensive-looking leather shoes. Naomi has no way of knowing what first brought him under-the-hill, if he came seeking a favor from the folk or just out of reckless curiosity. If he ever had a purpose here, Naomi can't imagine it's survived his ever-deepening spiral of sunk cost. Every night she's seen him play, he's gone full-tilt. Sometimes he wins a piece of himself back from a returning player, but never enough to justify the risk and usually less than he loses. If he ever won the favor, though, he could ask Magpie to restore him to himself, and maybe this is just enough hope to keep him from finding his better judgment. Or maybe that too was bet and lost before Naomi even encountered him. He isn't the only gambler she's seen haunt the game this way, but he is one of the worst off and seems unable to keep himself from returning.

Months ago, Naomi won his dancing. She can waltz very well now, do a half-decent tango and foxtrot. She also won his fear, which she joined another round just to get rid of, and all the poems he'd ever memorized, which she will keep because she likes poetry. It wouldn't do any good to feel guilty about this, and Naomi presses her heel firmly to the emotion when something under-the-hill does coax it out of her. Worse things have been bet and lost here. She once saw a pregnant woman gamble and lose her firstborn child. Blame the fairy tale that put that in her mind. *We are shaped by our legends*, Naomi thought, and then wrote that line down on the ride home. The game under-the-hill may be awful, but it shines with fascination. Say that Naomi is like a war photographer. Doesn't someone have to be loyal, first, to the preservation of the record?

Cupbearer's companion Naomi has not seen before. He's shorter than Cupbearer, broader in the shoulders, and more mundane in appearance, almost jarring in this setting. He's wearing a plaid button-down and his head is capped with curls that remind Naomi of a Jazz Age pinup girl's.

Menagerie shuffles the cards again, like snapping your fingers at a dog. "With what have you come to play?"

"With you," the boy says, confused and as if the answer is automatic. Cupbearer shakes his bare head, and shoulders past his friend. He performs a sweeping gesture, from his feet to his face.

Menagerie considers him. Naomi theorizes that the fair folk, much like apes, smile mainly to show their teeth. "With your own body and soul?"

Cupbearer nods.

"Seat thyself and fare thee well."

The strange boy, who is hardly strange enough to be interesting, is trembling a little. Naomi can see it in the ends of his hair.

"With what have you come to play?" Menagerie asks him.

"With my own body and soul."

Naomi winces. He must think that's the prescribed response.

After he's directed to sit, he leans forward to examine the goblet in front of him. Cupbearer covers it, holding it still even when the boy tries to pull it away and peer over the rim. The wine casts a gentle light on their skin, violet on Cupbearer's pale hand and softer in its small circle across the boy's nose, over his flushing cheeks. His curiosity, at least, Naomi finds sympathetic. He is cute in an exactly traditional way, like a puppy.

He lifts his face suddenly, and Naomi turns away. Usually the humans here try not to look at each other.

Once Magpie is seated, Menagerie spits the cards across the table. Three for each player; they're illustrated in bold, complex lines, all shaded in a single color. Naomi studies her hand. Black Hound, Black Cat, Blood Fool. The latter dances on one foot like the Hanged Man tarot card. The Hound and the Cat together can be part of a Menagerie or Sorceress hand. Menagerie is a valuable hand, only beaten by a Full Court, and it requires a Queen High and a specific retinue of animals, whereas the Sorceress can be filled out with an Oracle, Witch, or Changeling and any of the animal cards. Much more achievable and, being the fourth-ranked hand, still with a good chance of winning, that would be wisest. But the Menagerie is more exciting, an easy mistake for even an experienced player to make with a slight excess of optimism. So that is what Naomi will play toward, and how she will lose.

Risk management is key to Naomi's research under-the-hill. The game's stakes escalate with each round of bets—the more she plays, the more and worse she may have to forfeit. And since the prizes are incidental to Naomi's purpose here, winning big carries dangers of its own. Most of the human players seem to be drawn here by Magpie's promised favor, that personal miracle to salve whatever ache originally set them wandering through the world's strange, dark places. Naomi has yet to encounter anyone fool enough to win it and still keep returning. Like a fish goug-

ing itself on a hook, tearing free at the last instant and making off
with the bait in its bloody jaws, then reversing course to see if the
hook has anything more to offer.

Not playing isn't an option, they are only invited into the
hill for this purpose, and folding too often courts even more
attention—what casino likes a cautious gambler? So Naomi carefully measures risk against risk, and makes herself an acceptable
budget of losses.

It's easy enough, now that she's been playing for a while, to
cycle previous games' prizes back into the pot. Tonight: the knife,
Cupbearer's dancing, other minor sacrifices. However, she considers it wise to lose something of her own on occasion, not to seem
competent enough to game the system, though she wonders if she
might be, given the chance. Of her own things, Naomi has lost:
her left pinkie finger, the memories of her first kiss and of her sister's birth. The color red, a ring her father left her, and the taste of
blackberries with cream.

The game advantages new players. It's possible to bet small
things until you run out of small things. Naomi does miss
blackberries.

"Bets."

They begin with the woman on Magpie's right, whom Naomi
calls Oracle. Her hands whir softly as she lifts a previously unseen
cat from beneath the table, its body limp as a fur coat in her hands.
"Bet. My familiar." The cat, when she sets it down, arches its white
back without hissing, and blinks in a strangely lifeless way, like
one of those dolls with weighted eyelids.

The system here is imprecise, the value of a bet determined
partially by how interesting the item is to the others at the table
but also by what it means to the player to lose it. The most material things, the most replaceable, always fall early.

Naomi puts her knife down. "Call. Enchanted blade."

Cupbearer is squinting at his cards single-eyed. Probably, he is having trouble seeing. He motions, with his free hand, to his jacket.

Magpie considers him. The material of her face looks like something other than skin. The gold edges of her cards brush her beak. "Child, you undersell me."

Without hesitation, Cupbearer lays his cards facedown on the table and holds up his pinkie and ring fingers.

"Two fingers and the coat?" asks Menagerie.

Cupbearer nods.

The boy next to him presses a sound through his teeth. Naomi will need a name for him. Hound, perhaps, for those wide, pleading eyes. When it's his turn, he chews his bottom lip. "What can I—" he begins, and then swallows, puts his shoulders back. Naomi has always been unsettled by people who overflow like this, pour feeling uselessly from their faces and bodies. Here there's no quarter for that kind of human untidiness. "Call. What's living in my garden."

He is testing the betting system. Naomi remembers that, though she was more deliberate, wiser.

There is a folktale called "The Girl Without Hands" that frightened Naomi very much as a child. The story is about a man to whom the devil offered a great deal of wealth in exchange for whatever was behind his barn, where nothing but an old apple tree grew. He agreed, not knowing that his daughter was picking apples. Naomi would hope that whoever speaks so vaguely with the folk knows who walks in their garden.

Magpie calls and produces a small glass object from a fold in her feathered garment. She holds it up between two hooked black nails, lets the candlelight spark off it. "A vial of my own blood."

Naomi stares into the center of the table as Menagerie deals another round. The vial is the size of her thumb, and Magpie's blood in it is black as her feathers, with the same oily sheen. The plan had been to lose this game, then fold early in the second and third as if spooked into caution. This way she could observe most of the game without distraction. But the need for secrecy has made it essentially impossible for her to collect biological specimens from the folk. What could a chemical analysis of that blood reveal? A DNA test? Naomi's mouth waters. She picks up her cards.

Blood Changeling, White Death, Blood Serpent. Changeling and Serpent can both fill out the Sorceress hand. There is still time for Naomi to play toward that instead; she's done nothing to indicate a strategy yet. And she has a real chance at a mixed-suit Sorceress, which has a real chance at winning.

Is this a mistake? Is it a mistake that it is acceptable to make? Naomi presses her tongue against the roof of her mouth. She could always lose in the second round.

"Bets."

They will start with Magpie this time, and go the other way.

"Bet." Her voice is fascinating, a rustling susurration. Naomi would love to see Magpie's vocal cords. She sets a basket of shimmering fruits on the table, not too apparently different from the ones already laid out, except perhaps of higher quality, glittering with dew. *Sweeter than honey from the rock, stronger than man-rejoicing wine.* Fairy food won might be fairy food safe to eat. How many people taste something like that and ever get to go above the hill again? Naomi might be the only one living.

Next.

There is Hound's shaky intake of breath, uncertain. Cupbearer, beside him, begins to lean over, and Oracle says, without lifting her eyes from her cards, "Immediate forfeit."

Cupbearer sits back.

Naomi wonders about Oracle, whose name was not quite random. Of any of the humans, excepting, perhaps, Naomi herself,

she seems to have the best idea of what's going on, and a compo-
sure even Naomi envies.

"Bet." Hound looks down at his cards. "My first kiss."

Cupbearer taps the table with his knuckles. Naomi wonders,
suddenly, if he is unable to bet concepts now, constrained to those
things to which he can gesture. He motions with his hand toward
his throat, inhales two sharp breaths. His life? No, too early for
that. Hand drifting from throat to heart. Hound is leaning forward, as if he has come under the same impression, chewing his
lip, covering half of his face with his hand, like a child waiting for
a jump scare in a horror movie. Cupbearer holds up one finger.

"A year of your life?"

He nods.

Hound says, "Jesus fucking Christ."

What does Naomi value the same as a year of her life? Though
there's some question whether a year of Cupbearer's life and a
year of hers are worth the same. Based on a comparative survey
of behavior, she would say it's unlikely. Not that Naomi is pitiless.
At least, she does not think she is. Maybe she has a smaller share
of pity than she is supposed to.

"My hair, and all the French I've learned," Naomi bets. "And
what I know of dancing."

Farewell to the foxtrot. Cupbearer does not flinch. Does he
remember that it was once his?

"Bet," says Oracle. "A blood luck spell, lasting a month."

Naomi's fingers twitch. She has a pen tucked into her front
pocket, could scribble onto the back of her hand, *blood luck spell*.
What does that mean? Sometimes her skin tingles with how afraid
she is of forgetting what she learns down here. The difference
between a word and a real word is whether it's in the dictionary,
and by the same law, Naomi thinks, nothing is fully in the world

until it's been recorded. Not that it doesn't happen, but that in the absence of definition it can't be relied upon, can twist and blur and vanish, mirage-like, into something else.

It's fallen to Naomi to write the shape of this place, and Naomi has always meant to dedicate her life to serving one purpose very well. Scientists, journalists, explorers make a bargain with knowledge, and the best are prepared to sacrifice scrupulously. After you die, this is what you are reduced to anyway, Naomi reasons, if you remain at all, your contributions, the stars or little insects that bear your name. The thing to do must be to shape oneself, like those blind fish at the bottom of the sea, gradually discarding their vestigial parts. Naomi is probably more specialized than most, missing something in the way of some long-ago primate child, with a shorter tail than the rest. She has never been good at making friends, is in a perpetual chilly detente with her living family; has always had trouble dating, badly adapted to partners. But she's well adapted to this, sleek and streamlined with purpose; she goes under-the-hill like she would board a space shuttle, or a submarine, or go to live among the apes. This is why her, and why her alone.

It isn't ego, that she considers her work important.

"Swap," Menagerie says, like he is dropping a handkerchief to signal a duel.

Here the game becomes fay, in more than its symbolism and stakes. It's a game for much the same audience as Liar's Dice, or a card game Naomi was good at in primary school called Bullshit. One player names a card they are offering and a card they want. Another player may accept the trade, and neither knows until the cards have changed hands if they actually got what they asked for. Complicated in the hands of a species that may or may not even be able to lie, this portion of the game is conducted in absolute

silence, with only the cards' names spoken aloud. It is not technically lying, Naomi supposes, if you only say the names.

"Black Queen High," rustles Magpie. The house always goes
first. "Blood Witch."

Silence, one beat, two. Magpie points at Cupbearer. This is a
privilege of the House; if the card is in his hand he must give it
up. He shows her no expression. The fair folk have gifted him the
perfect poker face. He slides a card across the table.

Always better to gather the highest-ranking cards first. Naomi
has won in an accident before with a three-Prince hand. "White
Witch. White Death," she says.

Hound looks down at his hand, his eyes flicker uncertainly.
"I have—"

Oracle clicks her metal fingers, grabbing his attention. She
puts one silver digit to her lips.

Naomi cannot believe her luck. She beckons to Hound, places
the White Death facedown and slides it across the table to him.
The card she receives in return is, certain enough, the White
Witch. Slim odds, still, she'll need to draw the Magpie and the
Crow, but the small victory is sweet for its own taste.

Cupbearer does not make a trade, hasn't since he lost his
voice. He taps his three fingers a few times on the table and then
lets them pass him by, having already gambled away his own
chances.

When they've gone around the table, Menagerie deals them
their final cards. Naomi's fingers twitch a little as she turns them
over. White Magpie. Blood Consort.

Black Crow.

It's still only a mixed-suit Sorceress, not necessarily a winner.
Naomi does not cradle her cards close to her chest because she has
learned better manners than that.

"Rubbish and bets," Menagerie says, and Naomi discards her Consort and Fool.

Oracle folds.

Naomi's swallow pushes against the lining of her throat. She reminds herself that even if she does not win the blood today, she has still learned, can still write down, that they bet their own bodily fluids. "Bet." What does she value enough but not too much? "My first memory." She's not sure she can identify her first memory. Maybe her father walking her through the park by their old house, the blue lily-padded expanse of the pond, his fingers circling her fat toddler wrists. Naomi hopes that isn't it. Her father died when she was seven, she has few enough memories of him. Though once it's gone, she supposes she wouldn't know the difference.

Cupbearer's hand flashes in the air. Naomi does hope she doesn't win his fingers. That same gesture as earlier. Lungs, heart. *My life.* Three fingers, three more years.

"Bet something else," Hound says unpleasantly. Naomi is beginning to suspect that he's come down here trying to play savior. He seems, after all, more invested in Cupbearer's remaining fragments than Cupbearer does himself. In both tone and body, the boy is hunched all over and trembling.

Magpie smiles at him. When Magpie smiles, that plague-doctor mask curls up at the nose and Naomi can finally see her mouth. It is small and circular, filled with white, carnivorous teeth. What Naomi wouldn't do for a camera.

"Bet," Hound rattles out. "Anger."

Magpie lifts her cards high and then drops them to the table. "Fold."

"What?" Hound looks at Cupbearer, who does not look back at him. "I thought she was supposed to offer—"

"That"—Oracle raises a shining finger—"is later."

He must have thought he was playing for the favor. What does he have? Barely two scraps of knowledge to rub together, which makes Naomi ache for him, only a little.

"Read your palms," says Menagerie. They are capable of word-play, says a note that Naomi has already made. Read your palms. Put your hands faceup.

She turns over her Sorceress, with the Witch at the top and her zoo of animals behind her. Kept, presumably, for sacrifice.

Cupbearer has a Royal Family mostly in White. Queen High, Consort, Prince. And Birth in Blood. A little tragic, it beats the Sorceress if it's single-suit. But if both are mixed, the Sorceress wins.

Hound has nothing. He might conceivably have been playing toward a Black Full Court, the unbeatable hand. Four of the cards are there. Black Queen High, Consort, Fiddler, Poet. But the rest are rubbish.

Naomi has won.

"Take the pot, Fiddler." Menagerie nods to her, a liquidly measured gesture, Naomi can almost hear the *tick tick tick* of his neck turning, gears as fine as Oracle's hands. He smiles.

She puts her hand in the center of the table. The strange cat comes to her first. It climbs her shoulders, the weight of its paws strange and cool, and falls limp there as a mink stole. Naomi decides immediately that she will lose it next game. She reaches across the table to get her vial of blood, hot in her palm, her basket of sweet fruit, and this is when she remembers, in an unpleasant slap of sensation as a piece of Hound's mind pushes clumsily into her own.

Everything is very green, sweet-smelling in the way of trampled plants. Ari is sitting on a picnic blanket, really a sheet his sister Etta meant to throw out. The day's warmth is affectionate and beside Ari— beside Ari sits [ ], his face turned up to a sun he almost glows under. Reaching for his name is like slipping on ice, like an interrupted radio signal, like nothing at all, but the memory continues around the gap because what else is it to do? Even the empty space of him is fixed in Ari's mind. Wherever his name has gone, his body is here, his face is here, like it used to be, and he is lovely.

They've taken a day off their classes. [   ] hasn't worn sunblock and is going to burn soon, and peel, and complain. He's singing under his breath as he unloads food from the tote bag he brought. "Comfort for the comfortless, and honey for the bee. Comfort for the comfortless, but there's none but you for me."

"Where's that from?"

[ ] licks the corner of his mouth, and Ari tries not to watch the pink tip of his tongue. His pulse kicks irritably in his wrist "It's Irish, I think. A folk song. Wine?"

Ari shrugs. He looks impressed when he's told where the wine is from and pretends he's the kind of person who knows where wine should be from. It's not that [   ] is the first man Ari's wanted or even the first he's admitted to wanting, but he would be a lot of other, more concrete firsts. He certainly has the terrible finality of a first, a bridge Ari won't be able to get back over once he's crossed it.

"How long has it been since you've been outside?" [   ] asks. Ari opens his mouth and he scoffs. "No, I mean, really, since you put your work aside and got out of the city."

"We're in the city," Ari points out. The park all around them is sprawling but not so much as to obscure the greater forest of London imposing itself at the edges.

He lifts one sharp shoulder and considers Ari, with affection teasing at the corners of his lips. "You know what I mean."

Ari's had a squirming sense of anticipation since they left campus. [   ] can be so excessive in all his gestures that it's hard to be sure of him. "I'm here now," Ari says, quiet with breathlessness, and then sure as the next note in a song he's memorized, [   ] stretches across the sheet and puts a hand to Ari's face.

Ari has never been kissed before and that first time he can hardly focus on anything beyond the fact that it's happening at all, and so later he will assume that he was bad at it. Beyond the novelty, though, and the anxiety that flashes electrically through him, Ari does note that he is being kissed quite gently, as if by someone with great care for his enjoyment of the experience.

When [   ] pulls away, he's smiling. This will be worth remembering later, Ari. Remember him flushing, the shape of his eyes, put your thumb right against the crease at the corner, remember that particular shade of pink, that very specific gray.

"Why did you do that?" This strikes Ari as a sensible thing to ask, though he's been waiting all semester for it to be done.

"Love is not all: it is not meat nor drink," [   ] says, beginning a long pattern of Ari asking sensible questions and receiving insensate answers.

"What?"

[   ] levers himself upright again. "You're working yourself too hard." He opens a Tupperware, his hand shaking just a little. If Ari wished to list the things he accomplished today, he could begin with that shiver. [   ] hands him a pastry, little bits of mushroom in filo dough. Ari didn't even know he could cook. "Eat this," he says, "I made it to be romantic."

When Naomi swims up from the memory, her mouth tasting of mushroom and onions, Menagerie rolls Cupbearer's fingers unceremoniously into her palm. They're warm and damp as sausages, and there is a small callus on one knuckle. Bile washes up against the walls of Naomi's throat. She wants to scrape the memory right off her skin.

That poem Cupbearer quoted is Millay. Naomi would know it now even if she hadn't before. It ends like this: *I might be driven to sell your love for peace, or trade the memory of this night for food. It well may be. I do not think I would.*

There's a doubling in Naomi's mind. She's thinking, flatly, that at least she still has her sense of irony, and at once she is feeling a foreign outrage claw her stomach. She won that too, didn't she, Ari's anger? It vibrates in her. She looks down at her hands, and there are her own fingers. She is within her own body, still. This is just an emotion, and a fascinating one at that. Analyze it.

There are different flavors to the muddle of feeling. Her own indignation, fresh at the surface as she looks at Ari, whose name she would rather have kept on not knowing. How dare he drape his pain over Naomi's shoulders like that awful cat? But Ari is angry with himself too, and Naomi can still feel the shape of his mind over hers, its neat lines, its nervous organization. He's too smart for this and he knows it, coming to this game when he does not know its rules, spending scraps of himself for a chance at winning back what Cupbearer staked willingly. And he is angry with Naomi as well, for being here, for winning, for bearing witness.

His anger at the folk is righteous, and brittle as candy. He feels this place is like the inside of a pitcher plant, full of hooking, sticky trap hairs. He feels this like he is the first person to feel it. And then there is his anger with Cupbearer, spitting and snapping in its new home just beneath Naomi's lungs. That flattened, half-obliterated landscape of a face fills her with a gangrenous fury, bits of outrage rotting off to reveal something rawer and more dangerous.

"Libation," announces Magpie, in her crackling voice, which means their intermission. Menagerie unfolds himself from his seat and fetches a thin-necked pitcher, full of glittering violet wine. Ari is leaning across the table toward Naomi. There is absolutely nothing she could say to him right now that might prove both relevant and useful. She could tell him he is too smart to be here, but it's a bit late for that.

"What's your name?" He has the kind of smile that seems like it would be careful even if it wasn't forced. Naomi remembers the giddy anxiety in his body before Cupbearer kissed him, how he pressed his whole rabbiting heart against that kiss. It makes her embarrassed for him. Though he can't, any longer, be embarrassed for himself.

"Fiddler."

The smile tightens. "That's not your name."

Naomi nods.

Ari extends his hand across the table. Naomi is still holding his lover's warm fingers. He says, "My name is Ari."

What is it like missing that memory? It's so soft and so breakable, a mouse curled in some crevice of Naomi's brain. Her own first kiss, which she traded away some time ago, probably was not that kind. What is it like for him to be missing his anger? It's interesting, that he bet something so fundamental so early.

"You won my memory," he says.

"Yes."

"Can I have it back?"

Naomi would if she could, is the thing. She would like to.

"I understand that I bet it and that I lost it to you—" It would perhaps be better if Naomi called him Hound, still, because Ari is such an intimate name. She wonders if Cupbearer still knows it. "Fairly. But what could you do with it? You're human, aren't you?"

"Yes."

"And you don't need it for anything. It's mine, please. Is there a reason that I can't have it back?"

"It doesn't work like that."

Naomi has not touched the wine in her glass, but Menagerie pours more anyway, and she is glad enough of the interruption in their eye contact, a flash of bright violet. "Second round," he declares.

"Please," Ari says.

Naomi shakes her head. Does he think she wants these things?

His outrage and his memory playing in the theater of her skull, demanding, in that way a story does, that she involve herself. Naomi hates audience participation.

The cards are dealt. Oracle places a goblet on the table that fills with golden liquor before their eyes. Naomi hesitates a moment and then bets the familiar and Cupbearer's fingers. The hot, damp weight of both is beginning to nauseate her.

Ari puts on the table the taste of sweet potatoes, what a specific loss. Cupbearer opts for one of his ears; he only had the one remaining. Naomi won four years of his life. What is she expected to do with those? Will her own be longer, or does she only have the privilege of her name in some undefined cosmic record, stamped on the day of his death?

Menagerie deals again and Naomi picks her cards up. White Queen High, she notes, a shame she means to fold this round. A potential Full Court hand is difficult to resist, both for its rarity and its grandeur. But Naomi cannot afford to get competitive, or to play through everything that piques her interest.

"Bet," Ari says. "My four left fingers from the knuckle." He has picked up the formula of the language, for all the good that it's doing him.

Cupbearer wavers, a tight expression on his face that might once have been biting his lip, and flickers a gaze at Ari beside him before he folds. How many memories of his lover has he bet? Naomi wonders. Who is Ari to him now? The man who looks after him, strokes the curve of his bare head, resents him.

It's a usual curse for Naomi, to be unable to stop herself from thinking.

Ari does not know how to play this game, and yet he came here anyway. If he is not stupid, and he is not stupid, then that's a level of loyalty Naomi is not really capable of understanding. She could judge Cupbearer for forfeiting those memories, but isn't

Naomi the same woman who offered up her sister's birth, her late father, cut away her loved ones so she could fill that space with more objective kinds of knowledge? More important kinds.

Cupbearer folds. He is so bare that every part of him is intimate, the aching curve of his soon-to-be-severed ear against his skull. A good thing they haven't graduated to greater limbs yet. Naomi would not like to feel what Ari's anger would do in her breast at Cupbearer spread over the room like chopped meat. *There was no grass on Elkin Moor, no broom nor bonny whin, but's dripping with Child Owlet's blood and pieces of his skin.*

"Call." Naomi gestures at Ari with a short flick of her wrist. "His anger."

Oracle bets a cage of black salamanders with real fires flickering in their bellies. Naomi tries to focus her attention there, that wonderful strangeness. She presses her fingers to the joint of her jaw, feels it pop. She'd assumed that having a bad taste in one's mouth was not a literal expression, but her tongue has a rotten flavor.

As soon as the swap has passed and the last round of cards is dealt, Naomi folds. That will, at least, get his anger out of her. Which will help.

When terrible things happen under-the-hill, and terrible things do, Naomi doesn't interfere. Objectivity, but it isn't only about that. What power is Naomi supposed to have, as guest and observer in this underworld? This casino, like all casinos, is rigged in favor of the House, and the only lever with which a human might exert a little control down here is in the favor. Which has slim odds and is not a plausible plan of action. Considering it one, even thinking about what you might do with that power sparkling in your hands, is just nibbling the bait.

Naomi took a journalism class in her undergrad, when she thought she might do more conventional fieldwork. Here is one

of the things she was told: Never forget that your presence will
influence your subject. Never forget that your subject is respond-
ing to you. The bias of the study is really unfortunate enough,
but, furthermore, Naomi would not like to be in the way of her
subject's response.

Magpie spreads her cards flat on the table, and the bets go
twisting lithely around the remaining players. Ari looks down
at his cards, bottom lip folded between his teeth. "Bet," he says.
"Every song I know."

"Undersell," Magpie responds instantly, like a branch crack-
ing. "What is your name?"

"My songs and my singing." Is this canniness or determina-
tion? Naomi suspects that Ari has a lovely singing voice. There is
a slight, plaintive twang to his speech. Maybe he sang and Cupbearer danced. If Naomi won both hands, she could have been a
one-woman show.

"Raise," says Oracle. "The only secret I've never told."

"Call." Magpie taps her nails against the table. "An hour of
my magic."

Naomi cannot quite help herself from studying the minutiae
of Ari's face. She sees his expression cavern inward. When the
bets come around to him again, he folds.

White Queen High, White Magpie, White Serpent, White
Hound, White Crow, Blood Consort, White Cat.

Naomi's skin prickles. He is one card away from the Menagerie hand. He asked, in the swap, for the White Consort, and evi-
dently he did not get it, but that was not even the right card to ask
for. He could have gotten the White Fool or the White Steed, and,
in the absence of a Full Court hand—and one of the Queens High
has already been been folded—he could have *won*.

The game goes to Oracle, who takes back her unfeline cat and
then reaches for Ari's fingers. The severing is magical, done with

no blood. It doesn't hurt, Naomi knows from experience, but the absence is so sudden that it's almost the same as pain.

It's strange, that the sensation of Ari's anger remains even after it leaves her. The familiar and the outrage, Naomi surrenders both the burdensome little animals, but there's still the tension in her knuckles and her jaw, the burning at the back of her throat. The physicality of the emotion lingers, maybe. Or maybe it is Naomi who's angry.

More wine is poured and Menagerie shuffles the deck, cards flashing between his ringed fingers with a speed that might be magical and might be practiced deftness. Even in the midst of all this, Naomi's hands want for her pen, her notebook, the chance to keep record.

There's something about this place, or rather its inhabitants, how mathematic and perfectly selfish they are, that Naomi finds more sympathetic than the people she is often surrounded with. Or, no, *sympathetic* is not the word—more comprehensible. Say again that Naomi is like a war photographer, which means she is not like a soldier or a battlefield surgeon. Even the war photographers must feel twinges sometimes, but it doesn't do to live inside the twinge. Maybe, even, say Naomi is the camera; only here to click the shutter in her mind.

She looks at her cards.

Queen High, White, White Prince, White Oracle.

Well, fuck. Something bucks and lurches in Naomi's stomach, because she is holding part of a Full Court, an exceptionally good hand.

For her bet, Oracle tosses Ari's fingers onto the table in a clattering handful, and Naomi watches them roll. This is hardly the first or the most awful time she has played with pieces of somebody else. How old now is the firstborn child she saw wagered so many games ago, if it has even been born yet? Will he have any idea that he was cast onto the table? And yet this is not Naomi's business. If they are going to use this boy as poker chips, she may as well cash in. "Bet. His memory."

Cupbearer does not bother with the careful finger signs this time. He tips his chair back and lifts his leg onto the table.

The third round is when the favor is offered. It is when you bet high, bet early, fold late.

Perhaps Ari has noticed this. "Bet. My last name."

What will it be like for him to go without that? What will it be like for him, to not share a name anymore with his mother, or his sister, whose name in his memory was alight with fondness? The people that Naomi has given up pieces of, her parents, her sister, her first girlfriend, whose love she has excised from her body in bite-sized pieces; she does not think they would be surprised. She thinks that Ari's people would. Naomi has a mind for detail, and so it is the details that are unfortunate.

Naomi knows now that Cupbearer was not just beautiful once. She knows that he was smart, quick with his own words and other people's, vain, and too desperate to impress just for the sake of it. She knows that he took great pleasure in himself, his life, and Ari. She knows what it is like to kiss him, and to badly want him closer.

What would it be like to have yourself stripped away in layers? Memory and pleasure, thought and self-knowledge. Love. She didn't know the weight of that poetry when she won it.

"Bet," says Magpie. "Spell of healing."

If Cupbearer could speak, she could ask him what it was like. She's paid too much attention to him and Ari both, considered them too much outside the relevant context of the game, and now her mind keeps turning up questions for them. How did they get from the point A of that stolen memory to the point B of this night? What came between having and losing? *Let's say this is like an intimate interview.* Except that there is nothing actually important for her to learn from them, and it isn't like that at all.

Menagerie deals the next three cards.

White Horseman, Blood Oracle, White Cat. That's four cards now toward a Full Court. The bottom swoops out of Naomi's stomach.

The thing is, theoretically—

Theoretically, Naomi could play toward a Corruption hand, or Changeling High, or Treason, all these easy, inconspicuous things, which are plausible strategies for a cautious player but unlikely to win without impressive luck.

Or she could play toward a Full Court hand. Far more difficult, but an almost certain win, and this is the best foundation Naomi has had for one in the first turn since she learned the game.

And Naomi has learned the game. Naomi is good at it.

Imagine winning a favor from the fair folk. Naomi has a mathematical love for infinitesimal odds. Naomi has always, quietly, yearned to know if she could do it. And would it have to mean, if she did win—would it really have to mean she couldn't come back? Some winners must return, even if she has yet to observe them. Some fish must double back to the hook, because after all it did not kill them last time; last time they got away well fed. Couldn't Naomi be addicted to the thrill?

Imagine winning a favor from the fair folk, and the things she could do with it. Sometimes Naomi remembers that if she were to die down here her work would die with her, which is the most awful part of her decision to pursue this research alone. The favor could accomplish years of work; if by some slim chance she won it, wouldn't she be obligated to use it for that? To hasten and ensure the birth of this knowledge into the wider world? Wouldn't it be a crime, to spend the chance on anything more trivial than that?

"Bet," Magpie says, in that voice like snakeskin. Without

further description, she drops an amulet of vivid purple onto the table.

"Call," Ari says. Naomi watches his throat move, the way the structure of him pushes against his skin. She looks over at Oracle, who is down here so often. Do these boys, the fool and the fool who's come to save him, make her feel anything? Does Ari's anger move her, now that it's writhing in her body? What does? "My best memory this month."

Oracle's face is static and impassive.

Cupbearer performs that sign language again. He could fold now. Naomi does not quite let herself think, *Please*. He is pointing to his chest. Naomi can see his ribs through his shirt. He touches three of them.

Three ribs. Three ribs, a healing spell, a memory, a surname, four fingers, and anger.

Naomi puts Cupbearer's dancing back on the table.

Oracle points a metal finger at Ari. "His songs and his singing."

"Swap."

Magpie points to Naomi. She shivers, and she wonders what she did to draw attention to herself, or if this was random selection. Naomi needs to keep the White cards she has; if she loses one of them the Full Court will be impossible, and Magpie could just *take it*.

"Blood Poet. Black Consort."

Naomi takes a deep breath and slides her Blood Oracle across the table.

"White Magpie, Black Horseman," offers Oracle, and takes her card from Cupbearer.

Ari follows her, uncertainly, "Blood Fiddler, White Crow."

Naomi folds her lower lip between her teeth. Adrenaline is metallic in her mouth, and she has to keep saying to herself, *Sit down, sit down, this is still an experiment*. It is unlikely she will be able to win, and even if she is able she has not decided to, and even if she did win the favor. She could find a reason to come back. She could make it work. This is still, all of this, an experiment. "White Consort, White Cat."

Ari flicks his hand up, and a little of the air goes helplessly out of Naomi. She studies his face, plain and large-eyed and determined. Maybe Hound was an unkind nickname. *Will you help me?* Naomi thinks. *Are you able?* Surely it hasn't already occurred to him to bluff, but then again, whatever else he is, he is clever enough to have picked that up. Naomi tries to keep her teeth from sinking through her skin.

Ari slides his card across the table to her. Naomi turns it over.

She does not smile at him, but she would like to.

Menagerie deals the last three cards.

Naomi needs two White court cards. Two out of three White court cards.

Black Birth.

White Knight.

White Cupbearer.

Queen High, Prince, Consort, Knight, Oracle, Horseman, Cupbearer.

Full Court Hand.

It is not good practice in poker to let oneself smile.

Oracle folds.

Naomi bets, of course. The goblin fruit and Cupbearer's jacket she won two rounds ago, and her own pinkie finger. Why not?

Cupbearer does not fold. He bets with a sweeping motion, directed at his body like when he was betting years, but followed by no numbers, with the cockiness of a constant loser. Rage scratches up the sides of Naomi's torso and it takes her a moment to remember it cannot be Ari's.

It is a good thing that Naomi is going to win. The blood is celebrating in her veins, because it's such a validation, isn't it? A validation of the entire project of Naomi, that she learned all of this so successfully, memorized a ranked list of every hand, understood the rules well enough to win a game she was never really meant to.

Ari folds. Naomi glances at his cards. Black Cat, Blood Magpie, White Crow, Black Oracle, Blood Fiddler, pair of Fools.

Magpie produces another of those squid-mouthed smiles. "Raise. A favor from myself."

There are conditions implicit in the favor, the most significant being that though Naomi does not believe that Magpie could refuse the winner, there is nothing to stop her or her fellow folk seeking retribution against them. Safety might be a favor of its own.

"Call." Naomi returns the vial of blood to the table. Her stomach hurts, giving it over. She reminds herself that she will have it back. "And the boy's memory that was won to me."

Magpie shakes her head, slow half rotations that could be accompanied by the grinding of gears. Not enough. Naomi draws blood from her lower lip. She is going to win, she cannot fold, what has she brought with her?

"And my last name. And my right thumb."

It is enough. It is barely enough.

There is nothing left, Naomi realizes, for Cupbearer to bet. He is shivering, fine and frail, all up and down his body. Lost his leg and his rib and himself. Naomi wishes that she could spare him this part. *What lips my lips have kissed, and where, and why.* She does not love him, but she has loved him. He has bet his fear, so what is he feeling now?

He folds.

He makes, of course, no sound as his ribs crack from his torso. He crumples over himself. Sweat lies glittering on his featureless face. His body is stacked like steaks in a butcher shop, leg and set of ribs. Jesus fucking Christ.

Naomi waits for Magpie to turn over her cards. She must know, now, that Naomi has the Full Court.

"Raise."

Naomi startles, and then there is a cold, insectoid creeping over her bones. There is one hand that beats a White Full Court, and that is a Black Full Court. The Black Queen High, Black Consort, Black Prince, these cards have not been folded, nor have enough court cards that Naomi could safely rule this hand out.

"Free and safe passage from this place."

There is no arguing that this bet is valuable, but Naomi has never seen it offered before. She does not understand what it means. It is a threat of sorts, maybe. All of Magpie's teeth are so very white, and the inside of her mouth is black-bruised like a dog's jowls. It makes Naomi think of starlight.

"For you," she susurrates, "and any comrades. And your book."

And so she knows.

She's laid Naomi bare like a moth pinned to paper. Exact and scientific, all her research and all her doubts, and who knows how long she has known or what else she knows? Who knows what the fay are capable of knowing, and who knows if there has been someone fair sitting behind Naomi on her train home while she scribbled into her notebook? Beneath the electric terror she feels a pulsing, hot humiliation. She has thought herself clever, swimming away from the baited hook, but what hidden set of jaws has she been propelling herself toward instead? She has sneered, quietly and sometimes guiltily, though sometimes not, at the fools who wander in here thinking to turn the game to their own purposes, fancying themselves hero of this story. But who is she, who let herself believe that when she left whole and fat with knowledge, this was down to her own intelligence, her competence? Who did not stop to wonder if the fair folk might only be playing with their food? Safe passage away.

So there, and there, and that is that. To be allowed to do what they have done, and see what they have seen, and go free, remembering it. That is not one favor, but three, at least, and maybe more. Naomi knows that there is no way to balance this equation, with her life on one side and three of the folk's favors on the other. Magpie's eyes are like the black carapaces of beetles. Naomi does not know what she is thinking, what she wants. But then, what does Naomi know?

What matters is not always the value of the item, but the pain of losing it.

Naomi reaches into her bag and places her notebook on the table. "Call." Her throat is dry, her own body resisting. "Three years of my life." She would like to stop seeing Magpie's mouth. Menagerie leans over, with his hungry fingers like tubes of wax, and turns Naomi's pages.

And there are her words, her clippings, her bulleted lists, her hastily attempted sketches, her notes, and her notes, and her notes.

She is experiencing a state of grief and anxiety that makes her wonder, briefly, if she is going into shock. Probably not, though she is sure that people have gone into shock in this room. How often do these things, these mundane physical responses, disrupt the ordered flow of the game, where even the severing of limbs is convenient and bloodless?

Naomi should write that down.

Magpie turns over her cards.

Full Court, Blood Suit.

White Full Court wins. Naomi sees Magpie see this. Eyes like glass set in wax, but still, when she lays her hand down, Naomi sees the House see that it has lost.

Joy is sandpaper on the inside of her throat.

She reaches into the center of the table, with her hands all a-tremble, takes one of the peaches from the pot and bites it. *You cannot think what figs my teeth have met in.* How sweet it is; it wrings the dryness out of her mouth, and Naomi falls, closed-eyed, back into remembering.

[   ]'s head is in Ari's lap. It's hard to tell, now, whether he wants to be touched or doesn't care. He cannot sleep anymore. Sometimes he rises at night and makes the floorboards creak. He has no depth perception; he runs into things. When Ari leaves him alone, he stares. He looks lonely, but Ari isn't sure.

Ari still likes to be with him, which is probably pathetic. His nameless, lipless, eyeless— He has told his sister that his boyfriend, whose name he couldn't tell her anymore (does she remember? could he ask her?) is very sick. He doesn't know if she believes him, hopes she doesn't think he's so indecent a person that he'd lie about that just because he'd been broken up with. Though he is lying about it, assigning the suffering of disease to a man who elected his condition.

Is that unfair? Gambling can be an addiction. Ari does not know where the lines of his anger are supposed to lie. He should be sorry, anyway, for draping someone else's pain over his own like a couch cover. His sister has found and mailed him some of the books and pamphlets that are given to caretakers. She's sweet like that.

Sometimes Ari sings for [   ], quietly. He has not sold his hearing yet, and Ari does not know if he can still enjoy things like this, but once he very much liked Ari's singing.

"Comfort for the comfortless, and honey for the bee. Comfort for the comfortless, but there's none but you for me."

Naomi tries not to be too given to pity.

Here are the ribs, being slid across the table. Three ribs, music, a healing spell she wouldn't know how to use, a memory, a surname, four fingers, and anger she didn't want back.

Technical ownership over Cupbearer, though she still doesn't know his name. Her own name and the vial of blood and her fingers, safely kept, and passage out. And a favor. And her notebook.

And she can never return. Not now that it is all out in the open, her research butchered on the table, and the folk may seek novel ways of toying with her. Three years of study, and she still can't predict them with any certainty.

Three years of study, and this and many more things she will probably never learn.

"Fiddler fair," Magpie calls her, "what is your heart's desire?"

Naomi won Midsummer Switch with a Full Court hand. She could have anything now. She could demand that Magpie tell her everything she's wanted to know. She could make them let her come back, and give her a little chair at the side of the room, and let her take notes. At the end, Naomi could go down among unhuman things, and wrap them around herself, and come to understand them.

At the end, Naomi feels wrung out, hollow like her blood has abandoned her veins.

She points to Cupbearer, his empty, ugly face, his closed, single eye. She does not know what a person's life expectancy is with three ribs neatly removed, but he is still breathing. "Give everything back to him," she says. Her voice is clear, authoritative, and someone else's. Speaking into this hot aorta of the earth, at the end of the things Naomi can know. "Everything he lost. Give it back."

It's an entirely uneventful restoration. It feels as if there ought, at least, to be some flash and sparkle, something she could write down. Instead, there is just the fair face, and the pale hair, the gray glass eyes, and the long lashes. There is his open mouth, full of teeth. He stretches and rolls back both shoulders. At least he has the courtesy to tremble, as one before the grace of God. *That saved a wretch like me.*

"Vincent," says Ari, in a gasp.

Ah. That was the name. Vincent. Feels anticlimactic. When they go to embrace each other, Naomi turns away. She puts her notebook into her bag. She puts in the vial of blood, the peach with one bite out of it that will leave sticky juice all over the inside fabric. This day was a victory of sorts; it will be a little while before she runs out of things to write about. She cannot remember the foxtrot anymore. She has committed either an unforgivable waste or the first really good deed of her life. She thinks of the perfect machinery of the fay, Menagerie greeting every comer exactly the same, every time. She wonders, if you break a pattern once, and only once, does it change your place in some human taxonomy? Sometimes, Naomi's journalism teacher told her, you are writing one story and then you realize suddenly that you are writing another. "We should go," Naomi says.

The fay watch them with the still eyes of wasps. Who can even tell if a wasp is watching them? Magpie and Menagerie are frozen as if forbidden from movement. Behind her, Naomi can hear the grinding of Oracle's metal knuckles as she packs away her own things. Perhaps it is an exhibition of great emotion.

When they step out of the hill, sunrise has not come yet. It feels as if it ought to have, but they have not, after all, played through the night. The moon is still a lightless hole in the sky.

They are just boys, Naomi reminds herself, without looking over her shoulder. She knows they are following, and she is not so invested as Orpheus anyway. She can hear their ragged breaths as they come out of the hill, their crunching footsteps where the dew has frosted the grass. One of them is crying, and because Naomi does not recognize the voice she thinks it must be Vincent. They earned this all themselves, but they asked for none of it.

Closer than she thought, one of them puts a hand on Naomi's shoulder. She turns. Oh. Vincent has very fine fingers, long and pale, has a very fine smile, looks very fine with tears in his river-water eyes. *I already knew,* Naomi thinks, hating him, *how beautiful you are. Oh, Helen fair, beyond compare, I'll make a garland for your hair.*

"I owe you a debt, Lady." He speaks with faltering music; how used he has become to their language. He swallows, licks his lips. "Thank you. I—I don't even know how to. I was so—"

Naomi does not say, *Don't go back.* This is not how to thank her; she does not want his thanks. She wants to ask him if he thinks she made the right decision, but she has no reason to trust his answer.

She still does not like this boy at all. She can remember being in love with him, she can remember his long hands on her shoulders and his quickening breaths against her lips, and she can remember his hairless, shivering skin under her palms. She knows, for him, such new and tender love. She knows, for him, a little angry pity, because he is just a child.

"Don't touch me."

He takes his hand away, holds it against his chest like a wounded thing. He shakes his head. "Color," he says, eventually, looking past her over the river. "Do you know what it's like to forget color?"

Naomi follows his gaze for a moment, and then does not care to see what he sees. "I bet red."

He shrugs. One sharp shoulder, just like before he kissed her. She has one kiss from this man, now, that he has never given her, and that Ari has lost. She hasn't decided yet what she does and doesn't regret. "I bet everything."

Then he turns, and he is walking fast away from her, to the other side of the river. He is stretching his legs and his vision and his joy. He reminds her of a newborn foal. If she were to see him at the game again, she could call him Horseman.

"I don't know why you did that," Ari says. He says it suddenly and close to her ear, but Naomi jumps not even a little. He has, after all, been closer.

It's good, to take in some fresh air, after being under-the-hill. Going in and out of the ground, like a ritual of rebirth. Naomi breathes deeply before she answers him. "I can't give it back to you."

"What?"

"The memories, the songs." She reaches into the pocket of her bag, and she hands him his own fingers. Cooling a little now, but still soft to the touch. "You can have those."

He looks down at them, like maggots in the palm of his good hand. His bottom lip is caught between his teeth, the corners of his mouth curling up like Magpie's nose. "I—" He shakes his head, surprises Naomi by laughing a little. His curls bounce. "I'm right-handed anyway."

Naomi gets the ankles of her trousers wet crossing the river, soaks through her socks. She wonders what it was like for Vincent to walk back this way barefoot, when he lost those nice shoes. Will those be waiting for him at home, wherever home is, or have the fair folk technically cheated her over a pair of leather slippers?

She is trembling, and she is singing to herself, a venting of nervous energy. Naomi has always liked music. She has a lovely voice now, sweet and clear as anything. "Comfort for the comfortless, and honey for the bee. Comfort for the comfortless, but there's none but you for me." The song comes easily to her, melody tucked fresh and neat into her mind.

Ari pauses, halfway over the river, with the toe of his boot in the water. "I don't know that one."

Naomi sighs, a long exhale that feels as if it has been trapped in her throat for many years, and offers him her elbow. "No. You wouldn't," she says. And she helps him across.

Is This You?

You know it's going to be a bad day when you get up and find yourself already in the kitchen, seated at the table and eating Cheerios. The you at the kitchen table is thirteen, and she's eating the Cheerios straight out of the box by the fistful. Try to call her Maura. You are also Maura. Two people can have the same name, but two people cannot be the same person. A few Cheerios fall from Maura's hand and roll pinwheels across the tile. You tap your foot.

Maura doesn't look up, hiding behind the grease slick of her hair. Your hygiene at thirteen was awful—how often did you shower? Once a week? "Are you going to clean up after yourself?"

She rolls her eyes, slides off her chair, and swipes the mess up with a napkin. "Good morning."

If Maura is here it means your mother has published an essay. You ask Maura where it is this time, but she ignores you, licks her fingers, and then reaches back into the cereal box. The teenage iterations of you are the worst, though thirteen is not as bad as the years that followed it; angst-ridden, messy, uncooperative. There's a minor foam of acne bubbling on Maura's left cheek.

You turn to the counter to make your coffee. Looking at her is like looking at a photograph of yourself taken too long ago to remember the circumstances of it, recognizing yourself there, but being unable to recall ever inhabiting that moment. That's more words than you ever put to a photograph of yourself, but of course it's different when the uncanny feeling is made flesh, taking up room and air. Picking at her cuticles like you still pick at your cuticles, though you have the self-control now to stop before they bleed. She, tugging a pale strip of skin between her front teeth, autocannibalistic, does not. It's a kind of emotional headache, a knot of buzzing tightness forming at the base of your throat where your collarbones notch. You put your eyes back on the coffee grounds.

"I don't have time for this today," you tell her. "You're going to have to take the train to Mom's."

"I hate the train."

"I know." You put your coffee down, and go and get a banana. There's nothing else breakfasty around, you've been putting off shopping. The Cheerios aren't looking appealing.

"What do you have to do anyway?"

"Work. It's Thursday." That might be a real headache building in addition to the existential one; stress. It's only seven-fifteen. You're not late yet, though you are starting to fall behind, standing in the doorway half-dressed and without your hair brushed.

Maura raises a two-finger gun to her forehead, mimes pulling the trigger. "That's not funny," you reprimand her. It just sort of feels like you should.

*　　*　　*

It took you until Maura's third reprise in your life to realize that she came from your mother and not from some glitch in your own connection with reality. Your mother was publishing infrequently back then; you've heard it takes a while to get a leg up in publishing. And you were twenty-one, more than halfway to twenty-two, closing out the semester with straight As for the first time in your life and with a winter internship lined up helping to organize fundraisers at the local Planned Parenthood. When you took a step back from your life and looked at it, it was almost like you'd become an adult.

You found Maura in the bathtub that time—not taking a bath, though not having done anything else either. Lying there with her feet kicked up and her heels resting on the tile. She was seventeen, and could have passed for you in a heartbeat. It seemed possible she'd been sent to punish you for feeling well. At lunch, your friend April found you, and sat across the table from you and you. People don't ask you for an explanation. You still don't know why that is. She slides through the world conveniently, half real as she is. Other people don't need to be told to call her by your name. They do it automatically. "This is so absolutely fucked up," April said. And you nodded, laughing. It certainly was. She put her laptop in front of you.

On her laptop, she had an essay your mother had written about your suicide attempt. You did make a suicide attempt, when you were seventeen.

"Did you give her permission to write about this?"

"No."

While you read, you could feel Maura behind you. Not doing anything in particular, just breathing, twisting a nervous hand in her hair. You could hear the individual strands grinding together. "I didn't even know she wrote about me," you told April. Which was true. You didn't read your mother's writing. Because you didn't want to have to talk about it with her. Because sometimes it was about people you knew: your uncle, your grandfather, the neighbors. Because you didn't like the way she sounded on paper, much softer and more elegant. You didn't like how much you liked that person.

Your mother had spilled everything all over the page. Your ugly crying, things you said but couldn't remember saying, the way your skin divided neatly into two white walls between which blood spilled. You eventually had to block that article so you would stop rereading it; not the whole thing, just that one bit. The page unzipping, your skin unzipping, your blood, your mother.

*   *   *

If you are wondering what kind of child you were: You were a child terrified of your own body. You were afraid of the bird flu, of radiation poisoning, chemical warfare, poisonous plants, spiders. You nurtured up fear like a little green shoot, watered it, fertilized it, put it out in the sun. Encyclopedias, Wikipedia, library books. Mustard gas, Chernobyl, the rhododendrons growing in your mother's front yard. A video of snake venom injected into a petri dish of human blood, which bubbled, fizzled, and then congealed like Jell-O. The corpse of a black widow your mother smashed on the side of the front door; for three weeks you insisted on going out the back. Until your mother scooped you up in her arms, squeezing you around the ribs while you screamed, kicked, pounded disobedient fists between her shoulder blades. So afraid you nearly seized with it, she carried you out to the sidewalk. "See, Maura? It's fine. You're *fine*." That incident was what first put you on a therapist's overcushioned sofa. You were far too old to be screaming that way.

*   *   *

You shouldn't have been surprised by the accuracy of your mother's writing. Your mother took notes for most of your life. She was an organized woman. She carried a binder. People with severe health conditions—chronic, life-threatening, rare—have said this is what a person has to do. Have a binder for all the doctors, the operations, the diagnoses, the medications, the allergies. A woman whose memoir you read for some undergraduate class, a woman who nearly died of a very rare illness—orphan disease, that's the term for a sickness so particular no one could make any money off a cure—came to speak in front of your class once. Her mother had a sunshine-yellow binder, her mother kept every paper, wrote down every word. Some note about some allergy lost in a hospital transfer, that comprehensive thoroughness saved this woman's life. *You're giving her that? No.* The sound of pages flipping. *You can't give her that.*

There may be common knowledges between people who love sick people. Your binder, your mother's binder, that is, was blue, and had MAURA written across the front and down the spine in thick Sharpie letters. Once in a while you might imagine a line of mothers stood behind a line of binders, shelved front to back cover, in a long, neat library. Yours had print-offs from the pharmacy, pamphlets, scanned paperwork, chunks of parenting books and self-help books copied off and marked up with a highlighter, a calendar. Your mother always knew how far you were into a prescription. If you found yourself standing in front of the medicine cabinet, unable to remember if you'd taken your meds that day or not, you could count them, and call down the hallway to her for the right number. This was something you could rely on.

And notes, and notes, and notes. You always knew she had a memo pad in there, her pencil scratching away from a chair beside you. She used those little golf pencils, stubby as pinkie fingers. Why would you have thought to check what she was writing? You never asked to see the bills from the insurance, the emails she wrote when you missed school for a doctor's appointment, you didn't know your own Social Security number—there was a parental infrastructure, which you could count on like you count on the water to come out of the tap.

*   *   *

Three hours of Maura sullen on your faded office couch and demanding to play with your phone is quite enough. You skip out on your lunch hour to take her home. The noonday sun is pouring hot through your car windows, and you're tasting an apology to your boss because you know you're not going to make it back on time. You never do. Maura looks up from where she's lolling her head against the window and says, "She published a book."

You ease on the brake as you hit a red light, only look over at Maura once the car is stopped. She's leaning her forehead against the glass again, probably smudging it. "What?"

"Mom. She published an essay collection."

There goes your stomach, bottom dropped out. Like the feeling you get whenever your mother texts you. Every time, the stomach, and then a rush of cold from your fingertips up through your shoulders down into your rib cage. "When?"

Maura turns and looks at you, finally. God, were your eyes that big when you were younger? Are they still? Maybe she isn't quite thirteen. Her eyes are big as moons. "You didn't *know*?"

You don't know if she's making fun of you or if she's really surprised. Try not to ask whether Maura knows what she is, if she is anything. Someone behind you lays on the horn.

*   *   *

You go to the Trader Joe's and stock up on the expensive spiced tea you used to love, ginger and chai. You put Nutella in the cabinet. You buy a few puzzles, a stuffed animal, your favorite books when you were nine, thirteen, seventeen. Of course, you've tried being kind to her—you're not a monster—but this may be more prophylaxis than kindness. Keep her seen to, keep her busy. You walk two blocks to the bookstore. There is a stack of hardcovers on the new-releases stand, your mother's name stamped onto them in smooth raised letters. Almost unanimously, your therapists have encouraged you not to read her writing, but there are concrete realities to prepare for. Or at least concrete presences, even if their reality is dubious. Thank God for small mercies, maybe, that you did not wake up to twelve of yourself in the kitchen this morning, a Maura for every essay. That does not mean a promise for tomorrow morning. Take the collection off the shelf; the cover is simple but well done, a traditional family tree that, halfway up its trunk, shifts to a web of neurons like cracks in a plate. Clever. Your mother has titled the book *Parthenogenesis*.

*   *   *

Mercies or not, you don't get a long reprieve. One of the Mauras comes with you to therapy the next morning. She's eight. She perches on the back of the couch behind you, braiding your hair while you try to speak. Braiding it badly; she keeps pulling. "This is an invasion of privacy," your therapist says, as you extend the book across the table to her. She opens the book in her lap, and then shuts it again quickly. Maybe she doesn't want you to think she's reading about you. You two have already discussed this—*I want to hear things the way you want to share them*, she said.

Toward the end of the session she says, "Why do you worry so much what your mother thinks of you?" And you and Maura both break up laughing. She falls off the sofa, rolls across the floor, just nearly misses landing at your therapist's feet and instead bangs her shoulder on the little coffee table. "Shit," your therapist says, and you nod your agreement. You've got a headache setting in that grips your whole spine; you could almost mistake it for sympathetic pain. "That'll leave a bruise."

*　*　*

Does Maura know what she is? If she is anything. Does she know she isn't right? That she is written.

Last year, at the onset of an episode so bad you ended up having to switch medications, you went to the Getty. You love the Getty. If a museum could be your boyfriend, if you could run away with and marry a museum, the Getty with its sharp angled jaw would be second to none. Your flesh-and-blood boyfriend had lately left (bad communication), but that isn't what cracked you, you aren't that kind of woman. Or maybe you work hard not to be that kind of woman. The seasons going; the chemical sea change of the brain; maybe the sudden emptiness of your apartment; maybe the sudden fullness of it, when you woke up with Maura's spiny, pale body—like the hollow shell a sea urchin leaves when it dies—snuggled up to your side, her toddler face snuffling into your neck, companionate, inseparable; maybe the small boy who tumbled off the play structure at your school and then sat bleeding quietly on your office couch while he waited for the ambulance, a seismic fault line opened in his skull. One way or another, you were wrung out; like someone had broken your bones open and scraped out all the marrow.

When you want to feel something, an art museum is good for you, but it is very bad when you're sitting there inside it like a smooth shelled egg and you still can't feel anything. There was a little sculpture of the archangel Michael casting the fallen angels out of heaven, which you spent a long time walking around and bending over, studying the details. Not of Michael, an avenging baby in his flowing robe, but the funnel of hell-bound devils beneath him: a mass of grotesque faces and warped limbs, stumped shoulders, twisted necks. What kinds of art do you love and not want to love? Martyrings, beheading scenes, those still lifes of dead animals draped over tables, their fur lax, their glass eyes open. Sometimes a severed arm is as close as you can get to feeling real, the imagined thrill of pain. The sensation of being meat.

*   *   *

There are twelve essays in the collection. You count them; don't read them yet. They have titles like "In Loco Parentis," "Death and the Maiden." Sometimes you must have to wonder who your mother thinks she is.

Maura is around. Two or three more incarnations of her pass, more rapid-fire than you've ever become used to, but otherwise uneventfully. She moves things in your pantry while you sleep, uses your shampoo to run herself a bubble bath and leaves the bathroom floor wet. She puts your books facedown on the kitchen table so their spines bend.

A problem with having Maura around a lot is seeing your own body in motion. When you are in public sometimes strangers' eyes track her movements instead of yours. Her greasy hair, the sloppy sprawl of her posture, the paunch of baby fat you kept too long into your teenage years.

As a little girl—tiny; four, five?—the looks she gives you are so worried, and when she's a teenager her face is hateful, furious as the smell of blood on a barbecue. "We could at least try to get along," you might say. She pulls your lips back from your teeth.

"I don't like myself very much."

*   *   *

Some Mauras are stickier than others, do not disappear quietly in the night. You bring those to your mother's house. You usually stand at a distance, but the fifth Maura, who has been uncharacteristically docile, you walk to the door. She rings the bell for you. Take a breath. Hold still, Maura, it's just your mother.

Your mother opens the door, and she opens her arms. She takes Maura into them. She always does this. You've watched her do it from your car window, from the lawn, from your mind's eye. You often think of an anemone swallowing a fish. Maura exhales—might be contentment, might be impatience. It probably depends on the day, on the girl. She leans your forehead against her mother's shoulder.

"Hi, Maura," your mother says. Over her Maura's shoulder, so, to you.

"Congratulations on the book."

Her face does something bad, something like the feeling of watching another person walk precariously along the edge of a very high place. Don't apologize, but also don't put your fist in your mouth and bite your knuckles so you don't apologize.

"Thank you."

"It's impressive."

"It was hard to write."

You could ask her about the advance, how much she's going to make off it. Will you ask her about the advance?

She opens the door a little wider, as she turns her body and the version of yourself clasped against it toward the house. "Do you want to come in?"

"I can't."

Your mother looks back to you. When did her eyebrows turn gray? How have you missed these little details of her aging? "You haven't been answering my calls," she says mournfully. "I tried to tell you about it."

This seems unlikely. You may not know everything about publishing, but you are fairly sure there is a long stretch of time between deciding to write a book and seeing it on shelves. Still, it is true that you haven't been answering her calls.

You don't say anything. Your mother's face crumples up. She sighs. "Do I really make your life that hard?"

* * *

Sometimes, now that Maura is around more, you have to touch her, to relocate her hands away from something valuable, to catch the top of her head, keep Maura the sixth from knocking against the wall while she cries about flies that lay their eggs *under living skin*, cries because she's afraid of rotting. What's the name of that hole newborn babies have at the top of their heads? *Fontanel*, sounds like *fountain*. That soft place that your fingers could go in. The younger, smaller Mauras are the worst, the yous that are at the farthest end of the tether from you. You remember something you heard in a science class once, which may or may not be true, that the feeling you get when you find something cute lights up the same parts of your brain as the desire to crush.

* * *

What's that disorder—or syndrome? condition? you should know the difference between these three words by now—with the women who make their children sick on purpose? It's a German word, it sounds like a kind of sausage. There was that true crime show you saw a few years ago, about the terminally ill girl who killed her mother, and when they found her it turned out she didn't have any of the diseases she was supposed to have and she was five years older than her mother'd told everyone she was. You've never been able to get out of that Wikipedia-diving habit. It's supposed to be something a woman does because she likes the attention—like what people say about teenage girls cutting themselves. By the time you were seventeen, which was the first time anyone could have plausibly called your situation life-threatening, your binder was thick and heavy as a textbook, and the Sharpie had faded and been written over again. When you finally started managing your own appointments, how surprised you were to learn that there was hardly any paperwork at all.

But you're not being fair. While it was happening, there was hardly any attention. While it was happening, a Xanax prescription would manifest periodically in your mother's medicine cabinet, and then disappear, and then come back again. While it was happening, not even you could have accused your mother of enjoying a moment.

*   *   *

That first Maura, that ghost of your suicide attempt, ended up being one of the worst Mauras to have around. She was awful. You kept having to take your knives away from her. She bit her own knuckles until she bled, and the blood got on your sheets in thin pink streaks. She took all your roommate's aspirin and threw them up next to the toilet. Every time she opened her mouth, she cried. You had to wonder if you were being punished. Did you believe in God, or karma, or any sort of divine intervention? Did it matter? You believed in your ability to deserve punishment. You kept having to take your hand away from your mouth, so that you would not bite into your fist like an apple. Maura left one of the kitchen knives on the counter, with her blood still on the tip. You walked in on her in your bedroom, up on one of your chairs and knotting your bedsheets around the ceiling fan. She looked at you, shiny-eyed. You looked back. Your bedsheets were patterned with little sailing ships, done in blue outline. You shook your head. "Seriously?"

*   *   *

You did ask your mother not to write about you. When you were sixteen, after your grandfather died, and you read what she wrote about him. The person he became on paper and the person she became on paper, too solid and too fragile at once. "Please don't write about me," you said after reading it, when she wanted you to say something kind. When you should have said something kind.

You don't get to read the copy of her collection you bought. You learn that she wrote about this conversation, too, when you come home and find yourself sixteen, gritting outrage through your teeth and burning ripped pages over your stove. You snatch Maura back by the hair before she can burn herself. Your smoke alarm goes off.

* * *

Part of your job involves dealing with parents. And it is mostly mothers you deal with. Mothers who come to hand you paper-work, to complain to you about grades or detention like you can do anything about it, to shoot apologetic looks at you while they wait to pick up their unruly sons. They ask you where the coffee is, they remember your name and bring you chocolates at the end of the semesters. Some of them are your age; why is it that they sometimes feel like a different species? Like they've sprouted claws or a horn from the center of the head. You'd like to think you'd be a good mother.

Every year at the start of school the mothers come to give you medical forms, which is when you learn the fragilities of their children, their antibiotics, their antidepressants, their EpiPens. Maybe sometimes you want to say, *Oh, escitalopram, I was on that too when I was ten.* Would that be comforting, who knows? It's also when the vaccine exemption forms are turned in, and you have to process those and not say anything. The women who hand these to you often look like your mother, waspish and WASPy. One of them has a button clipped to her purse strap that says "Mothers know best."

A couple years ago you were visiting your mother—just for the afternoon, you only ever visit for the afternoon—and there was an anti-vax rally on local television, which you were watching instead of talking to each other. The reporter was talking about those parents who'd brought smallpox back to California—brought, like they were carrying it on their backs, in their purses, in jugs, in jars, in BabyBjörns—your mother's forehead kept scrunching up, making worry lines. "What?" you said. She chewed her lip. "What?"

"I wish they wouldn't use that tone," she said, and you restrained a scoff. Your mother gave you a baleful look, as if she'd seen the scorn on you anyway, and folded her hands up so tightly her knuckles went white.

"You don't know what you're talking about, Maura," your mother said. Which was true, you didn't. On the TV, a woman lifted her baby into the air, maybe so that the camera could see him, but for one absurdist second you thought she might toss him into the crowd. Your mother was quiet for a moment too long and you braced yourself, as you had learned to do against a certain kind of silence. You glanced around the kitchen for the remote, but couldn't find it. Looking past you, at the screen, your mother murmured, "It's terrible to have a child."

You raised your hand to your mouth unthinkingly, the tips of your teeth resting against your knuckles. "Don't do that, Maura," your mother said. And she sighed, pressed her palm against her forehead. "I hate it when you do that."

*　　*　　*

For a year or so, part of fifteen and part of sixteen, you would sometimes have crying jags so violent they made you throw up. Maura is on her knees on your bathroom floor. You've got an awkward fistful of her ponytail, strands of hair still falling ragged into her face, coated in bile. When she sobs, it convulses her body so badly that you can't really tell when she's gagging and when she's not. You're squatting with your own, smaller body seizing between your knees. "Jesus," you hear yourself say. "Fuck." The sounds she makes are like trying to drag a blunt knife through cloth. Ragged, tearing. There's some puke on your sleeve. Take a deep breath. Resist the urge to bash her head forward into the toilet to make the sound stop. At least in the moments you want to hurt her you only want to hurt yourself. Say something comforting, in the silence between her hitching breaths. That's what that silence is for. Come on, think of something comforting.

*   *   *

A week after your mother's publication date, you're on your eighth Maura. You're pretty sure it's your eighth. So, assuming one for every essay in the book, then at most you've got four Mauras left, right? You say that like you can safely assume anything, like you know how this works. You're feeling soft on Maura eight. Or maybe you're feeling guilty. Maybe there isn't a difference. Do you think you'd make a good mother, Maura?

You take her to your favorite waffle place. Her favorite waffle place. You've outgrown your sweet tooth, but goddamn did you love those waffles. Your mother called a prohibition on them when you were fourteen, along with most sugars and fats. Your waistline was expanding, encroaching. You've always occupied too much space.

She gets a pecan streusel waffle, caramelized sugar crusted at its edges. What would you call this pleasure you feel at watching her dig in? Whatever the opposite of schadenfreude is. She's got a little bit of whipped butter on the tip of her nose. A lot of the Mauras your mother sends you are sad, but not all of them are.

"Is this your daughter?" the waitress asks. Maura catches your eye over the lip of her orange juice glass. What a messy eater she is. You'd like to think you'd teach your daughter better manners than this. But then, your mother tried with you. Maura swigs back her orange juice, and then mouths, *Old lady*, in your direction.

*   *   *

While you're asleep, Maura goes through your laptop. She's gone by the time you wake up, you don't even have to drive her home this time. But you pull open your computer in the morning and there are photos of you, photos of you beside your mother, photos of you beside your friends, photos of you from thirteen through today. She's emailed three of your middle school friends, how did she even find their emails? You can hardly bear to read what she's written except it starts with, *I miss you*, and then, throughout the paragraphs, *Do you remember? Do you remember? Do you remember?* She's opened a bunch of your mother's essays in your browser, left a comment on one calling her a bitch, which you delete. You don't need that phone call. She's been reading Wikipedia, has articles open with titles that look like the runup to a joke. Folie à deux, how a baby forms in the womb, the Freudian uncanny, Death of the Author. There's definitely a punch line coming here.

*   *   *

Sometimes your mother calls you in the middle of the night. She doesn't do it often. She does it just rarely enough that you can't excuse not picking up. She could be stuck on the side of the road somewhere. She could be in the hospital. You're estranged, but you are still a daughter. Something still happens in your rib cage when you think of your mother dead.

On most of these calls, she will talk to you like she hasn't called you in the middle of the night. The neighbors' health, your

job, have you been to the local farmers' market, have you had your
flu shot, she's doing the NAMI walk this year, have you thought
about it, the cookies she's making. Like it isn't twelve-thirty, one,
two. "Mom." Does your voice waver? Maybe a little. "Mom. Mom.
It's the middle of the night."

And she'll sigh. She'll say, "I feel like we never talk anymore."

Once, though, last year, one-fifteen, you'd been having trouble getting to sleep anyway, holding a cup of tea between your cold
palms, seven weeks since your boyfriend left you. Some of his stuff
was still piled up by the door; was there something wrong with
the way that closeness happened to you? So you couldn't sleep.

And then your mother's tear-stained voice on the phone, out
of nowhere, like God saying, *Yep.*

You took a long, deep breath. "Are you all right?"

And she said: "Did I do enough for you, Maura? Could I have
done more?"

*   *   *

"There is a syndrome called Capgras delusion, the sufferers of
which believe, wholeheartedly, that a person they love has been
replaced by someone else pretending to be them." You're lying on
your back on the sofa, with the book held up above your head.
You've shelled out another thirty dollars for a new copy. You're
reading aloud. Your mother's author photo keeps winking at you
from the inside cover whenever the pages sag to reveal it. She's got
her hair in one of those crown-type updos that you never learned
how to do. You could've asked her to teach you. The ninth edition
of you is lying on her stomach on the floor, chin resting on both
her fists. She might be ten. This isn't the kind of thing she should
be hearing.

"It's extraordinarily rare, usually comorbid with paranoid
schizophrenia—comorbid is, by the way, the word they use to

tell you your child is suffering from the symptoms of more than one disorder. It's a word that sounds right. All around the world, there are myths about children replaced, changed, made wrong by some external force. The common horror of parents feeling that the thing they love most is not right."

Maura's started to cry. When you look down at her, her eyes are so shiny it's a little like looking at a cartoon. "Shit." Get off the couch, take her in your arms, let her huddle up to you. Her body is small and warm, soft and warm, you can feel each of her individual bones. That feeling that sweeps over you, like holding a friend's baby, like holding a half-starved kitten, like feeling the articulated bones in a bird's wing. "Hey, shh." Swaying back and forth there on the floor, rocking her in your arms. Of course she's crying, what did you think would happen? "Shh. It'll be all right."

*   *   *

Tuesday of the next week, you're driving home from work and Maura is with you, which means that technically you're driving her home from a school, the sun on both of your heads and the crossing guard smiling at you like you're her mother. Maura the tenth is talkative, and that's how you learn your mother was wrong about something. Because Maura's fourteen and since you're driving her home from school she's talking about school and she starts talking about being bullied. She's really specific about it too, she's got this look like she's trying to be casual but she wants you to be worried. You hate that look because you know that's something you still do, where you'll say something like it's nothing, but you know it's bad, and what you really want is for someone to say that it's bad, to say that it's awful. But Maura tilts her head like she's talking out the window, and says that Ashley in her chemistry class called her a "saggy cunt."

You stare at her.

"I'm just repeating it," she says, folding her arms sullenly across her chest. Like you're upset about her language. The thing is you don't remember Ashley from your chemistry class but you're pretty sure if someone had called you a saggy cunt when you were fourteen, or ever, you'd remember. It's hard to ask Maura questions because at this age you were kind of a bitch but eventually you realize that your mother thought you were unhappy when you were fourteen because you were being bullied.

"Do you remember Mr. Shelbert?" you ask. She doesn't, though, you can already tell. Your heart is doing something lovely in your chest, achieving liftoff. Your heart is singing.

When you were fourteen, a man who was sort of a neighbor, not on your street but two blocks from your street, burned down his house with his family inside. His family was a woman and a little girl. You cannot believe your mother forgot this. Or maybe just thought that it did not sink into you, even though she always called you a sensitive child. You'd never met the man, but you imagined that you met him. You assigned him faces and put him in crowds, like the devil.

Something in your chest came unhinged after that, and some silvery essence poured out of you, some faith that the world was basically good. What put you out of sorts when you were fourteen? You smelled smoke and could imagine that was what burning hair smelled like. Seeing people on the street, you kept wanting to unlock their faces and get at what was behind them. Bad things just happen sometimes. In the month after that you felt like the apple lying next to a rotten apple in the barrel, picking up its mold. Absolutely none of this is happy, there is nothing happy in this story, except that across from you with her brown little eyebrows drawn together, Maura doesn't remember a word of it. Like she was written up by someone else.

It's a surprise your mother didn't remember Mr. Shelbert, really. That house burning, that would've made a nice backdrop. Thematically appropriate.

*   *   *

You buy a pregnancy test. You definitely aren't pregnant. It's been months since you had sex. Of late, especially, you haven't been in the mood. Maura is still in the backseat of your car. There's an essay in your mother's collection titled "Gestation." You buy the test anyway, take it home.

You pee on it, and a little on your fingers. Even if you were pregnant, a not-so-virgin Mary pushing out your own childhood, you could get an abortion. Maura is sitting on the edge of your bathtub. She's eight and wearing her hair in braids you're almost tempted to undo for her because you know your mother does them too tight. You imagine you're at the park with a baby and someone points at Maura, the other Maura, and says, *Oh, that one looks just like you.* Obviously the pregnancy test is negative and you throw it away, and when Maura asks, "Why do you have to pee on it? Why don't they have one for your mouth or something?" you ignore her. You're not sure it's ethically possible to justify having children right now, the weather is changing and the inhabitable land is shrinking, Congress has passed a bill that deregulates something, though you've already forgotten what and just how bad it is. Sometimes when you try to think about the future you have panic attacks. Is it fair to give a child what the world has left? But you do think you'd be an all right mother.

*   *   *

When you drop that tenth Maura off, your body is still tingling with not being fully known. After your mother sends her inside, she looks you up and down, takes in the longest breath, and lets it out in the longest sigh.

"Why can't you just keep her for a day or two?" she says, shaking her head at you, like you're heartless.

You're not heartless. "I shouldn't have to."

Your mother opens her mouth.

A hand up to stop her. A long breath, in, out. "She isn't mine, Mom."

"She's you." Your mother's eyes are your eyes are Maura's eyes, big and hurt. She could look so pleading.

"We can't both be me." Why do you say it that way? In that way that leaves room for your selfhood to be displaced.

Your mother shakes her head at you. "Did you even read the essays?"

"I already know what happens in them."

*   *   *

How's this for a metaphor? You're sitting at a table with your mother and each of you has one palm curled half around the white shell of an egg. The egg is organically perfect, round and smooth and cool as if it has just come out of the fridge. You want to put the egg whole in your mouth and swallow it, shell and all, let your throat swell like the body of a snake to accommodate it. Your mother keeps telling you that if you want the egg and she wants the egg that's fine, things can still be fair. She'll take her side, and you'll take your side, and you'll both just pull.

The hardest thing to explain to someone is something they should already know, so you're trying to tell your mother why, like a baby, you can't split an egg in two, but she gets up to walk away with her side and out spills the white-gold heart.

More a fable than a metaphor. Sometimes when you're daydreaming you imagine writing one very long, important essay, to eat all your mother's essays like a row of eggs. Maybe you don't want to be a writer but you can still hook something clever on the end of a sentence. A story is like an egg, because—

No. A memory is like an egg—

No. When you have an egg in your hand—

You're still thinking about it over a half-written email when you remember that there is a kind of egg that splits and when it does it makes a twin.

*   *   *

Only once, purposefully, did you make the mistake of reading the comments section under one of your mother's essays. You know the universal laws of the internet; you don't read comments sections. There is someone promoting a get-rich-quick scam, and someone saying that if you're going to give your child psychiatric medication you might as well have them stick a fork in an electric socket, same brain damage. There's also a woman who's written, "Jeanne, thank you so much for writing this. It expresses so much I haven't had words for about raising my son. So glad I found your work."

*   *   *

It must be the eleventh Maura, the one where you wake up and you see yourself, your now self, your exactly yourself self, staring back at you with your eyes already open. You were wrong about the suiciding Maura, this one is the worst one. She walks half a foot behind you. She brushes your teeth while you brush your teeth, and when you spit into the sink she spits onto your bathroom floor. She finishes your box of Cheerios. She listens while you call in sick to work. She kicks her feet up on your table and sings your favorite songs, she logs in to your laptop and tweets about your headache.

Babies are born with all of their teeth already in their heads, wedged up high above their mouths in double rows. First the baby teeth come down, painfully, through the gums, and later their shadows follow them. The permanent teeth erupt and knock their used-up counterparts aside. They have both been there all along, side by side. This is the kind of thing you think about sometimes.

By the end of the day you want to scream at Maura. You want to grab her by the shoulders and buckle her. *I'm alive,* your body keeps trying to say, but no one's listening. *I'm alive, I'm alive, I'm alive. I'm real.*

You're pretty sure you haven't spoken when Maura swivels her head toward you, your head toward you. "Are you sure?" she asks. "Are you sure your version is the right version?"

*　　*　　*

The first and last time you tried to say something really profound to Maura, she was fifteen. This was well before the litany of selves. You were twenty-three, you'd just gotten your job at the school. You were younger, comparatively, though that is always true of the past. You wanted to get her away from your boyfriend, even if he didn't seem to mind her, notice her, you didn't like the past and the present breathing so close to each other. But you still wanted to be kind to her. You took her to the park. Like, what did you think you were doing, taking a fifteen-year-old to the park, but you just wanted to sit outside in the sun somewhere, and she sat on the bench beside you. This is true about you, Maura, that you wanted to be kind to her.

"Listen," you said, "listen." You put your hand on the upward jut of her shoulder. It quivered a little. She felt made of bones and

bad eyewitness accounts. Her skin was warm through the cloth,
which was warm from the sun. That was maybe the fourth Maura
you'd ever gotten, and you were still astonished by the fact that
she'd disappear sometime soon, sometime by the end of the day
probably, and she'd go . . . wherever she went. Maybe she went
nowhere, but she was there next to you then. "Listen," you said. If
you ever had a daughter, she might look like this.

"It's going to be okay," you said. Was that really all you could
come up with? Was that the best you could do? But you didn't
have anything else. You couldn't comfort this girl, and you weren't
sure you understood her any better than any adult understood any
child. You only had the insufficiencies that you wanted to hear
when you were fifteen, but that you wouldn't've heard if someone
said them. You are sure, at some point, your mother put her arms
around your shoulders, rocked you against her chest, said, *It's
going to be okay.*

Maura bit her lip. You noticed, as she flicked her gaze upward,
rolling her eyes without quite rolling her eyes, that the color of
those eyes was lovely. The color of your eyes may, apparently, have
always been lovely. Your self looked up at you like the wrong end
of a joke. "Is that all?" she asked.

"Yes," you had to admit. "Yes, that's all."

*   *   *

"This happened to me too." That was what your mother said, the
one time you yelled at her for the essays, which was after the one
about your suicide attempt. You hadn't yelled at your mother in
years; it wasn't productive. Knowing every action is documented,
perhaps you have tried to restrain yourself to those you could
account for. Yet you were crying on the phone, your hands were
shaking, you were folding up the crumpled sheets that Maura had
resigned to you after giving up trying to hang yourself with them.

That's what your mother said on the phone. "This happened to me too, Maura. You aren't the only one this happened to."

*   *   *

The last Maura of the collection arrives infant and squalling in your bed. You awake with her on your chest, like the warm bodily weight of a cat. You awake with her screaming in your ear. While you make your coffee, you rock her. And while you start the car, you sing to her. And you brush her little baby hair, so thin, so soft, out of her red baby face.

When your mother answers the door, you hold the baby out to her. Wrapped in your T-shirt so she won't be naked, waving her little fist in the air. Your mother looks tired. "Maura," she says.

You shake your head. "I can't take care of this for you."

Your mother bites her lip, the way Maura bites her lip, the way you bite your lip. She looks at you with fathomless sadness. "I've always loved you so much, Maura." Her voice is damp. You're not heartless. "I only ever wanted you to be happy."

You hold the baby out again. Your arms ache from the small, squirming weight of her. Poor Maura. This smaller, poorer Maura. You wait for your mother to put her arms out, and wait. When she does, you lay the baby in them, and there is just a moment when you are both holding her, the hot aliveness of her, the newborn smell of her, between the two of you. You think of telling your mother that you've been considering having kids, lately. You think of asking your mother if you'd be a good mother. "I can't hold this for you," you say, instead. "This is yours."

Fruiting Bodies

We all have ways of eating our lovers.

I like mine over rice with vegetables and a hint of balsamic vinegar.

In the evening, in our kitchen, Agnes stood naked with her hands laced behind her neck. I knelt beside her, and cut a mushroom from the back of her knee with a small, sharp knife. I dropped it into a red plastic bowl. The evening light slid like syrup down Agnes's body. By this point, I had learned some of the topography of Agnes's mushrooms, their patterns. Her chest will sometimes grow truffles. The backs of her knees love death caps. I raised myself to a squat, and took hold of the next mushroom, growing at the base of her stomach. I held it firmly as I slid my knife through the stalk. The trick, as with a straight razor, was to cut close to the skin without nicking her.

We had rituals for looking after each other's bodies. When I worked construction in the summer, I would come home and lie on my stomach and let Agnes's hands smooth the knots out of my muscles. If I made hurt sounds, she would touch my chin, the side of my face. "Hush," she said. "Oh hush, listen, you're home now." At home, now, Agnes's skin bloomed mushrooms and I trimmed them.

The red bowl was for poisons. Blue was for edible. We kept our illustrated guidebook on the kitchen counter. We'd had the guidebook before. Agnes was a botanist. Sometimes she still liked to go walking in the woods, and would come back with berries, and herbs, and wild-growing apples. I guided the knife along the curve of her hip, cut away a small grove of destroying angels with their bulbous white heads. Agnes's skin was soft, where the mushrooms grew and where they didn't. "Get the one between my thighs," she murmured. "It's chafing."

A patch of hedgehog mushrooms gave up with barely a tug of the knife and I put them in the blue bowl. I stroked her bared thigh like the flank of a horse. I have always been the one who cooks, in our relationship, who does the nourishing. This comforts me; a need and the ability to fill it. The first meal I made for Agnes, she moaned like she had never tasted food before, like I had just introduced her to the very concept of eating. *This is a good woman*, I thought, *this would be a good woman to love.*

Mostly, I buried the poisonous ones. In our garden, under the dark earth. Better there than in the garbage, where raccoons might get them. We were so careful. Everyone has heard stories of those amateur mycologists who could not tell an orellani from a chanterelle. Orellanine poisoning takes two to three days to manifest. Flu-like symptoms, followed by kidney failure, followed shortly by death. You would never imagine you were sick from something you ate days ago. Once, Agnes called poison control over my entirely ordinary flu. These things make you afraid, love and proximity to the unknown.

* * *

Before the first mushroom appeared, the doctor called us. He said *abnormal mammogram result*. He said *come in right away*. A pale lump in the meat of her left breast. While we waited for the doctor, I took Agnes's shirt off for her, her bra, folded them on the blue-rubbery covering of the cot behind her. I slid my hands up her sides, passed the silk of her body through my palms, and stopped at the crease of her breast. I had been worrying the little knob of flesh for days, whenever she let me, my fingers going to it always, pressing, pinching. The lump was distinct, solid in the softness of Agnes's breast. It felt like, with enough pressure applied, it might pop like a zit between my nails. I squeezed it, asked, "Does this hurt?"

Agnes shook her head. In scientific places, Agnes tended to look in charge. People approached her to ask where things were: elevators, restrooms, the maternity ward. She did not dress like a nurse, but she had a face that could be as smooth as a rounded pane of glass, the shape and color of those windows medical students watch surgeries through. I think people understood from this that she had knowledge of secret anatomies, that she could open things with her hands.

This time, under the LED and the antiseptic smell, Agnes looked lost. The worried line between her eyes, the gooseflesh rising on her arms and chest. She looked estranged from her insides, like they might do something they weren't supposed to. She reached for the paper gown to put it on. "These things are an exercise in humiliation," she said.

I reached up to pet her hair. A little greasy, because she hadn't showered that morning. "You should at least tie it in the front, like a robe. They're looking in your breasts anyway."

"That's not the way it goes on," Agnes muttered. She rubbed her cheek, gestured one-handed to the gown's open back. "Here, Doctor, look how fat my ass is. Do I have cancer? God." Her voice went deep and damp as a plunge into wet earth. I was holding the strings of her gown, ready to tie it around her shoulders. She could wear it any way she wanted. "Give that to me." Agnes took the strings.

She had to pull the gown away from her body to reverse it, and so I darted quick as a weasel between her and the paper, so she held it behind me, and caged me in her arms. "Geb." Agnes put a hand on my shoulder. "I'm all right. Let's just—" She stopped when I bent and put my mouth to the seam of her breast. I had intended just to kiss her there, but the tumor pressed against my lips and Agnes shivered, so I put it between my teeth. I pressed my teeth into it, just a little. When Agnes did not seem to feel it at all, I pressed harder, as if I might really bite the cancer off her, and then the tumor did, somehow, come off in my mouth.

I stumbled back a step and spat into my hand. "What?" Agnes said. Baffled, I shook my head. I looked down at what I held.

"What?" Agnes said again, setting the gown aside, putting her hands out to me palms first, like she was afraid I'd hurt myself.

"No, no." Between my thumb and my forefinger, the bit of mushroom cap was so delicate. Its gills brushed, feathery, against my skin. I went back to Agnes and spread my hand on the side of her breast. There it was, in the valley where her skin was pressed from the wiring of her bra and earthy with her sweat. I took the mushroom carefully between my fingers. Like pulling a tick out, have to get the whole of it. Agnes gasped.

I held my hand out to her. "Look." The mushroom lay in two pieces in my palm, half shiny with spit.

"Where—" Agnes began, and with my other hand I rubbed at the skin beneath her breast, which was smooth now. "Oh."

She took the halves of the mushroom from me, cupped them in the palm of her hand. The bright light shone down on both of them, Agnes and her body. She laughed an airless laugh. "Champignon," she identified the mushroom. A beautiful thing about

Agnes, how readily knowledge came to her lips, like she licked answers off the backs of her teeth. "It's an edible one."

Agnes didn't let me eat it, then. "Hold it," she said, and gave the mushroom to me. "Don't crush it any more."

"Do you want to wait for the doctor?" With my other hand, I was already handing her her bra.

"No." Agnes smiled, stretched her arms back to do up her own clasps. "I want to take this home."

*   *   *

After I trimmed back the last of the mushrooms, Agnes decided to go for a walk. She had always liked her walks in the woods, and used to enjoy following the road into town, even if the walk took longer than her visit. She used to be friends with people near the top of that road, people she would mention to me. A hermited artist, a young couple living in a trailer, the children who ran up to the edge of the woods like the lip of the ocean. When Agnes went out now, I sometimes worried she would go back to town. Fully in bloom, Agnes's mushrooms bulged cancerously against the limits of her clothing. It would not have been so bad freshly cut, though as often as not the mushrooms did not come away from Agnes perfectly clean. They left fragments of stalk like scar tissue. She scratched or pulled or squeezed at herself, like a teenager with acne, trying to make herself smooth again, and left her skin red and gaping in little open-mouthed sores.

Agnes liked to examine her body as a measurable quantity. Though our extra room was always intended as her office, she never used it much before, preferring to stay late in the lab, with the precision of the instruments, the climate controls, the rooms full of green things. Sometimes I would meet her there, and if it was empty she would take me into her glassed-in worlds, small farms and rain forests and flower gardens grown between windows. Once it was warmer outside, I thought I'd like to build her a greenhouse. Now, her office was filled up with samples, with sketches and notes and slivers of mushroom on microscope slides. On spare pages of her sketchbook, she drew rabbits with clubby mushroom paws, deer with antlers of branching fungi.

I brought her strands of her hair I'd picked off the floor, a pillowcase she'd drooled on, a nail clipping, collecting pieces of her from all around the house and returning them. She would look at them through the lens of her microscope, hum through her teeth, take photographs. I liked how closely she looked at herself now. It was a beautiful way to live.

In her absence, I cleaned the fridge and swept the floors. I put the rent check in my wallet, so I would not forget to bring it to the post office. Now, Agnes wrote articles for glossy periodicals, *Nature*, *National Geographic*, *Scientific American*, which appeared regularly in our PO box, with Agnes's words printed finely beneath someone else's pictures of a breaching dolphin or a foreign sky. I picked up jobs at construction sites, as a dishwasher, moving furniture, though I preferred more and more to stay home, when I could. I did not like to leave Agnes alone.

I washed the day's dishes in the hot sink, sponged the building grime off the counters. I liked to end my day with some amount of cleaning. Outside, the afternoon was sliding toward the night, the sky a purplish flush. I turned the lights on, so that when Agnes came back the cottage would be glowing for her. I took the mushrooms outside to bury before it got too cold.

Our garden is bordered by an unsteady white fence, beyond which the woods are a tender green in the evening light, veined with deer paths. The fence is a porous boundary. Agnes's strawberry plants push through to the other side, and when we dig along it we find roots that aren't ours.

I dug deep and close to the house. Though Agnes said it was silly, I feared the deer and the squirrels turning things up. They wouldn't eat the mushrooms, Agnes said. She said, "Animals know what things are poison. How else would they live?" I preferred caution anyway. I dug the hole deep and narrow, and into it I poured all the poisonous ones. Agnes's death caps, her false morels, the destroying angels.

Close to me, the ground creaked under the weight of a body.

Living in the woods, you come to a taxonomy of sound. You learn how entirely alien human movement sounds from anything else. And living with another person, you learn their noises too. Their pace, breathing, the register of their voice. The body in the other room.

I mean that I did not mistake the sound of breaking branches for anything besides what it was. A gait heavier and clumsier than Agnes's, someone unused to navigating in wilderness. It's easy to listen for that, the slide of tennis shoes in mud, the complaints of birds signaling the potential threat.

I pushed dirt over the hole, and kept my back to him.

"Hello?"

I stayed where I was, crouching. The earth fell dark on the backs of the mushrooms.

"Hello?" His voice was deep, impatient, with a consistency like tree bark.

"Hello."

He grinned at me. He was perhaps thirty, with a carved, angled face and sweaty hair hanging over his eyes. He looked like he was trying to look like a hiker. I had not been grinned at recently. Agnes didn't grin. I examined the several white squares of his teeth, like Chiclets buried in his gums. He was leaning awkwardly against the fence, propping nearly all his weight on it.

"Please don't lean on that."

"Sorry." He steadied his elbow on the post, and the wood creaked. Agnes and I had laid that fence ourselves. Me holding the hammer and her hands steadying the wood. "I'm hurt." He levered his socked foot up onto another post.

He seemed to have punctured himself, deep into the ball of his foot, and a vivid gem of blood welled from the hole in his sock. I am not a doctor. I could not be expected to know a serious wound. But if he was trying to get himself to the road, he seemed to be in trouble. Briefly, I imagined the hole in shoe, sock, foot, and the things that might pass through it, bits of leaf and twig, the casings of insects, the dirt. We were over a mile, perhaps two, from the kind of road an ambulance could drive on. Agnes and I followed a bike path when we needed to go to town.

"What are you doing all the way out here?"

He gestured to his foot. "I fell on—there was a fucking nail in the path, and I stepped on it. Can you help me, please?"

"A nail?" That looked like a lot of blood for a nail, though I supposed it mattered of what size and where. There had been more buildings in this area, once, and the occasional rusty builder's nail did make itself known on the ground.

"A *big* nail." He gestured emphatically at his foot. "Please."

I wasn't sure what he expected me to do about it. His sock must have been blue once, was now soaking a deep purplish color, and had the miniaturized embroidery of some very expensive hiking line.

"Are you going to do something?" he snapped. His was a loud voice, where I was not used to loud voices, or, rather, was used to mine being the loudest.

I considered the smear of mud and blood. "I could bring you out some bandages. Or"—I knew that I was supposed to offer; I did not want to—"you could come inside."

"Yes." He smiled. "Thanks. That one. Can you help me?"

I went and opened the gate for him. He pushed through, and then steadied himself with a sudden hand on my shoulder. His palm was slick, not just with sweat, but with dust and sap and his own blood. My tank top strap, thin and rough under the ball of his wrist, ground into my skin. He was perhaps eight inches taller than me; I am not tall. I would guess forty, fifty pounds heavier. His arm came down across my shoulders, against the soft back of my neck, and I ducked out from beneath him before he could get a grip on me.

He fell. He landed with his shoulder in one of Agnes's planters, which I had built. The wood groaned under him, and he groaned, his eyes closed. I stepped back from him, resting my heels in the soft dirt. "Please don't touch me."

He opened his eyes. They were blue, that human blue which is not like the water or the sky or flower petals, only an eye. His mouth was slack and his face pallid, and I noticed then, in an absent way, that he was handsome. Beneath the beard and dirt, he had an easy, masculine kind of handsomeness, like a face carved from oak. Sweat stood out on his forehead in individual droplets, as if startled from his pores. I pointed at the door. "It's just there." He had made it this far.

When he at last got to the couch, he collapsed without waiting for me to offer it, so I went into the kitchen and got the old dishrag. "Put this under your foot," I told him. The couch was not new, but we'd kept it in good condition. "And take off your shoes."

"I'm Arthur," he called after me, even as I went out of the room.

I came back with the first aid kit. When you lived as we did, the distance from town and undrivable roads, you had to be prepared. The usual gauze, butterfly bandages, disinfectant, and aspirin. But also glucose, sutures, nasal airway tubing, a clotting sponge, rehydration salts. A bag of solutions to our bodies, even the secret parts of them. So that if I needed to I could pull Agnes's skin together, reach down into her lungs or her bloodstream. I had added, lately, atropine, which is an antidote for muscarine, penicillin for amatoxin, activated charcoal, and an emetic to induce vomiting.

Arthur had raised his foot on the arm of the couch, but had not put the dishrag down. Instead, he was wiping the sweat from his face. I tucked my fingers under the lip of his sock, and peeled it back, against the resistance of scabs loosening from skin. He shouted, and tried to pull away from me, so I caught his ankle and held him while I finished it.

I cleaned the sole of Arthur's foot with wet wipes, blood and dirt coming away in quick, neat stripes until I could see the hole clearly, narrow and deep. "Stay still," I said, but he wouldn't, kept squirming and shifting his leg, a muscle spasming in his thigh. I let the wet wipes fall in a crumpled pile on the floor.

"You need to come forward." I pulled him so that his foot was off the fabric of the couch, while he hissed at me. I could see the smear of blood and dirt where he had been.

"Jesus." His eyes were closed, his mouth pulled into a thin wince. "Sadist."

I dribbled disinfectant over the wound, watched it puddle on the floor. The only satisfying part was the bandaging, blinding that little bloody eye with cotton, and then circling all his skin around and around in the white gauze.

"What's your name?"

"Geb."

His laugh sounded like a branch being stepped on. "Were your parents hippies or something?"

I tightened the bandages, and taped them closed.

"My parents were hippies," he said. "Reformed hippies."

When the bandages were done, I gave him two Advil from the first aid kit, and went and sat in the wicker chair. The cushion was starting to spit up feathers, which poked into the bare skin beneath my shorts. Agnes and I always used the sofa. The wicker chair was for guests, but we hadn't had guests in a while.

"Do you have someone who can come and help you?" I didn't think that, even with Agnes's help, I would be able to carry him as far as the road. A little distance, maybe, but it was more than a little distance.

"I was hiking alone."

"There isn't a hiking trail near us."

His left shoulder crept up toward his ear. "I must've gone off."

Far off. A couple of miles off, at least. "Do you have someone you can call?"

He stretched his bad leg on the sofa, dropped his foot on the cushions with his muddy shoe still on, and then shook his head. "I saw some deer tracks, so I wandered off-trail."

"Are you a hunter?" Of course, that wasn't what hunters did, not good ones. If he was a hunter he might have a gun, but not one small enough to conceal in his backpack or at his side. He would have had to leave it behind in the woods.

"No, no." He waved a hand. There was dirt settled into the lines of his palm. "No, you know, I'm not really anything. I just wanted to see some deer. Some wildlife, you know? My buddy said he saw a mountain lion up here."

Mountain lions don't go where people are, not unless they're starving. They keep to their own. Even the sound of human voices frightens them.

"You won't see a mountain lion."

He gestured to his foot, baleful but still smiling, a gesture that said, *Shucks, what can you do?* "Probably won't see any deer now either."

"Can you call your buddy?"

He shook his head. "Went back to Florida a couple days ago. Hey, do you have any stronger painkillers?"

I would have told him that we didn't, though we did have a few pills left over from Agnes's wisdom tooth surgery two years ago. They might or might not have been expired, but in either case I didn't want to give them to him. We might need them one day.

I would have told him this, except that then Agnes came home. Agnes moves like her own big cat, transferring her body slowly from step to step, nearly silent except that she sings. She sings songs first sung by rusty-voiced men: Johnny Cash, Bob Dylan. *If I could only turn back the clock to when God and her were born.*

Arthur looked up at the sound of her voice, which anyone would have. Ill-suited to the songs she loves, Agnes has a voice like clear water passing through cloth. His eyebrows went up when he saw her. He shifted his jaw, as if tasting his own tongue in his mouth. Agnes stilled halfway through the door. He looked like a dirty old coat tossed over the back of our couch, like a dead lizard in our bathtub. Because I would have hated it, I braced for her to hate it.

"Who's this?" I watched her eyes go over him, chronicling, leg braced up, mud on the couch, greasy hair flopped over his eyes.

I curled my lip. "He hurt himself."

"My name's Arthur." He sat up, finally taking his white-wrapped ankle off the back of the couch. "I was hiking."

"Oh," Agnes breathed, and her face relaxed into gentleness. Of course she did not hate it. Agnes has always liked hurt things. I scraped the sofa stain with my fingernail, and dirt bunched up thick against my cuticle. "What happened?"

"Stepped on a nail," Arthur said. He made a pained face, his eyes bright and large. He extended his foot.

"You poor thing." Once I found Agnes a sick rabbit. Limp-legged from an infected bite. She fed it with a syringe. Holding its shocky body close to her chest, wrapped in a towel, her thumb braced at the hinge of its jaw to force it open. Animals do not want to take the things they need. Agnes rocked that rabbit so, so close, stroked the soft puffball of its skull. Rabbits are one of those animals that can die of fear. When we were eating the stew that night, I asked her if she ever wanted to have a baby. It seemed like she might.

She knelt on the floor, took Arthur's ankle between her palms, held him steady as a doctor would while she examined the sole of his foot. "How deep was it?"

Arthur shrugged. "It was a big nail."

Agnes hissed air through her teeth, and she rubbed her thumb over the heel of his foot, stopped at the arch where the bandage was just beginning to pink. "You poor thing." Again. "It might've hit bone."

Arthur lolled his head against the back of the couch. There was a line between his brows, as if he had a headache, or was considering something deeply. "It might have," he said. "I think so." He laughed low, and pushed back a strand of hair sweat-stuck to his cheek. He had the kind of hair that makes a man look like a dog, tawny and lying close to the lines of his face. "It hurts like a motherfucker. What do you think?"

Agnes shifted, curled her hand to better support his ankle. Some people are very earnest. Agnes was sometimes so earnest that it was like being stupid. She wants everything to be all right for everyone. She touched even that joint where he was not hurt with such tenderness. "You should really see a doctor."

"What's your name?"

"I'm Agnes." She reached to shake his hand. Agnes's hands were small and rounded, like the hands of a doll. Wrapped in anyone else's, even mine, they disappeared. With the other, she pointed at me. "That's Geb."

"We met." Arthur directed a broad, warm smile at me. There was sweat, still, standing out on his forehead, making his skin look slick. "What sort of name is that?"

"My name."

"I was just asking your friend"—Arthur turned to Agnes—"if you have any stronger painkillers." I watched the corners of his lips tug like he was trying to make his smile go wider than it should. I am always wary of that kind of person, who can tell within a few sentences who in the room will give them things.

Agnes touched the dip in her chin with one finger. "I think we do." She turned to me. "Don't we, Geb? From my wisdom teeth?"

"Maybe."

She smiled at me.

I tipped my head toward our bedroom. "Probably in the medicine cabinet." I wanted to speak to her alone, but she wasn't moving.

"Would you go get it, Geb?"

I went and got it.

When I returned, squeezing the little orange bottle in my hand, Agnes had pulled the wicker chair up across from the sofa, and they were talking about getting Arthur back to town. "Y'all don't have a car?" he said, in a tone that suggested he'd already said it once.

Agnes shook her head, apologetically. "We bike."

"How far could you walk, do you think?" I asked. Arthur just grimaced and gestured to his foot, stretched out again on the top of the sofa. "How far did you walk to get here?"

"I—"

Agnes lifted the pill bottle, showing me where the label had rubbed off. "Do you remember what these are?"

"They're for pain."

"Yes." Agnes held a pill up to her eyes, and turned it between her nails, squinting. "But what are they?" She paused. "Maybe Vicodin?"

"It's fine." Arthur held his hand out.

Agnes sucked on her lip, considering.

"It's fine."

She handed him the pill, which lay small and circular in his hand for a minute, before he swallowed it. "Give me two," he said.

"I don't think that's a good idea."

"It's for pain," he said, but Agnes capped the bottle and handed it back to me. I closed my hands around it. Arthur's face contracted briefly, canine in his anger, upper lip curling toward a snarl, before he dropped his head onto the sofa's armrest and exhaled a whistling breath through his teeth.

"Cars can't come up here," Agnes explained, gracious enough to ignore his ingratitude if she had noticed it at all, and lapsing, as she often did, back into another conversation. She had pulled the wicker chair perhaps two feet from the couch, within reaching distance, so I leaned against the top of it while she spoke, and idly extended one leg into the space between the two of them. It relaxed me, somewhat, to act as a border. "There used to be a road, but nobody can drive it now. Definitely an ambulance couldn't."

"Well—" Arthur began, and I interrupted him.

"Search-and-rescue will have something. An all-terrain vehicle. Or they could helivac him."

Arthur hissed.

"What?" Agnes's hand lifted. "Your foot?"

"No." He pressed two fingers to his forehead, a gesture like shooting himself. "I don't have insurance."

"Oh." We, all three of us, considered this.

"How much does an ambulance cost?" I hazarded. Agnes put her pointer finger between her teeth, and worried at the flesh on the edge of her nail.

"Probably more, if it's a helicopter."

Arthur stretched out on the couch, letting the bones of his back crack. "I don't want to impose," he said. "Don't let me impose."

*   *   *

Agnes decided that I should make dinner while she and Arthur talked about what to do. I always made dinner, but I did not like the way that Arthur looked at my hands as they moved over the food, the pots, the measuring spoon. On the couch, the two of them leaned their heads together. The electric light slicked up Agnes's platinum hair, so it shone like butterfly wings.

I wanted to make her something simple and warm that night, mushrooms over rice. I sorted out the cremini mushrooms, round as tulip bulbs, and dropped them sizzling into the buttered panned. A thick, earthy smell rose over us as they cooked. Arthur was telling Agnes about his job. He did design work for an ad agency, he said, "but that's boring. You don't want to hear about that. I don't even want to be doing that. It's temporary. I went to art school." He smiled at her, like a slice in an apple.

Out of the deep wicker chair, Agnes leaned toward him. "I draw, actually." I dumped the mushrooms out of the pan and set them aside, poured in the rice.

"Do you really?"

"I'm not very good."

"You are."

"Oh, I'm sure you are," Arthur said at the same time, speaking over me.

"Well." Agnes bowed her head a little. "Thank you." She

turned around in the chair to look at me, resting her chin on its woven top. I opened my hand over the pot and dropped in the green onions, sliced in thin, fine circles. "That smells great. Do you need help?" She poured herself sideways out of the chair, starting to rise.

"Actually"—Arthur raised his head—"do you think you could get me a glass of water?"

"Oh. Sure."

Agnes knocked her hip against mine as she slipped into the kitchenette. I bunched the fresh thyme in my palm. Under the bright kitchen light, the sweat on her back glittered, a sleek expanse of white like the skin of a seal, with the straps of her bra and her dress pressing into it. Agnes is self-conscious about that, those places where her clothing sinks into her body instead of lying flat against it, but it's always made me want to run my finger under that strap, smooth those red marks.

I looked back at Arthur. He was looking at her too, at the soft slopes of her shoulders, the roundness of them. He met my eyes, and turned his head away toward the windows.

When the food was done, I dished a plate of just rice without the mushrooms. I handed it to Agnes. "For your friend," I said. I had cut our mushrooms from her body with my small, sharp knife, held them in the cup of my hand, mated their sweat with the sweat of my skin. My heart rested high in my throat at the idea that she might make me explain this, the lurching, doubting second when I wasn't sure what was understood between us. I touched two fingers to the inside of her wrist, where her pulse lived.

She turned on the heel of her small brown sandal and swept back to Arthur. "Here," she cooed, smiling like a nurse with a child. "This one is for you. Do you need help sitting up?"

I took our plates to the little table, which had the convenience of being behind the couch. I got our pitcher of sun tea and our glasses. Agnes sat Arthur up against a few of our pillows, and handed him his plate again, and put a napkin on his chest.

Only after she sat down with me, and I poured her tea, did I start eating. I roll my first bite on my tongue like some people say grace, the mushroom perfect as a small planet or an eye. Sinking my teeth in and thinking of Agnes's ankle, the inside of her thigh, the damp crease of her elbow. My love bore fruit, our permission to live apart from the world.

"Oh," Agnes groaned, from the depth of her throat. "Geb. Delicious. That's so good."

"It is very good," Arthur said. "Who taught you to cook?"

"I added more garlic this time." I reached over and speared a mushroom off Agnes's plate affectionately. "Do you like it?"

"It's great."

Arthur had rested his chin on the top of the couch. "What kind of things do you draw?"

"Oh." Agnes chewed and contemplated. "Little surrealist things, you know. Just sketches. Animals. Things I see in the woods."

Arthur levered himself up on his elbow, his face smooth and sincere. "You shouldn't undersell yourself, you know? I think women sometimes undersell themselves."

Agnes hummed around the fork in her mouth.

"Would you like me to take a look?"

"That's all right." She shook her head, so the pale tips of her hair dusted her shoulders. She dabbed her napkin against the pink corners of her mouth. "I don't think so, but thank you."

"I used to be into figurative stuff like that," Arthur said. "You know, stuff that really draws on nature?" He paused, holding up his plate in my direction. "Hey, do you have anything else to eat?"

"No."

He tilted his head at me a little, again like a dog, wanting a treat. "It looked like there was more."

I got him an apple.

He pointed his finger at me. "You're the best. Anyway . . ." He seemed to be having trouble sitting up, the pillows slip-sliding a little beneath him as he shifted his body to compensate. "I'm getting more into, you know, earth art lately. Have you girls ever been out to Spiral Jetty?"

Agnes shook her head.

"Oh, it's amazing. It's"—he held his hands a little apart; his palms were big; his nails were not clean—"this great big installation. When the tide goes in and out"—he turned one of his hands palm down, slid it back and forth—"it covers and uncovers the art, yeah? The earth breathes, and the art changes."

Just slightly, Agnes changed the angle of her face, so that I could see the razor's edge of her smile. I covered my mouth with my hand, but not subtly.

"It's beautiful," he said.

"Are you done with your plate?"

"Oh, sure. Anyway . . ." I took the plates back to the sink, rolled up my sleeves. I used to do dish duty in a lot of kitchens, finding work here and there, and have always liked to run the water so hot my skin turns red. With the sink on I could ignore their voices, which was nice and then unfortunate, because as I turned it off Arthur said, "Maybe I could stay for just a couple of days, while it heals."

I went to the kitchen island, and put my elbows on it. I tried to find Agnes's eyes across the room. Her expression looked guilty, flushed with an antelope anxiety.

"It could have gone into bone," I said. "You might need surgery."

Agnes thinned her lips. "Geb."

"It could get infected." I gestured to the white space of the bandages, the seeping blood. They'd need to be changed soon. "We don't have enough antibiotics. Or what about tetanus?" A new thought, but was it even a wrong thought? The builder's nail rusting and jagged in the middle of the path, if it had been in a path, if it had been a nail. "You get that from rust, don't you?"

"Well." Agnes tipped her head, that voice, thoughtful and lightly impressed, that said I'd actually thought of something she didn't. If Arthur had not been here, dragging her focus off, there would've been a soft little curve of her lips. "Have you had your booster shot?"

"My what?"

"Your tetanus booster." Agnes would have made a good doctor, I think, though I am not sorry she didn't become one. Too many strangers, too much of her self with them. When she buried her heart in rotting leaves, at least, it always came back up. "You need one every ten years. That's a no?" Arthur shrugged, and it reminded me of a child. Sullen, exaggerated.

Agnes touched her lip thoughtfully, the dip just above the cupid's bow of her mouth.

"If I don't stay, what else am I supposed to do?" Arthur gestured to the window, palm open, fingers spread wide as if to encompass the night. "Walk?"

"Of course not." Agnes got up, went to the window, as if she might see the headlights of a car through the trees, a helicopter landing. She rocked a little on her feet.

"We can just call 911," I said. "They'll have something."

"I said I don't have insurance."

I glanced down at Arthur, splayed flat on the couch like a deer in the road. "When you die from tetanus, your jaw locks. Your muscles go rigid. You can seize so bad your bones snap."

"Geb," Agnes repeated, her voice a little sharper. I looked

steadily back at her. I've often thought that Agnes and I were so close we could have our own silent language. Agnes does not always consider every possible risk. I clenched my jaw. Some mushrooms grow very quickly, some appear overnight.

"We don't have to let you stay here."

Arthur widened his eyes at me, and then turned the look to Agnes, whom it was really meant for. "I can't walk on it. I can't."

"But—" Nine-one-one had to come and get you, I was sure, even if you didn't have insurance.

Arthur touched the corner of his eye. "I think I'd pass out. It hurts a lot. Walking here I almost threw up."

Nervously, Agnes tugged on the strap of her dress, resetting it on her shoulder, revealing the small red trail its elastic had bitten into her. "Maybe . . ." She pressed her lips together. "Maybe you can just stay here tonight. And we can talk about it more tomorrow."

*   *   *

"I wish you wouldn't be so hostile," Agnes said.

Sound traveled fleetly in our cottage, the walls were not thick. I sometimes pictured our tight arrangement of rooms like the curled shell of a snail, the bathroom, our bedroom, Agnes's office, the living room and kitchenette. Once, shortly after the mushrooms began to grow, Agnes was angry with me and asked me to sleep on the couch. I lay there on my back all night listening to the sound of her breathing.

I lowered my voice. "He just showed up here. Out of nowhere."

Agnes crossed her arms. "He's hurt."

"But what's he doing here?"

"He's hurt."

I sat on the edge of the bed and tugged my socks off, looking at the floorboards instead of Agnes. Sometimes my face did things she didn't like. "We're miles off the hiking trail."

Agnes was wriggling out of her dress, shimmying it over her stomach, and I turned around to watch her. She still undressed with her back to me sometimes. Like she didn't want to see me see her. "Not miles," she said, with the fabric over her head. "It can't really be miles."

"At least a mile. I think it's two."

"Well . . ." She shrugged. Her hair fell feathery over her back. Her bra and underwear pressed lines into her body. The shape of her around them. "He said he got lost."

"He said he got lost," I agreed. In impatience, she turned to me, and I pulled my tank top over my head. A neat way of avoiding her gaze, and when I met it again, her smile was gentler.

"You can't be so paranoid all the time." But as if to soften it, she came over to me and put her hands on my shoulders. She hooked her fingers under the thick straps of my sports bra, ran them down its seams, paused, stroking at the center of my back. "You can act so jealous."

There is a way Agnes has of saying something that is both teasing and not.

Jealousy was a kind of game between us, once, when we went to Agnes's work parties, when she had work parties to go to. She would drift, leave me in corners so that I could watch her laugh and disappear into other people's conversations. There was an ache to it, but also the knowledge that if I went to her, and put my arm around her waist, and my chin on her shoulder, she would lean against my chest, or touch my hair. Because there were limits, there were lines.

Maybe Agnes missed parties.

I reached around her back and took her bra off. In the valley of skin between her breasts, a miniature grove of enokis was sprouting. I pinched their stalks between my fingers.

"Oh." Agnes looked down at them, at their small white faces. "Really?"

"Yes." I took two of the slim mushrooms and tugged.

The slight, clever curve of her mouth, and she plucked at the elastic of my bra. "I don't make a habit of walking around naked in front of strangers."

She was beautiful, but I wanted her to be serious. I put my hands on her hips, and held her at a distance. "He's going to see."

"You worry."

I put my forehead on her shoulder. "I do." I had worried since that first champignon, since we walked out of the doctor's office. I had worried every time she left the house, even with the mushrooms newly shaven, that they might burst forth and betray her, that if she walked down a public street, head after head might swivel to follow, hungrily scenting her strangeness. I had worried even before there were mushrooms at all.

Agnes sighed, and her hand slid up her chest, where she took the enokis between her thumb and forefinger. Her sleek fingers holding that small grove of white trees.

"Is it that you want me all to yourself?" She slid her other hand down her hip, tracing the lines of herself. "Is it that you would like to keep me?" There was a certain twist to her mouth, to the way she straightened her body. I am not always the best at telling what people mean.

"How long is he going to stay?"

"Until he can leave." Agnes shook her head, her bright hair falling mussed around her face. "Let's just not fight, all right? I don't want to fight with you."

I thought of Arthur, through the thin skeleton of our door, lying on the couch with the sinking pits of his ears open. Listening. But Agnes said, "Take your bra off," and I did.

Naked, Agnes was a body carved from damp wood, porous, soft, replete with the surfacing noses of her mushrooms. "I don't want to fight." She took my hand and put it in that space where the enokis were blooming. Their heads were slick eyes on my knuckles. Agnes stroked my flank as one gentles an animal. I felt like an exposed nail bed, like skin that was never supposed to touch air. I put my mouth between her breasts, and closed my teeth on those rice-noodle stalks, held them tender in the moment between consumption and severing. Agnes's hand slid into the waistband of my shorts; the silver berries of the enokis lay in the hollow of my throat, and I bit.

I ate of my lover between her breasts, and held the little heads of the enokis in my mouth for her to taste. I ate of my lover at the musty crease of her belly, where the smallest frill of oyster mushrooms had begun. "My beautiful thing," I said, while I pulled her underwear down to her knees. "My agar wife."

She laughed. She kissed her palm and then lay it on my shoulder. "Mushrooms don't grow in agar," she said. Agnes laughs during sex, this giggle, gasping and disbelieving; she is always startled by something. "Just bacteria."

"I can't believe you want me sometimes," she said, when I kissed her stomach again.

"Why wouldn't you believe that?" I said, and leveled the heel of my hand above her clit. "My damp wife, my rotten-log wife, my mushroom wife. What's unbelievable"—I lowered my head to her thigh, and nipped the yellow head of a chanterelle—"about any of this?"

Her nails pressed deep into my scalp. "You are," she murmured, "so good to me."

*　　*　　*

Agnes needed more sleep than I did, ever since the mushrooms began to grow. It was as if some of her energy went into birthing them.

The next morning I unwrapped the blankets from myself and laid them over her again. I could hear Arthur in the living room, the sound of his body on the creaky sofa. I did not want to go out, but I also did not want to leave Arthur alone any longer in the small cavity of our cottage. I wriggled into sports bra, jeans, tank top. There is a safety in simple, narrow clothes. I have always liked my body, the promise and the tool of it.

Arthur was still on the couch, his head lolling back across the pillows, holding a notebook over his head.

"You can walk a little, then," I noted.

"Good morning." He put the book down on his stomach. When I opened the fridge door, it obscured me from him, but also him from me. Agnes had started the overnight oats last night, and I took them out, the strawberries, the brown sugar from the cabinet. "You look nice today," Arthur said, while I stretched to reach the box.

"You got up this morning."

Laughing, he raised one hand over his head. Like I was pointing a gun at him but he wasn't very impressed by it. "Sure did, Officer. I didn't want to wake you girls up to help me piss."

What an unpleasant thing to say.

I laid strawberries on Agnes's oatmeal, with their points turned out like a flower blooming. I put a small, perfect well of sugar in the center of it. "Do you think you'll be able to leave today?"

"Do you think I could get some of what you're making?"

Agnes came out while the coffee was brewing, after I had given Arthur some oatmeal, in the hopes that he would put it in his mouth instead of talking. She was singing to herself. Sleep-easy and glowing in her blue silk robe, which draped lazily over fawnish shoulders, revealed the fine bar of her clavicle. I wondered if she had forgotten Arthur was here. I wondered if she hadn't.

"Agnes!" he said, and held his arm up with the book in his hand, held so tight that the pages bent down around his fingers. "I've been looking at your sketches."

Agnes stilled. She pulled each silky blue side of the robe closer over her chest and tightened the sash. Her flush was a blotchy pink up to the roots of her hair. "My sketches?"

"Yeah." He peeled the book open, one of his fingers smearing over pencil lines, showing us Agnes's deer, with its fecund horns of thriving mushrooms. On the next page, Agnes's own face, blooming with fly agaric bright behind her ears, with an overhang of lovely red coral fungus above her brow.

"Oh," said Agnes, "those really aren't ready to be looked at." She tried to take the book, but Arthur caught her quickly by the wrist and tugged her down on to the couch with him. He tucked his legs back, so there was enough space for her to sit without touching him, but barely. He laid the notebook in her lap.

"Really." Agnes moved to cover the drawing with her palm.

"No." Arthur grabbed her hand again. I thought of the beak of a crow, pressing sharp through flesh, picking a morsel away and exposing bone. "Look," he said, and pointed at the drawn Agnes's nose, "you have a wonderful line quality, but, I think"—he shifted his finger along the plane of a cheekbone—"your features aren't quite properly set. You have the individual components down, but I'm not sure you have a grasp on the underlying structure."

"When are you leaving?" I pictured a knife, and skin gathering like cloth at the end of it, creating a valley in the body.

Agnes shook her head at me, an aggrieved weariness on her face. Like it was me.

The body on the next page was mine. My body naked, my ribs in the lines and shadings of her pencil. Agnes drew me in motion, stretching on the hardwood floor in the morning, the strain of muscle in my arms, the plane of my stomach and chest, the dark fuzz of hair, down over my scalp, my neck. My body as if it, itself, were carved from hardwood, sleek, shining, knotty; the perfect effigy of myself.

"You model for her?" I watched Arthur measure my shape, compare it to the sketch.

"She does," Agnes said, with my body dangerously visible in her eyes.

Arthur was still looking at me, at my arms, the skin of my throat, the places where my blood flushed. "You must be very close. You know"—he clicked his tongue against the roof of his mouth—"I ran this figure drawing workshop at my community college. It's a skill, posing a model well, working with them." He fluttered his hand toward Agnes. "This is good."

His palm landed on her arm, on that bruisey flush of skin at the crease of her elbow, and he paused with two fingers pressed over her soft skin. "What's this?" he said, and pinched a bit of her flesh, where a pale bump was rising.

*   *   *

I went into town that day, to do the grocery shopping. Of course I did not want to leave Arthur alone with Agnes, but of course we could not live on mushrooms alone. She was working on one of her articles in the office when I left, and Arthur was on his back on the couch.

"Isn't there someone you could call?" I said, as I passed him.

He levered himself up on his elbows. "Geb," in a voice like a foot in dry leaves, "have you thought about why you feel the need to be so confrontational with me?"

When a body is put out to rot, bacteria begin to break the cells down, and the enzymes in the pancreas cause the organ to digest itself. Fluid leaks from the mouth and nose. Maggots use their hooked mouths to spoon up the body's liquids, as they squirm in through the skin, out through the eyes. Carrion birds up above take note.

"Don't bother Agnes," I said, as I turned toward the door. "She's working."

The ride into town was long, a pleasure with the sun on the back of my neck. I liked those fleet moments when Agnes was a fair maid closed in a tower and I was a knight running her errands, with a favor wrapped around my forearm. Town did not always seem so estranged from us. Agnes used to go in more than I did. She used to go to her book clubs, to her work, to her parties. The first time she asked me to come with her, I had to ask her if she thought that was a good idea.

She laughed. "It's fine." And shook her head with all the ease in the world. "They're scientists, they're not like that. Maybe some people around here are, but they're not. It's fine."

It was fine, then, though the gentle pressure of her hand in mine had seared me, her skin, like overheated metal, seeming to produce both heat and over-bright light. Still, then, it was fine.

In town, I bought everything I could carry in the bike's basket. I weighed the round tomatoes in my palm, and found them not quite ripe enough. I thought it would do good to make Agnes a particularly excellent meal. I went to the farmers' market instead, to find ingredients that were sufficient.

By the time I came home, the light had a silken, pre-evening quality. The cottage lay stormy against the trees behind it, with the evening flowers beginning to show interest in the back garden.

I parked my bike next to Agnes's, where the first layers of dust and small leaves, those articles of disuse, were collecting on its blue paint. When Arthur was gone, I should take her into town. I should take her to a coffee shop, or to a dinner party. I should take her to another town entirely. We would rent a car. We would go dancing. I would insinuate my leg between her thighs, and buy her frilly, expensive cocktails. I would take her hair down, and hold one hand at the sweaty back of her neck. I would eat her out in the seat of the rental car, with her back pressed right slick to the foggy window, mushrooms growing up against the glass.

When I opened the door, Agnes's expression turned rabbit-like. Small, and caught. Arthur's foot was in her lap, his dirty toes like the spotted heads of chestnut dapperlings. She was unwinding his bandages, stripping down to the wood-polish stain of his blood.

He spoke animatedly, with both his hands suspended in the air, and in the confidence of Agnes's hand resting on his ankle. "I think I lost a lot of direction around then, you know? I don't know if you've ever had that happen. Have you ever lost something, where it feels so much like you'll never come back from it that you just stop crying, and you let yourself get . . . really isolated, really adrift, you know? I'm still trying to figure it out, I'm still trying to—"

Agnes must have squeezed his ankle, because he looked up sharply, first at her and then at me. Have you experienced that, the moment in which someone who is supposed to be your ally is suddenly allied with someone else?

"I was just changing Arthur's bandage," Agnes said, as if she had to make excuses to me.

The chestnut dapperling contains the same kind of toxin as the death cap, amatoxin. Amatoxin inhibits an enzyme necessary to RNA synthesis. It perforates the plasma membrane of the cell. Fatalities usually come from damage to the heart or the liver, where the amatoxin stops the body from repairing itself. The cells, and then the organ, dissolve.

Agnes unwrapped another layer of bandages. The skin of Arthur's foot was pink and vulnerable, like the new skin of a baby rat. It looked to be healing well.

"Could you get me a damp cloth, Geb?" She turned her lids down sweetly. "With warm water, please."

"Do you have any other roommates?" Arthur aimed the half-hearted grift of his smile at me. "Or is it just you two here?"

Agnes took the cloth, and stroked it over his leg. That nursing quality. Once, when I strained my back at work, Agnes lay me down on the bed, covered me in hot pads, fetched me tea. She rubbed her slow soft hand over every muscle in my body.

"It's just us," she murmured.

Arthur tipped his head back on the sofa. "Must get lonely."

"If you don't go to the hospital soon," I said, "you might die seizing," and then I left and stood in the hallway. I opened and closed the door of our bedroom, so that they would think I had gone in, and waited. It felt as if there were small copper wires wrapped around each of my muscles, coiled very tightly, and constricting.

"It seems to me," Arthur said, "that Geb doesn't like me very much."

Agnes sighed. I could see that sigh in her, without seeing her. The way it would pass like a slow roll of water from her shoulders down her back, the way that she would lift one hand, duck her head a little, and tuck a strand of hair out of her face. Even if there was no strand to tuck there, she would make that phantom movement anyway. "Geb can be very territorial."

"I think anyone would be territorial over you."

A hesitation, a quiet hesitation, and not even the sound of Agnes breathing. "I'm not—"

Arthur laughed. "I know. I know. Sorry. That was too much. I'm too much sometimes."

Agnes liked it when people called her beautiful. Not because she was vain, or if she was vain who could blame her, but because she was entirely unconvinced that she was. I wondered if it had started to matter less from me, because I said it all the time.

"I just hope I didn't offend your friend," Arthur said.

Agnes was quiet. She was quiet like she was choosing her next words carefully. "Geb and I are very close. I think that, sometimes, she can be very dependent on me."

There are fungi that keep tree stumps alive. They attach two trees and can transfer nutrients between them. Occasionally, then, when one tree falls, and can no longer catch the light with its own leaves, it is still fed by the others, bonded to them by that quiet underground web.

Of course, if the connection is severed, there is nothing the tree can do for itself.

"She's jealous." Arthur sounded pleased. "Of me."

"I'm going to get some more bandages."

I didn't try to move as I heard her coming into the hallway. I waited. There was no surprise on her face when she saw me, but the plum of her mouth pinched together, rotted, and I thought, *Please, oh please, don't be angry with me.*

"You were listening," she said.

"Yes."

She slid past me into the bathroom. She came out with the bandages.

"Maybe I am jealous," I said, hushed and sharp and small, Agnes's body insinuated close against mine, me trying to stand in her way, without making myself visible in that open arch of doorway. "Maybe I am jealous about this."

"Don't be," she said. I reached out to grab her shoulder, but she leaned away, this small, quick motion, which was not enough to be out of my reach, but enough to signify that she wanted to be. So I couldn't touch her. So I could do nothing, because sound carried in our little house, and she slipped around the corner, and back out to him.

*   *   *

When Agnes came to bed that night, she lay facing away from me. "Don't be angry," I said, to the raised mountain of her back, the line of white mushrooms, the destroying angels of her back. "I love you, don't be angry with me."

She turned over to look at the ceiling, and then she guided me toward her. My cheek against her chest, against the ridge of her collarbone. "I'm not angry with you." Her voice had a stillness to it that made me think of empty clearings, of fairy rings, of being spirited off to some far, awful place. *Hush*, I wanted her to say. *Oh hush.* "It isn't healthy, though, how suspicious you are. It isn't healthy how the only person you love is me."

"That's not true."

She sighed, and touched my hair, pressed her nails into the back of my neck like I was a dog. "Who else do you love?"

"Why is it a problem that I'm loyal to you?"

My father is dead. I don't talk to my school friends anymore, and had few to begin with. I never got along with people at work. It's a miracle that I met Agnes, but I have, anyway, always been a one-woman creature.

Her breath shivered in her throat, a sound like that small, rustling beat of wings. "Is that what you think, that I'm not loyal to you?"

"I didn't say that."

"It's fucked up," she said, "that you think me caring about other people implies that."

I lifted my head off her chest. I opened my mouth, thinking to say something.

"Not even caring about," she said, "even being nice to."

"I don't like him."

Agnes sat up then, sharply; her shoulder knocked into my chest. "I don't care if you like him."

"Do you like him?"

She shook her head, hard. She looked like a schoolteacher when she did that. I wasn't sure whether this was an answer or not. "He's hurt. What do you want to do?"

"I don't care," I said, because I didn't. If he was going to die in the woods, then I thought he ought to die there. I thought it would be a generous use of his body to feed it to crows. There were people who asked to have their body fed to crows, when they died. They called body farms about it.

"Do you think I'm going to cheat on you?" Agnes asked. There was an angle to the question, to position it as the farthest possible thing.

"He keeps touching you."

She touched her forehead, the crease of skin between her eyes. "I don't want him to touch me."

I started to sit up, feeling a spreading heat, an elastic outrage. "Then—"

Agnes cut me off. "He's just being nice."

"He's *not*."

"You can't keep me locked up here," she said. She had lain back down again, settled herself on the pillows. She was staring up at the soft whiteness of the ceiling like I had built her a prison. "I miss people, Geb. You aren't the only person."

I'm sure it won't surprise you that he did not leave after one day. He lounged on the couch. Agnes changed his bandages for him, her fingers like spider legs over his ankles. He talked to her around me, when I cleaned, while I cooked. "I wish I could help you," he said to me, while I wiped down the coffee table where he had been resting his foot. Arthur told Agnes about his art, stories from his office, about his buddies, and their hiking trips. He made her laugh.

I knew he got up when neither of us were in the room. It was the small things. Two or three books rearranged on the shelf, his phone charger plugged in on the other side of the room, a bowl of oatmeal, or a glass of water, already at his side in the morning.

Agnes did pull away when he touched her. She did sit far on the other side of the couch from him. She angled her shoulders to avoid his hand on her back. He was casual, expansive. I took care never to pass by him closely enough that he could reach for me, because he would.

"Stop," I said, when his hand grazed my hip. "Stop. I don't want you to touch me."

And he lifted his palm, held it up to me as if in surrender. "Sorry, sorry, Officer. It was an accident."

I walked away, but he was still speaking to himself, to Agnes in the room with him, her head bowed over her laptop, writing up one of her articles, maybe listening and maybe not. "Didn't know I was over the legal limit, Officer. Sorry about that."

I made him rice, tomatoes, pasta. "I wish I could help you," he said to me again, from his seat on the couch, with his foot atop it, lying in the stain of his own blood. "What are you two eating?" he would say, when Agnes and I had our dinner. "That looks good."

*   *   *

Agnes let me trim the mushrooms again on the third day, because their small knots were already showing through the cotton of her

long sleeves. I roused her in the dark of the morning with my
hand on her side. I got the bowls from the kitchen cabinet, and
my paring knife, going softly past Arthur on the pads of my feet.
Agnes lolled in her pink cotton romper. She hummed to herself
with her voice still sleep-gummy. "Tell the rambler, the gambler,
the back biter. Tell 'em that God's gonna cut 'em down."

I undid the buttons on her chest, and knelt between her
spread thighs. She smiled down at me, and I slid the jumper off
her shoulders. The grooves of the hardwood pressing into the thin
skin of my knees.

Agnes laid her hand on my shoulder. The corners of her
mouth turned up. "Well, my goodness gracious," she sang, "let
me tell you the news. My head's been wet with the midnight dew.
I've been down on bended knee, talking to the man from Galilee."

"You're like an old man." I made my back a bow curve, arched
my neck up to kiss her. Some things are just so lovely. She rolled
my bottom lip between her teeth and then bit. "I need to take your
underwear off," and she stood half up to let me. There was the
comfort of a still, empty room, the light between us, the dark outside. Have you noticed that, how when you turn the lights on in
your house at night, space decreases to the size of the room you're
in? It becomes the only room in the world.

"There's a horn of plenty growing from your back," I told her,
and then licked into the black velvet trumpet of its mouth. I cut it
away. I shaved mushrooms from her shoulders. I untangled them
from the slick curtain of her hair. I trimmed an ivory funnel quick
and easy from her thigh.

"As sure as God made black and white," Agnes sang, "what is
done in the dark will be brought to the light."

"Do you think he's really injured?" I sliced the velvet pioppini
from her ankle.

"You saw his blood. You bandaged him."

"Do you think he's as injured as he says he is?"

Agnes shook her head. "I don't think you should assume people are lying."

"Have you left him alone in the house at all?"

"Why?"

I stopped, with the knife above the oyster mushrooms on her shoulder. "Because I don't want him going through our things."

"I don't think—"

"Your office door doesn't lock."

Agnes exhaled, lifting her shoulder into her knife, and that moved me, that she was so trusting in my hand on her, and did not believe I would even accidentally hurt her. "I don't really want to talk about this," she said. "Not right now, this is just for us."

She put her hand in my hair, and dragged my head back, turned my face up to hers. "I love you," she said. Her eyes were the clear pale gray of nestling feathers. I could see the lake of each freckle on her nose. She lay her palm on my cheek. "This is just for us."

*   *   *

We went back to the living room together, with my mouth tasting of mushrooms and Agnes's tart body. We were of a piece in that moment, my hand at the crest of her waist, that small possessive tense. This is just for us, this was just for us.

Arthur had his feet on the coffee table, angled to greet us with the opening eye of his blood on his bandages. He was holding Agnes's sketchbook again, at a contemplative distance from his face, and he lowered it at the sound of our footsteps.

The grin on his face was canyon-deep.

"I wondered," he said, "where you got the mushrooms from."

He gestured at Agnes, his hand taking her in, taking in her body, the whole of her. "So that's what they're about."

Like a straight razor, I slipped my body in front of Agnes's body. "What?"

A word you might have used to describe Arthur is *guileless*, in the broad openness of his body, in the easy way his shoulders rested on his frame. Some people have a way about them. He gestured out the window. "I went out for some fresh air."

"Oh." The small black coin of Agnes's open mouth.

"You said you couldn't walk."

Arthur stretched his back, bringing his arms to meet slow and languid above his head. He wove his fingers together, his back cracked. There was a smear of fresh dirt on the bandage Agnes had wrapped for him. "I can't walk far."

"It's none of your business." I wanted to put Agnes away. In another room, in a tower, in a castle, in a place where only I could reach her, and also in a place where she could not sweep my feet out from under me, trying to be kind.

"I didn't say it was my business," he said, making that awful gesture again, the hands raised, surrender.

Gyromitrin is the toxin found in mushrooms of the genus *Gyromitra*, like the false morel. Poisoning leads to liver necrosis, your organs dying in your body. Symptoms begin in as little as two hours. Vomiting and diarrhea. Followed by dizziness, involuntary muscle and eye movement. Death occurs within five to seven days, as the kidneys and liver fail. In severe poisonings, there is a terminal neurological phase. Seizures, delirium, coma, death.

"I just think it's really amazing." He reached both his hands out, as if to take Agnes's body between them. "How did you do it?"

Agnes shook her head, and I loved her for her unwillingness to explain even if it came from inability. Arthur sat forward on our sofa. The threads would be matted with his sweat, the stink of him and his blood. "Did it just happen?" He rested his elbows on his thighs, a casual authority to his posture, in this place where he was not welcome and had not been invited. "Who have you talked to?"

"No one," Agnes said. She lifted her hand halfway into some uncertain gesture, and then let it fall again. "I'm not sure it would be a good idea."

"Why not?" The easy, inquisitive cock of his head. I stood halfway between them. I could have reached forward, hooked my fingers in his mouth, and pulled until those white teeth abandoned their sockets. "Don't you want to know what caused it? What it means?"

"She's studying it," I said, though I knew as soon as I had spoken that I should not have given him any handhold. He exhaled, a half laugh or pure animal satisfaction, looking past me, as usual, at Agnes.

"I'm just desperate to know," he said, with awful honesty, "if you'll tell me."

I looked at Agnes's face, and, horribly, I saw an opening there. A floral expansion. Her poor scientist's mind locked up so long. *Let me tell you*, her face said, *oh, let me tell you.*

She sat down beside him, perched on the raised back of the couch. "It started a few months ago. I don't know why. I did do some work with the mycology labs, but not extensively. I thought it was cancer, initially. That is—I found a lump. They told me to go in for a mammogram." She pushed her hair out of her face, and then, just like that, she told him everything.

He kept leaning nearer as she spoke. And she would lean away from him. Not far, not obviously, but like those plants that curl themselves inward when you touch them. Her shifts in parallel to his. "That's amazing," he kept saying. "That's fascinating." He licked his teeth.

*   *   *

Muscarine is a nerve agent found in many mushrooms, including fly agaric and the ivory funnel. Though it does not deliver the surest death, it is the quickest. A headache sets in after as little as fifteen minutes. The ivory funnel is sometimes also called the sweating mushroom, but victims cry as well, and drool. Usually an asthma attack, then, or several. As the heartbeat slows, and the blood vessels widen, blood pressure drops, and circulatory shock sets in. Death can arrive within nine hours.

It was hours before I got Agnes alone again. Every time she stood, there was something. Arthur's hand on her arm, another question she could not seem to walk away from, Arthur's voice demanding, "Where are you going?"

When she came, finally, into our bedroom, I was waiting. My back against the headboard, my legs crossed in front of me. I thought of my body like the swaying curve of a charmed snake. Agnes was pale and tired. I held the ivory funnel up to her in both my hands, stroked my thumb along its stalk.

I saw the moment that Agnes knew what I meant, when some sleeping animal in her mind turned over and cracked a pupil. "No." She held one hand up, and took a step away from me. "Geb."

The ivory funnel is a meaty white mushroom, with a head like the face of the moon. Chopped up and cooked, one white mushroom could look much like another.

"Bury that," Agnes said. "Geb, you're supposed to bury those."

If you ever find yourself in a situation like this, I will tell you that at least you'll learn from it. How quickly you come to a willingness to kill, and how quickly your lover will believe it of you.

There are so many ways to find out what you will do when there is no one else to help you.

"He saw you." There are things I think Agnes has always failed to understand. Lack of kindness being one of them, and also that a person can both behave kindly and mean harm.

Agnes's hands flew up. "And?" She lowered her voice, leashing the bird of her anger. "And you think that means we should kill him?"

I nodded, and her hands went up again. Like they were trying to escape her body. "*No!*"

"He saw you." I didn't know how to make her see danger when she didn't perceive it. When she gave herself to the danger, and let it in her home, when she spoke to it about mycology. I wanted to take her by her shoulders and snap her like a whip. I wanted her to understand.

"What do you think he's going to do?"

"He could tell someone," I answered plainly, because I knew already that if we let him leave he would. Knew from how amiably he had let the idea lie when she rejected it. Knew because she had told him her drawings were not to be looked at, and the next morning he had found her sketchbook. Where had she kept that sketchbook? Even as we spoke, I thought of Agnes's office door, which did not lock because until his arrival we had not needed locks within our little cottage, and the gallery, the buffet of her body's fine phenomena tucked just behind it.

"Who's he going to tell?"

I shook my head in one quick jerk. "Someone in town. A friend. Someone he meets on his trip home. A newspaper." The magazines that Agnes wrote for turning hungry on her, a photograph of her skin, pitted with life. Worst of all, that it would not be her who wrote the words beneath it. "Anyone, someone."

"All right, all right," Agnes said, in that voice she used to soothe wild animals, the deer and the rabbits and me, born low in her chest and rasped against the roof of her mouth. She reached for me, slowly. "All right. What are you afraid of?"

I pulled away. My tongue was a snake in my mouth, snapping against the walls of it. "I'm afraid that someone will hurt you."

"*Who?*"

How to explain to her that terror that was nonspecific but certain? Did you know that, once, witches were identified by a devil's mark secreted somewhere on their bodies, which would not bleed when pricked? But the mark was not always visible, and for the task of uncovering it witch-finders carried special needles. Once, Agnes and I went to a diner together, and as we sat down the woman in the next booth said something quietly to her son, and then they both got up and went to sit on the other side of the restaurant. And when I mentioned this to Agnes, she shook her head as if to clear away a bad dream. *No*, she said, and, *Really?* and, *I'm sure there's another reason.* But when she closed her mouth I thought I could hear the small creak of her teeth pressed too hard together. I could not imagine making a present of Agnes to the world, I could not imagine handing her to it gift-wrapped.

I could not imagine that Agnes had ever really lived out there, even if I had met her in the world and plucked her from it. Surely she grew in these woods. Surely we had always lived in this little house together, and that was why she was not afraid. I reached for her and she let me, so I unbuttoned her top. I showed her her chest, and all the secret bumps on it. I pressed my thumb on the raised head of something under her skin.

"Historically"—I swallowed, I pressed my tongue against the roof of my mouth; I swallowed again—"has this gone well?"

She opened her mouth, but I did not want her to speak yet,

so I put my finger over her lips. The softness of her skin there made me panic-sick. I could not bear for Agnes's body to enter the body of knowledge, to be offered for public consumption. I could not stand for anyone but us to take the sacrament of her. "You're wrong, you're strange, and what do you think—what do you think"—I flexed my hands over her shoulders—"someone who isn't me is going to say?"

With the glossy look of a shot bird, she stepped away from me. I reached after her but stopped before I could touch her, unwelcome. "I love you so much, Agnes, I know how to. But what about the people who won't?"

Agnes shook her head. Her face was stone and set. "You can be so dreadful, Geb. So dreadful and so selfish."

I wanted to speak. Maybe there were worse things she could call me, but I could not think of any. Had I been selfish with her? And how, and when?

"Your problem"—she spoke so definitively that I could only imagine she must know—"is that you really want to be the only person who loves me, don't you? You would rather I be alone, and unhappy, as long as I'm with you."

I put my hands over my ears. "That's not true."

"You want there to be something about me that only you could love."

"There are things about you. Like that." I did not take my hands away, or look her in the eye. Perhaps I couldn't. That she used to like to make me jealous, because she knew that I would let her, and maybe this was still true. That when I brought her the wounded rabbit, she held it wrapped tightly in the towel and close against her chest, even after she had cared for it all she could, even as it struggled, and, dying, stretched its wild head away from her. That she had wept, afterward, but closed her eyes, savoring, when she tasted the stew I made her. That if I learned how to really say no to her, I do not know if she would love me so much. "But not the mushrooms."

Agnes took a step back from me, one that was measured. I inhaled, wanting badly to explain myself, to tell her that these things were true but it was true also that I loved them completely, that I loved her as I loved her mushrooms, benign and poisonous alike, with hunger aching sweetly in my jaw. But Agnes shook her head, and took a second step away.

"I'm going to make dinner tonight," she said, "and until he leaves. I don't want you preparing any food," and she shook her head at me, slowly, the way that one looks at a dying animal. I found a deer corpse one day, while hiking through the woods, that was dissolving under the worms, the fungi, the beaks of the crows. The pale antlers lying against the earth. One of its eyes was still partially intact, with the socket just beginning to pull away, and a sheen of once-white liquid. Do you imagine expressions on the faces of corpses? It looked desperate. "Not his," Agnes said, "and not mine."

*   *   *

I slept in the backyard that night, and not much at all. I looked at the clusters of the stars, watched a spider stringing up webbing in our rosebush. Perhaps it was not necessary for me to go back at all. The cottage might close itself, become the perfect yellow shape of an egg containing only Agnes and Arthur, and his large hand with its chapped knuckles smoothing over the seashell curve of her body. How well they could fit into each other, those archetypes of masculine hardness and feminine softness, and how little place there was for me between them.

Agnes left the red bowl for me in the morning, so I woke lying beside the poisonous mushrooms. I buried them without being asked. Maybe I dug the hole shallower than the others, imagining that I would have cause to dig them up. Maybe I patted the dirt over them softly, lightly, with my own two hands. You cannot blame me for hoping.

I still had, also, that small, sharp knife. I could hold him down and turn it around the sole of his foot, peeling and peeling the skin away. Did he really splinter bone, was infection festering there, what was the secret injury down at the heart of him? There are only simple answers to a knife.

But I imagined Agnes's face. I let the knife be.

When I came into the house, he was eating her mushrooms.

It was the plate I had made before we fought. Swiss brown mushrooms with pasta. Garlic, cheese, onion, butter, the heat of the stove on the undersides of my wrist, and the face Agnes always made when she put the first bite of my food into her mouth, which said that I cared for her so well.

The mushrooms, which had grown in a small grove at the back of her neck, like miniature trees. I had bent my mouth to one, and sucked it.

Arthur held a square of mushroom on his fork. The fat dripped onto the plate. When he saw me, he lifted his fork, in a cheers gesture. The slick body of the mushroom caught the light, and then he closed his mouth around it.

I could hear him bite from across the room.

"You can't." My voice sounded sharp and lonely, a crow shrieking its rage outside. "You can't have that."

"Why not?"

When Agnes came into the room, I can imagine what she saw on my face. What I saw on hers was nothing, the flat capstone sliding into place in a wall. When ancient builders built houses, did you know they would bury a man alive beneath them? To ensure the stability of the house.

"You can't have that," I said again, thinking that she had said she loved me, that anger did not kill love, or that, if it did, it killed it like amatoxin. Over a long period, with several lapses and relapses. This is just for us, Agnes had said, had agreed, had upheld. This is just for us.

"Geb." The flat line of Agnes's mouth fell on me like a floorboard. "Geb, stop it."

And Arthur took another bite.

*   *   *

Even inside loss, or the curled serpent of its potential, things have to fill the day.

I cleaned, I made no food. I paced circles in the garden. I took my bike to the road and did not ride it anywhere.

There was one beautiful place. Our small stone house, and the two of us inside it.

Inside, Agnes sat next to Arthur on our couch. She smiled at him, and maintained that careful foot of distance.

She showed him a sketch she had done of him, and he turned it around and showed it to me, resting on his laurels. She had drawn him, the fine knots of each of his muscles, the open collar of his plaid shirt, his golden retriever hair flattened against the sides of his face. He had started to smell, from several days on our couch, and his hair was greasy slick, but she had managed not to draw that. She had drawn him with a loveliness.

For lunch, Agnes served all of us leftovers. Arthur stood from the couch and loped over to the table. "I think," he said, leaning at me over his plate, "that you're quite a loving person, Geb, deep down, but I wish you would work on some of this toxicity."

Agnes caught my wrist. "No," she said, "no."

"See?" Arthur said. He pushed two greasy strands of hair out of his face, and then he laid his hand heavy on my shoulder. There was the slick of his sweat. Frogs breathe through their skin. Imagine, being cupped in someone's hands, and suffocated. "This is what I mean."

And then Agnes put her hand on his wrist. "You shouldn't touch people," she said, "without their permission."

I had fancied myself, before, Agnes's tame animal. Until the sun went down, I measured the here and there of our yard like a dying dog. I thought of places that I could bury a body if I wanted to bury a body. The woods are full of places like that. The woods know what to do with a body. When Agnes came to the door to call me, I did not raise my head.

"Will you come in for dinner?"

"No."

Agnes sighed, pushed a phantom strand of hair from her face. "Can you not," she murmured, "act like the world is ending? For once, can't something be the right size for you? He's leaving soon, and I'll still be here. Will you come in and eat dinner? I cooked."

Her hands were small knots in her skirt. She looked teenage, and the evening was opening its arms for her. She looked like she might touch the back of my neck, and soothe the thorns of my hair there. I went inside.

She'd made that simple dinner again, mushrooms over rice. With zucchini and carrots, and the hint of balsamic. The way that I liked it. This might be called a peace offering, except that she served it to us both.

I want you to know that before this, there was a moment when the meal simmered, when the plates were laid out, when Arthur was looking at Agnes's sketchbook, and Agnes was away in the bedroom, when I could have dropped something into the pot. Perhaps I could not have gone fast enough to the garden, and dug up a death cap or an ivory funnel, and slipped it secretly into the meal. But perhaps I could have. I want you to know that there was a chance, and that I didn't take it.

I closed my eyes. I pressed the mushroom to my tongue. I tried to think of the place on her body it had grown, and then could not bear to, with Arthur next to me, also thinking of her skin. And the damp pop of the mushroom in his mouth.

"My God," he said. "My compliments to the chef."

We ate mostly in silence, all three of us swallowed in the moment, in the different weights that hung from its different arms. Closing my lips around the last mushroom, I met Agnes's eyes. The gray of them had darkened in the evening as if under rainwater. Her mouth was slightly open. *What do you want?* I would have said, if Arthur wasn't there. *Tell me anything you want. It doesn't matter what. Tell me what you want, regardless, and I will give it to you.*

Beside me, Arthur started to cry.

He did it soundlessly, with a quiet catching breath. So startling, that for a moment I imagined he was sorry.

He swallowed, and his throat bobbed, muscles sliding under skin. There was a thick sweat shining on his forehead, I noticed, and beginning to trickle down his face, a drip suspended from the tip of his nose and then falling. His hand lifted, trembling, to his throat.

I backed my chair away from the table. "I didn't." Shaking my head already. "I didn't." I would go for the phone. I would call whoever needed to be called, the helivac that should have come in the first place. There are no things that cannot be forgiven.

"What?" Arthur's voice a low rasp over gravel. "What?"

Agnes caught my wrists in her hands. Holding my arms like we were children, the two of us swaying against the shift of the world. "I did." Her blown pupils, her strange dark eyes. "It's okay. I did."

"What—" Arthur tried again, and his breath was a narrow little wheeze.

"Panicking . . ." I said, "panicking doesn't help."

I could see him trying to make himself level, trying to make his voice stable and flat, and his body, in its panic, looking for somewhere to go. He tried to rise, too suddenly, and gasped. His poor foot.

"What did I eat?" he demanded. "What did you feed me?"

Agnes's palms were slick. When I released her hands, just for a moment, she flinched in the absence of me, a tremble that started in one single vibration, like a quake splitting the earth, and then didn't stop. The glisten of sweat on her cheeks was like silver. I freed one of my hands from her grip, and touched my own tongue. "Not me, right?"

"No." And she fell against my chest. She buried her breath in my shoulder, fixed her arms tight around me. In the background, there were Arthur's gravelly little sobs. "No, not you."

*   *   *

It was a gruesome thing.

I put Agnes to bed, because she was shaking, and because there are some things we do for the people we love. In the case of the ivory funnel, the estimate is that there is enough muscarine to kill a man in one large mushroom. Agnes had put three or four, perhaps, in his dish, drizzled with balsamic. I got up from time to time to check on her. She lay very still in our bed, not weeping, watching the ceiling. I have always known my lover to be very sure in her choices. I kissed her, and I ate the shiitakes from her clavicle. I went back to Arthur, as the shock set in.

The heaving, jerking motion of Arthur's body, like a frog on hot stone; I did not feel nothing about this. But if my hands trem-

bled they still did the work of being my hands, which was all they
needed to do. I gathered his things. His phone and its charger, his
shoes, his torn and bloody sock. Arthur watched me, or at least he
turned his head in my direction, and his eyes rolled in their sockets like a horse's eyes. He had been talking earlier, but wasn't any
longer, the wood under his cheek shining with his own sweat and
spit and tears; his mouth opening and closing, his square white
teeth. There are good poisons to die from; muscarine is not one of
these. But we made do with what we had, and I would not be any
crueler than Agnes had decided, and I would not be any kinder.
At last, I went and opened our kitchen windows, so that the cool,
sweet air poured in.

When he was done, I went and got Agnes up. She tilted her
body to my hands on her shoulders, though she was still too far
from me in the new morning light. "This could be a very bad
thing we've done," she said, and I nearly wept that she said we,
instead of I.

"No." I slipped my finger behind her ear and stroked her
there. "No."

Agnes took his feet, and I took his hands, and we took him
off into the woods. We carried him to the damp places, where the
leaves decay, and the mushrooms grow. We laid him in a clearing,
at the center of it, with the woods growing up around him, with
his eyes open. Open, and in perpetual observation of the sky. The
woods know what to do with a body.

Only then, after we had walked away from him and started
downhill, back toward our bike path, our clearing, our cottage,
did Agnes start to cry. Her wet face in my shoulder, her body
swaying to my body like a vine around a tree, she cried. I think it
was from relief. Certainly I was relieved.

I stroked her hair. "Hush," I said, and Agnes's breath hitched,
shuddered. A rising, irregular lump on the line of her jaw rubbed

sweetly against my throat. "Oh hush. Listen." She hushed, silent and shivering, in the moment of stillness right before a sob breaks. "Listen," I repeated, and pointed up toward the sky, though we could see nothing there yet. "The crows are coming."

And they were.

Endangered Animals

I drove Harry from L.A. to Michigan the same summer that California burned down.

California burned down every year, of course, and had all my life. Fire was one of the only seasons we had. But it was getting worse in a way you could see. In May, I'd driven to CSULA to take my last final of the semester with the smoke so thick on the highway I had to turn my headlights on. Here and there, ash fell at the sides of the road.

The fires had raged through mountains and down hillsides, eating up landmarks and houses and trees. It wasn't like they were that big a part of my life, really, though during the last Topanga fire Harry and I worried that the Getty Villa would burn down. We'd both taken field trips there as kids, and returned a summer ago, back when we were sleeping together again, had gotten told off by a security guard for making out on the lip of a big mosaicked fountain. The fountain was a reproduction of one from Pompeii. The museum didn't end up burning.

Harry loaded her old Camry to its limits with boxes, and together we strapped a black roof bag to the top. The little cactus she'd spent a year tending on her dorm windowsill was wedged into a cup holder, and her hamster, named Emily Dickinson, sat in a white wire cage belted into the backseat. Harry was going to the University of Michigan to get her master's in social work. It was a good school for that, she said, the best.

I still had a year of undergrad left, and was flying back after I helped Harry settle in.

We passed through miles of burnt hills in our first few hours. There was something beautiful about the pitch-black ones, which looked like lava rock or certain descriptions of a woman's hair. But more of the burning was patchy, an uncertain patterning of char against the summer's usual brown grass. Harry had her music up as high as it would go and was singing along. Recently she liked Joan Baez, so that was what we trailed out our open windows, her long, sweet melancholy, and Harry's own untuned voice. Harry sang like someone who so, so badly wanted to sing beautifully.

There was the occasional tree still standing against the ash, some of them black through, raising their branches and twigs against the blue sky like paper cutouts, and some inexplicable survivors, scattered, a dusty, living brown, amid their burned brethren.

"It looks like another planet," Harry said. "Like Mars."

"Mars is red," I reminded her, looking away out the window. It wasn't me leaving California, but I felt like it was, I wanted to look at these hills like I'd never see them again.

"It'll be gold again next summer. Amber."

It felt too generous to call that patchy brown and yellow after anything you might use to make jewelry. Most summers, our hills were like the set of a Wild West movie. They had filmed some westerns out at Vasquez Rocks, actually, the spiny, sloping formation of stone that my father used to take me to climb as a kid. As well as some movies set on Mars. I took Harry there once, and we got drunk sharing a bottle of raspberry rum and made out, lying on our sides on a wedge of stone, until Harry's shirt rucked up and she told me, laughing, "I'm getting gravel down my pants." You could still see the stars pretty well from Vasquez, and the moon was bright, which was good, because we hadn't brought flashlights. We kept stopping, on our stumbling way back to the car, where we'd sleep, that night, to avoid driving the hour back to school. Harry clinging to me and me wrapping my arm around her waist and saying, "Don't fall off," and Harry pointing up at the night sky to tell me, "Look at that, Jane. Holy shit." Amazed each time by our new angle on the stars.

Harry and I had both lived in California all our lives. When Harry looked at grad schools, she mostly applied out of state. She said she wanted to go somewhere green. She was going to freeze her ass off in Michigan.

We'd decided to make an event of the trip. It was the last time we were going to see each other for a while, and I wasn't sure how well we would stay in touch, if we would, once Harry was absorbed by her new city, new school, new people. We were going up the coast first, stopping on the way in our favorite cities, and then driving through Glacier National Park, up the Going-to-the-Sun Road, before we began the long blank journey through the Midwest and finally to Ann Arbor, and Harry's tiny, waiting apartment. I would spend a few days there, help her unpack, settle in, buy furniture from the used shops. Then a flight back to California in time to set up my own dorm.

"It'll probably burn again next summer," I said, and flicked my hand at the countryside.

"God." Harry sighed. "Don't say that."

"Would you roll up the windows? I can taste the smoke." The fires along the freeway were out days ago, but something was burning somewhere. Harry rolled up the windows. Joan Baez, louder now that she was trapped against the glass, sang "Sad-Eyed Lady of the Lowlands."

Harry drove with one hand on the steering wheel, and her head leaned against the driver's-side window. She looked like some kind of desert animal, short, big-eyed, arranged out of angles. Like a pocket mouse, tiny and staring, with quick knobby knees. Her hair was a ragged twist of sandy curls. All of it made her look younger than she was. The car wove minutely side to side with her steering. She was a crappy driver, but she loved to do it. "Did they ever cancel school for the smoke, when you were a kid?"

"Oh sure."

"I won't miss that," she said. "Or waiting for the big one."

I leaned over and knocked her on the shoulder. "Don't be so sure yet." I loved Harry's shoulders, which fit perfectly in my cupped palm. "We're driving right over the San Andreas."

When Harry laughed, she tipped her head back, and I could see the tips of her teeth. It was beautiful, and also something I think she did because she saw women do it in movies. Sometimes, even when trying very hard, Harry didn't manage to seem original. "You're such a dick," she said. "You're gonna be out there for another year. If either of us is gonna get eaten by an earthquake."

"Guess I'll die, then."

"Ugh." Harry held her free hand out. I dropped a handful of shelled pistachios in it, from the bag I was holding between my knees, and she shoved them into her mouth. "Don't die, I'd miss you."

"Sure you would."

"Sure, I would. I'd miss your sweet temper."

From the speakers, Joan Baez sang her last, mournful note. "Dylan wrote this for the woman he was with after Joan," Harry told me. Harry talked about artists she liked like they were her friends, with first names. "The woman he married."

When we finally came down out of the hills, to the long straight highway that would smell like cows for the next hundred miles, Harry whooped and slammed the accelerator. On these empty roads, she drove like a teenager who wanted to die. The car lurched so quickly toward ninety that I could feel the world narrow.

*   *   *

I met Harry in my second semester of college, on the steep staircase that went from the cement island of our campus downhill to the boxy white dorms. In the spring, the one stunted cherry tree that grew on that hillside flowered pale pink, and the concrete steps filled with hundreds of black caterpillars.

At their largest, they were about the size of my thumb, and covered in a layer of bushy black spines, so that each looked like a bit of wool dropped on the ground. I didn't know where they came from, or why there were so many of them, but they showed up every year. For days I couldn't walk down the steps without seeing ten or fifteen, and more of their crushed bodies underfoot, smeared like roadkill on the sidewalk. Hardly anyone even looked to avoid stepping on them. It's amazing what college students can ignore, especially by the middle of the semester.

That day, I saw Harry bent over at the base of the stairs. She had a stick, and she went down on her knees, and coaxed one of the caterpillars off the cement, then flicked it into the grass. And she climbed a couple of steps, spotted another one, and bent down for it. I watched her do this for almost five minutes. She was getting in everyone's way, and her face was very serious, puckered, her hair pulled back in a ponytail. I'd never tried to pick up a girl I didn't know before. I wasn't sure how you were supposed to do it. I started at the top of the steps, and began collecting the caterpillars as I found them.

When we met in the middle, I held one out to her in my cupped palm. The caterpillar was curled into a tight ball, even more like a stray bit of yarn. Harry looked down at my hand, then up at me, and grimaced. "Oh no," she said, "I don't like to touch them. They're kind of disgusting."

I blinked at her, and then, obediently, tossed the caterpillar off onto the hillside. I wondered how many of them actually survived out there, didn't crawl back onto the steps to be crushed, or else get scooped up by birds or infiltrated by parasites. "Then why are you picking them up?"

Harry winced, and tugged on the long fringe of her ponytail, a nervous gesture she would have up until she lopped it off. "I just feel bad letting things die."

There would always be something compulsive and anxious about Harry's kindness, which made me think sometimes about the difference between not being bad and being good.

That spring I had a single, because my roommate had moved home and hadn't told housing services, and Harry had a girlfriend who she said she was in love with. The girlfriend was tall, coltish, a criminal justice major. She had that unfortunate verbal tick that articles are always warning women about now, where you qualify all your statements saying, *I think,* and *As far as I know,* and *This is just my opinion, but,* when you don't need to. Saying, *I'm sorry,* whenever you start or stop speaking.

*   *   *

Our motel the second night had two twin beds, which was the beginning of a pattern. It was a toss-up, in every one, as to whether we'd get one bed or two. We hadn't fucked on the trip, and I didn't expect we would, but when there was just the one bed we slept in it together. Harry said that she'd forgotten to call the places that didn't have an option when you booked online. I wasn't sure if the hotels where she got to choose were the ones where we shared the bed or where we didn't. I decided not to ask.

None of the motels allowed pets either, but Harry always snuck Emily Dickinson in. I told her the hamster would be fine in the car overnight, but she wouldn't have it.

The nights were nice. We knew how to live in each other's space, and had for a while. If there weren't two beds, one of us would sit on the floor, or go play with the hamster. Both of us quiet with our headphones in, or me reading my book, which was about cannibalism in the natural world, while Harry tapped thoughtfully at her keyboard. I was trying to read more about science, and thought something a little macabre might keep my attention better. Harry liked to go on Reddit and give relationship advice to strangers. I didn't get it. Sometimes she'd lift her head and tell me whatever crazy shit she'd just seen. "This guy used his girlfriend's savings to buy a five-thousand-dollar dog."

"What?"

"A five-thousand-dollar dog."

"What kind of dog is five thousand dollars?"

She waved a hand. "One of those fussy purebreds with all the health problems."

Or I'd close up my book and say, "This guy thinks climate change might make people eat each other."

Harry would look at me with very wide eyes. "Why?"

"Famine."

"Oh."

And then she'd go back to typing for a while, telling the man on the internet what to do about his fussy dog and his girlfriend he robbed, and I'd go back to my book, and descriptions of prion diseases. Later, we'd share take-out food out of greasy boxes, flipping through the channels on TV. Ghost-hunting shows and late-night History Channel documentaries about aliens. Harry leaned

on my shoulder and then, sometimes, climbed into my lap, and I
put my arms around her body. She was so skinny, but her stomach
was still soft, still stuck out a little. We talked about the things we
were both excited for. Driving along the coast, Powell's in Portland, the explorer myth of getting to see glaciers.

Harry was the first girl I ever hooked up with. Because she
climbed into my lap like that, and took my hand and put it on
her stomach. We were watching TV in my room, under a blanket
that my roommate left behind. I never got to know the roommate, but think she moved home because she was afraid of killing herself. For a few weeks, I wouldn't go on her side of the room
at all, which was empty except for her cheap sheets on her cheap
mattress. Then I stripped her bed and spread myself out as much
as possible, trying to crowd her presence out. Harry angled my
hand until my fingertips were in her shorts. I could feel the thick
elastic waistband of her underwear, and a few coarse curls of hair.
I asked her if she was sure. We'd known each other for maybe
three months then, made out a couple of times, drunk, and hadn't
talked about it. She was still with her girlfriend.

"Yeah," she said. I remember my uneven heartbeat, and the
sensation of having half swallowed something I couldn't get down.
I remember that I only really thought of her girlfriend because I
was thinking that I'd never touched anyone but myself, and Harry
had probably been fingered plenty of times. I remember feeling
like the shape of her skeleton would be imprinted on me for the
rest of my life.

*   *   *

In Portland, we stopped at Powell's, where Harry darted off toward
the true crime section and left me holding her hamster. Emily
Dickinson was tucked in a little denim purse and squirming violently against my hip. I wondered if she was frightened, having

been moved around so much all of a sudden. It was ridiculous to
me that Harry insisted on bringing her. Hamsters only live about
three years, and Harry'd already had Emily Dickinson for nearly
two, cage hidden in the closet of her dorm. Her parents would've
taken care of it, I'm sure, but she insisted. She didn't want it to
be alone, she said. Or she didn't want to be alone. One of those.

I slipped my hand into the purse and tried to pet Emily Dickinson's fragile little skull. She bit me.

When Harry got the hamster, I drove her to pick up an old
cage from her parents' house. I carefully neglected to ask her how
many furry residents had lived and died in that cage over the
course of her childhood. That was the only time I met her parents.
She introduced me as her friend Jane, which was true because
we'd stopped sleeping together at the time. I was fucking women I
met on Tinder, who I made sleep on the couch if they stayed over,
because I couldn't stand sharing my bed, hated unfamiliar limbs
sweating on my body. It felt like the thing to do to make these
girls breakfast in the morning, but I never learned how to cook,
so breakfast was microwaved packets of oatmeal or a rubbery egg
on toast. Harry said she was taking a break from sex for a while,
with anyone. She didn't want to talk about what happened with
the girlfriend.

That's when I was thinking of getting a tattoo. A girl I'd been
hooking up with told me that tattoos were a good way to feel in
control of your body. Her body was covered in them, and firm
and blunt as a knife hilt, very within her control. I thought maybe
some poetry. During classes I would screenshot stanzas here and
there, add them to a folder on my laptop. That bit of "Wild Geese"
that goes, "You only have to let the soft animal of your body love
what it loves," except that I always misremembered it, until I
looked it up, as ending with "want what it wants."

Harry would flop down on my bed, on her stomach, and click

through my selections. "This is nice. You should get this," she said. I never ended up getting any tattoo. I had a particular anxiety about them, that anything permanent would embarrass me eventually. But I heard Harry repeat those lines later, and mistake the author. *The soft animal.* It's possible that Harry named her hamster Emily Dickinson because she didn't know who Mary Oliver was. I didn't correct her, in the moment or later. For Harry to be innocently wrong about something was sweet.

I wandered. In the science section, I read about why the bees were disappearing. And they were disappearing, not just dying. Colony collapse disorder is when the bees abandon their hive in the middle of the night, leaving their queen behind and their larvae pupating in sealed waxy cells. Against my leg, Emily Dickinson had finally, blessedly, calmed in her little denim bag. I was also pretty sure she'd pissed in it.

When I eventually went looking for Harry, I found her picking through a wall of cookbooks. She couldn't even reach the second-highest shelf standing on tiptoe. "Which one do you want?" She pointed, and I handed her a beginner's guide to French cooking.

"Thank you, stranger," she said, and swayed, smiling against my side. "That's very chivalrous of you, stranger." My chest ached. I kissed the part in her curls. If either of us were a man, or even if we'd been a little older, we wouldn't have tried to actually be friends after we stopped having sex the first time. Not right away, at least. We went to a big school, and could have faded seamlessly out of each other's lives.

"I think I'm going to become a woman who cooks," Harry said. "Like, really cooks."

"You cook." There was one month in that same fall when she came to my dorm and made dinner for both of us once a week, and left me a mountain of leftovers, sealed in Tupperwares that overtook my tiny fridge. I'd said something about how my TV dinners were making me want to shoot myself. There was one grocery store within walking distance, and it sold pouches of soup that you had to shake, frozen, out of their bags before you could microwave them, and burritos that got so hard at the corners they tasted like you were eating part of your paper plate. Harry's food had been simple, maybe even a little bland. Chicken-and-rice dishes, pasta, the kind of biscuits that you squeezed out of a cardboard tube and then put in the oven. Warm comfort food. It was the tenderness of her doing it at all that got me. I hadn't known she thought about me that much.

"But like *really* cooks," Harry said, and showed me a book on making different kinds of pies. The index revealed that there were more kinds of pies than I'd formerly known about. "I think I'm going to become someone who hosts dinner parties, and brings in macaroons for my coworkers, and has a spice drawer."

"I think you could do that," I agreed. "Maybe not very big parties." I'd seen pictures of her apartment.

"Don't harsh my buzz."

"Your hamster pissed on me."

"Oh. Good girl, Emily Dickinson."

I snorted and handed her Emily Dickinson's purse, and she put it back on.

"The best part of moving," Harry said, leaning against my chest, "is getting to reinvent yourself. I'm going to be someone who cooks. I'm going to buy new clothes. Maybe I'll go by Harriet again. Or Etta. Or one of those names girls make up, like Bunny or Goldie or Mouse."

"I've never heard of anyone doing that."

Harry shrugged. "You read the wrong books. I'll dye my hair. I'll learn French. I'll stop using my contacts and get glasses. I'll make all-new friends. Next time you see me, I'll be somebody else."

She was still leaning against me as she said this, the blade of her shoulder pressing my breastbone, my exhales stirring the shining thicket of her hair. Whether she'd meant to needle me or not, I didn't want to start anything by calling her on it. From this angle, I couldn't see her face, and the air above her head smelled like my shampoo because she'd borrowed it this morning. After a moment, I leaned down to collect her stack of books, and she lifted Emily Dickinson's purse to check on the hamster inside, wrinkling her nose at the unmistakable smell of urine. Between Harry needling me and Harry failing to consider me, I was trying not to think too much about which I'd prefer. But, God, sometimes Harry just said shit. I settled her books against my hip, and gestured toward the exit. "We should probably get back on the road."

*   *   *

In the mornings, Harry's alarm would wake us both up. She would refill Emily Dickinson's food, if it needed it. I would put on coffee. She'd start packing our things while I went down to the continental breakfast, if there was one, and brought up not-quite-expired yogurts and dry bagels. Harry's jaw popped when she chewed. Sometimes she put on lipstick. I swallowed my meds with coffee, two white circular pills. The antidepressant I'd been taking for over a year had stopped working, slowly, and then all at once, so I spent last winter in a low static. I read a lot of essays online by people who wanted to kill themselves. Everyone on my mother's side of the family had attempted suicide at least once, except, so far, for me. I wouldn't call us unhappy people. It's just that these things run in the blood. During lectures, I'd look out wide windows and imagine my body hanging in the frame of them, swaying and purpling. I performed gruesome mental surgeries, picturing myself flayed, my organs on display, quietly amputating a limb in my mind while I talked to people.

It's maybe not a surprise that my sex drive was low, haunted as I was by imagined mutilations. The one time Harry and I ended up in bed together that semester, her body was a skeleton straddling my thighs, so beautiful that I actually wanted to puke my guts up. I thought about a sharp, calm blade removing slabs of flesh from my stomach, hips, my wide shoulders, the breasts I kept tight behind a sports bra, like slices of deli meat. Until my naked body looked something like her naked body.

"You're not really into this right now, are you?" Harry'd asked, taking her hand away and wiping it on the bed.

"No," I admitted. "I don't think so. Sorry."

"That's okay." She flopped beside me on her back, and bumped her forehead against my shoulder. I told myself I was a jealous bitch. "You don't apologize to friends."

We hadn't tried to have sex since then; it just didn't come together. When she told me she was going away, in January, I think she resented me for not having more of a reaction. We'd just come from the Women's March and were tucked into a Starbucks, drinking Frappuccinos, sweaty and coming down off the high of our anger. A sign someone had handed Harry was wedged in next to our bags on the floor. It said "We don't have time for denial" in blocky green letters. I was so tired I could barely lift my head. On a list of symptoms I'd written to show my psychiatrist, I had scrawled, "When I'm around other people I don't feel real." When we made papier-mâché sculptures in elementary school art class, and they had you paste the paper and glue over a balloon, and then pop the balloon. That was something like the feeling, like whatever was usually under my skin had all gone out at once. "So," Harry said, and kicked the base of the table, "I got into the University of Michigan."

My stomach rocked briefly, a boat going over a rough wave. I think I said, "I'm glad you're going somewhere with seasons."

Once we shoved our dirty clothes into our suitcases, I went to check us out and Harry snuck Emily Dickinson back to the car. Between Portland and Glacier National Park we had a couple days of just driving, scenic route. I asked Harry to find somewhere other than the cup holder to put her stupid cactus. My arms were longer than hers and I was worried about shoving my elbow into it. She ignored me. After hours of plains, there was something breathless about the mountains we passed into. The clusters of trees, from even a little distance, were like crumpled velvet. I could smell lake water. Harry looked up from her phone and said, "This guy on Reddit threw out all his girlfriend's clothes and replaced them."

I laughed. "Holy shit."

"The internet always makes me feel better about how shitty I am at relationships."

When the new medication finally started to work, it was like the tide washing out. I'd felt for the last few weeks like I was catching my breath, standing on the damp beach of myself. I have always known I am getting better when things that are beautiful start to feel relevant to me again. The trees green and rich against that slap of vivid sky, all of it still and unreplicable. The truth was that even despite everything with Harry I was doing better than I had been in months. Sadness is different when it is coming from a place you can make sense of.

Harry wanted me to tell her she wasn't shitty at relationships, but I wasn't going to. I was looking at the trees. Later that year the Amazon rain forest would be burning, which doesn't really have anything to do with anything.

*   *   *

We were both looking forward to Glacier National Park. With Portland behind us, the first day of driving had been long. I was beginning to feel so dreary about the rest of the road that the park seemed like the last beautiful thing I was ever going to see. Harry had started talking more and more about school. The classmates she'd been emailing with, the courses she was excited for. I pulled out my phone and swiped through Tinder just to have something to do with my hands. Funnily enough, there were not that many queer girls in this part of Idaho, or at least not that many with Tinder profiles.

Harry was still driving one-handed. I minded it more than I had the first day of the trip. "You're weaving," I said. She ignored me.

I wanted to think that Harry and I were a matter of timing. That we both regretted something. After her girlfriend broke up with her, she wasn't dating, and then she said she wanted to try men for a while. "I usually get along better with other women," she said, "but I don't know. Maybe it's easier with men. I think men expect less from you, as long as they're getting sex."

I told her I didn't think that was how it worked. I told her, "At the risk of saying 'not all men,' I don't think that's even most men." I told her if she went into it with that attitude she'd end up with someone who treated her like shit. There was a boyfriend for a little while. He was fine. I think he broke up with her. I think it was before we started having sex again, in the last weeks of classes pre-summer. Harry making flash cards on my bed, wearing just her underwear, leaving smears of brightly colored ink all over her bare legs and my sheets. But she vanished on a backpacking trip for the first half of that summer, and we didn't keep the habit up. And it wasn't like I waited in the wings. I dated, and decided I was too busy to date, and hooked up with people who weren't her, and dated again.

That semester I met Harry was spring 2017, and the inauguration had happened a month or so before. There were protests every few weeks. Our school sent out emails promising that the administration would do its best to protect undocumented students, but it didn't say what its best meant. One of my classes got derailed into debating whether a nuclear missile could reach us from North Korea. "I heard they can reach New York," a boy on the other side of the room kept saying. "If they can reach New York, they can reach us." This led to the realization that a lot of us didn't know where North Korea was. When I visited my mother, she sent me home with iodine tablets she'd bought online, meant to mitigate radiation poisoning, and I kept them in the bottom drawer of my desk. And Harry was there, and we had a lot of sex. These things didn't really have anything to do with each other, except that it always felt like something was on fire in the next room.

We pulled over at a rest stop and Harry leaned into the backseat to poke her finger between the bars of Emily Dickinson's cage. "How are you doing, baby?" she cooed. "You sweet little thing. How are you doing?" Emily Dickinson was a ball of white fur, with long orange teeth and rheumy pink eyes. I sometimes thought about killing that hamster. Harry craned her neck to look at my phone. The girl whose profile I was looking at was blond, ruddy-cheeked, smiling. She was nineteen. She had a face that made you want to take someone dancing. "You kind of have a thing for girls with small tits, huh?" Harry said.

I clicked the app closed. "Come on."

"I'm just, like, saying you have a type. I'm your type. It's not an insult."

She was twisted up, weaselly and golden in her seat. Pretty and small and the same live animal whom I'd gotten in a car with just because she said, *Come with me.*

"You're kind of a cunt."

"What the fuck?" Harry started laughing, and then stopped in the middle of it, which left her mouth open, bottom lip curled so I could see the flat white tips of her teeth, the slick of her spit on her tongue.

There was something dry in my throat that I had to swallow around, something like a ball of chalk. I was so tired. "You heard what I said." I hadn't raised my voice yet, but I would rather yell at her than cry.

"Where did that even come from?"

I shrugged. "From you kind of being a cunt."

Rest stops are such beautiful liminal spaces. A long way below us the lake was so bright you couldn't look right at it. There was a quiet wind, as there always seems to be at rest stops. Maybe cars make it. The parking lot was empty, except for one beaten sedan parked in a far corner, glittering indifferently where streaks of paint had been scraped from it. There was no way to tell if it was abandoned or not.

"What crawled up your ass?" Harry demanded. "What do you care what I say?"

"Never mind," I said. I had the sensation of something bubbling in my chest, like those mouths that open in the earth and spit sulfur and steam, venting themselves into the sky. If I had shouted at her then, I probably would have shouted a lot of things. At this point, though, it didn't feel worth anything to argue with her. Five days and a long empty road from Michigan, it felt both early and too late to air our grievances. "Forget it."

"*No.*" Harry was petulant, outraged, and she twisted over the center console. "You don't get to just sudden—" She cut herself off halfway through the word, sucking in a breath so abrupt and high it sounded like a scream, and clutched her arm back to her chest.

I startled. "What?"

"Fuck!" Harry inhaled again, sharply. "Holy fucking fuck! Jesus!"

"What?" I looked around the car, frantic, but also wondering, a little, if this was a joke at my expense.

"I put my hand on the fucking cactus!" Harry shouted at me.

This did not register with me right away as a thing that could happen. I looked at her, at her arm, which was indeed lit from the base of her palm up her wrist with tiny golden spines, and then at the cactus, innocent in its cup holder. My breath made a hitching sound, which was not quite, but almost, a giggle.

"What the fuck?" Harry snapped at me, clutching her arm in her other hand. "Shit! It isn't funny. Christ. Do something, whore!"

This time I did laugh. I couldn't help it. I did see her pain, wrung into the raised, canine set of her shoulders. I didn't want to make fun of her. It was just that, *Do something, whore*, was the funniest thing anyone had ever said to me. I dropped my head between my knees.

"Jane!" There was real hurt in Harry's voice. I bit the tips of my fingers to stop laughing. It didn't quite work.

"Shit," I said, "Shit. Okay."

We were lucky that Harry plucked her eyebrows, I guess, because I only had to go into her makeup bag for tweezers instead of trying to unpack anything. I went and opened the door, and she leaned forward out of the driver's seat, swearing continuously under her breath. "Does it really hurt that badly?"

"*Yes*."

The light was watery and indifferent, Harry's arm resting on her knee too much in shadow. "You need to move forward," I said softly, "I can't see." I put a hand on her waist and urged her toward me gently, until she was holding her palm in the sun. "Okay," I said. My legs were shaking a little; I knelt down on the asphalt.

"It smells like cow shit out here," Harry complained.

She was right. I picked up the tweezers. "Hold up your hand."

She did, until I was within kissing distance of her knuckles. I held her still by the bare tips of her fingers. I caught the first spine between the tweezers, and pulled.

Those little thorns were so thin and so many that they looked like a layer of fur growing over her arm. It took me nearly an hour to get them all out. Neither of us really talked, except when I would say sometimes, "Hold out your palm." Or, "Turn it this way." And Harry would do as I said. It was meditative, the sound of our mutual breathing, the way our bodies kept the air between us warm, the layer of sweat dampening the places where I touched her. Her lashes, casting needle shadows on her cheeks, were almost the same color as the cactus spines.

When we were finally done, Harry said, "Jesus Christ," her voice like a strained muscle. She stretched out her legs, and got up to walk in a few ginger circles around the car. I took her seat, still warm, and let my eyes shut, tipped my head back to stretch my neck. It wasn't fair to blame Harry for my being here, when she'd put no more pressure on me than an invitation. I'd come because I would miss her, because I could guess she didn't want to make the trip with her parents, because it didn't seem likely we'd stay in touch once she was gone. Because she'd asked me to. I got up and checked on Emily Dickinson, who was chewing up the cardboard of a toilet paper roll, then plucked the cactus from its cup holder.

"Where are you taking it?" Harry asked, leaning against the Camry's side.

"I'm going to leave it here."

"No, no," she said, and reached her hand toward me in protest. "I want to keep it. It's not the cactus's fault."

I shrugged, and got into the driver's seat, while Harry went around to the back and began rummaging things around, wincing occasionally when she used her sore hand. When she got back in, she curled up on the passenger seat, and pulled the blanket that we had put there for napping over herself. As we turned back onto the freeway, her voice was sedate: "This person on Twitter was talking about a mouse we drove extinct."

"Hm?"

"Or a rat," she said. She'd pulled out her phone. "It's called the Bramble Cay mosaic-tailed rat. It went extinct in 2015. We drove it extinct." The *we* she used was very personal. "Because the seas rose."

"Oh." I wondered who on her Twitter feed was talking about dead rats.

"Do you want to see a picture?" I was driving, but she held her phone up in front of me anyway. It was a rat. Big-eyed and sandy brown and curled over itself. It felt strange to be looking at a color photograph of something that didn't exist anymore, though I guess lots of photographs are of things that don't exist anymore. The rat looked a little like those desert mice which I always thought looked a little like Harry.

Harry sighed and tucked her phone away. "Isn't it so sad?"

*   *   *

The morning before we drove the Going-to-the-Sun Road, Harry made us stop at a gas station because I admitted I had forgotten to eat breakfast. I chewed at a granola bar, feeling slightly sullen, and watched her stretch out her legs in the parking lot, pacing back and forth among the cars. One of the side effects of my medication was decreased appetite. I knew a side effect was nothing to be particularly proud of. The granola bar was stale.

When Harry got in the car, she handed me an apple. "Do you know what makes a glacier different from regular ice?"

This was something I definitely should know, but I paused for a moment because I wasn't sure I did. "A glacier is permanent."

Harry beamed at me. "And it *moves*. That's one of the criteria."

"Really?"

"Yeah. I looked it up last night. I think I must've learned it in like fourth grade, but I forgot."

I laughed. "Me too."

"It's because of the weight they put on themselves. All of them are crawling all around the world."

The Going-to-the-Sun Road wound up around the body of a mountain, looking down over a white river and a glacial lake and a valley that bled so richly green it looked like the earth's opened artery. Harry kept rolling her window down and then closing it again, pressing her face to the gap and then the glass. "Why don't you leave it open?" I asked.

"I don't want Emily Dickinson to freeze."

Her knees, her elbows, her sharp little chin, all of it squeezed against the glass like she wanted to hurl herself into the open mouth of the sky. I took the bends carefully, and mostly kept my eyes on the road. We pulled over at the first outlook, and Harry touched the inside of my wrist where my hand was on the steering wheel. I got out of the car, and came and stood at the side of the road with her, and looked over the edge of the world.

"Oh." The sound came from somewhere deep in my stomach. The valley was as vivid as a place no people had ever been. And there were those spots where the trees gave way before the stone tops of the mountains, gray rock exposed like the earth's wrists and clavicle, vulnerabilities that were not vulnerable. "God." Harry leaned over, knocked the top of her head against my shoulder. It was the kind of beauty I didn't even try to take pictures of, because I knew they wouldn't matter.

"Just imagine how it'll be when we get to the glaciers," Harry said. "How many people get to see glaciers?"

"Probably fewer and fewer," I said.

"Don't say that."

We got back in the car.

All the way up the mountain, Harry was quiet. When I turned my head to her, she was looking at me like I was part of the landscape, just in that brief moment. Like I was something too wide-open and heart-wrenchingly colorful to be photographed. Harry's nose was red and her face was pale from the cold. I had a brief, obscene thought that I could fuck her for probably the last time I would ever fuck her on the Going-to-the-Sun Road. In her car, looking out over the green vertigo of the canyon.

And what? Why? To have done something memorable, or important, or probably get arrested. Quietly, Harry said, "Where are the glaciers?"

"I don't know."

She sat forward in her seat a bit, rewrapped her blanket close around her shoulders. We were pretty far up the mountain. "Shouldn't we have seen them by now?"

I shrugged, helpless. "I don't know."

We passed a shuttle parked by an overlook. It had its roof open, and there were tourists hanging out, resting their folded arms on metal that must have been freezing cold.

Harry licked her lips. I could almost hear her tongue moving, we were so close together in that car. "Did you look up if they were still here?"

"No," I said. "Did you?"

She shook her head slowly. "We would know, if the glaciers here had melted. Right?"

I blinked at her, confused. How on earth would we know that?

"Maybe they're farther up the mountain. Maybe you can see them from farther up the mountain." Her voice going just a little shrill, finding a brief common note with the wind.

"Maybe."

We passed more tourists, clustered in their bright jackets on ledges. We passed little waterfalls and streams and a wall that wept snowmelt, which was in fact called the Weeping Wall. I'd heard you could rent cabins here. I wished we'd gotten a place to stay overnight. I wished I had come alone, so I could focus on this singular emotion, just me and this place that looked like a different planet because it looked so much like earth in picture books. Harry had said she wanted to go somewhere green. "Even if we don't get to see glaciers," I said, "it was worth it to see all this."

Harry's mouth was a somber pink line. "Definitely."

The wind made a sound like we were pulling something out of it that it wanted to keep. "They can't just be gone," Harry said. "Can they?"

"I don't know."

There were occasional pockets of ice, muddy and melting. And there were wide, discolored swaths of rock, where ice had been and was gone, had left its ghost on the earth. I pointed these out to Harry. She bit the heel of her hand.

"It's called Glacier National Park," she said. "Shouldn't they have to say if there are no glaciers?"

And, "That can't really have already happened."

And, "It's not fair. That something can just already be gone."

"No." My hands were tight around the wheel. I felt full of the kind of mourning that comes with moving away from home, even though it was Harry who was moving away from home, and I was going back.

"Stop!" Harry shouted when we rounded a corner, and I hit the brakes thinking an animal had run out into the road. Harry opened the door and ran. She stopped at an outcropping of rock that looked over a sharp slope downward and, through a grove of trees, to mountains in the distance. "Jane!"

"What?" There were a lot of people gathered at another observation point ahead of us, in their brightly colored jackets. I was a little distracted by how close to the edge Harry was standing, the fact that her knees trembled under her.

"Look," she said, and I followed her gesture to the two peaks opposite us and far away, snow-topped, which had a blue triangle of ice nestled between them.

"There's one," Harry murmured. I stepped in closer behind her, and she leaned back against my chest. I could feel each of her breaths in the hitch of her shoulders. I thought of the first time I held her in my lap. "There's one."

We walked the rest of the way to the observation point, where the other tourists were. Some of them had binoculars. The glacier was far in the distance, cold and small. Harry stood right up against the railing, and looked at it in silence for a long, long time. There was a sign next to her, with a photo of a man standing astride a glacier, like an arctic adventurer, in 1938, and a picture in 2016, of the place where the glacier had been. Lake water, and a few chunks of dirty ice. The sign told me that in fifty years, 85 percent of the ice had melted. The sign told me that they expected it all to be gone by 2030.

I told Harry this, with my voice lowered. "Just in time, I guess," I said. The mountain air was cool all around us. Under the ambient shriek of the wind, I could just barely pick out the sound of Harry's breathing, coming fast and sharp through her half-open mouth, touching in its smallness. I let my hand fall lightly on the crest of her spine; I was pretty sure she was crying.

"Don't touch me right now," she said, and then, "Sorry."

"It's okay." I went over and stood on the other side of the observation point. The ice was far away from us. I tried to estimate its size. Two miles? Three? I was not good at guessing these things at all. Maybe it was twenty, maybe it wasn't even half. I felt still and very small, like how everyone feels in the presence of

beauty. If I brought children here one day, they would not see this.
It would still be beautiful. I would find myself trying to tell them
that something was missing, and then unable to describe why it
should be so important to see a particular triangle of ice. Because
you never can, now. Now you couldn't if you wanted to. I was
twenty-two. I was a baby. There was the glacier that had inched
its long slow body over the surface of the earth, and shaped stone,
and settled here in Montana. I would outlive it.

Harry and I were both dry-eyed when we got back to the car.
But I did hold her, sitting in my lap, her body clutched into mine,
tight and awkward, her pulse pounding against my skin at several
points. And not there, where it felt sacrilegious, but a little farther
down the mountain, I did kiss her, and she did kiss me back, and
it did taste like something old that wasn't gone yet, and we probably would have had sex if we weren't both so cold by then, but
we were. So we kept driving.

* * *

When we came down off the mountain, we ordered slices of huckleberry pie at a restaurant with a touristy wooden sign out front.
"Huckleberry Pie! Huckleberry Shakes! Huckleberry Ice Cream!
Huckleberry Jam!" It had a stuffed bear reared up in the middle
of the dining area. There was a fake fire in a fake-stone fireplace.

Harry hadn't said much since she'd climbed out of my lap,
just a soft, "God, please," when I'd pointed out the restaurant's
sign. She hadn't cried again, that I could tell, but she was drawn
into herself, her purplish lip caught between her teeth, one hand
buried in her little canvas purse, though we'd left Emily Dickinson
sleeping in her cage. I felt tender toward her, with shared emotion,
with the knowledge that I'd miss her very much. But nothing I
could think to say felt right for the moment. Harry's other hand
pushed a bite of her pie around her plate with her fork. It was hot.

And really good, touristy or not. It tasted like the cobblers my mom made sometimes when I was little, which meant it tasted like sitting at the gray-marble-topped kitchen island with the chandelier my mom always hit her head on, the lights off in the rest of the house, and the sound of whipped cream hissing out of a can.

Also like huckleberries. Tart and sweet.

On the TV, mounted on the wall, California was still burning.

"Let's get married," Harry said.

"What?" I had taken a bite too quickly, and scalded my mouth, and so sat there with my tongue hanging out a little. Harry's hair was limp around her face. Another thing that gave her a hungry look, as so many things did. There was a purple streak of pie filling on her cheek, and she was still holding her fork in midair. It dropped crumbs when her hand shook.

"Let's get married," said my ex-girlfriend who had never been my girlfriend. "Let's have kids. Let's go to Italy and France and Spain. Let's fuck a lot. Let's—" She put her fork down. "Let's have a lot of kids. Let's live in a cabin, with a lot of kids and a dog and—"

"Let's eat pie," I agreed. I think I was smiling, because my mouth hurt.

"Every day."

The difference between a Shakespearean comedy and a Shakespearean tragedy is whether there's a marriage at the end. Here whatever has come before is answered with love, which means sex, which means children. Let's fuck and be plentiful. That's how you send death out of the room for a while.

"You're beautiful," Harry said, looking at me very intensely, like she wanted to swallow me into the centers of her eyes. But her gaze also kept flicking away, toward that television. I touched her cold hand, briefly, with mine, and she put another bite of pie in her mouth.

"Is it burning anywhere important?" I asked. I'd sat so I could

see her and the window and the mountains outside, but not
the TV.

"No." She licked the huckleberry filling from the corner of her
mouth. "Just by my old elementary school."

I felt so tired, tingling like a limb after the blood has rushed
back into it. Harry rubbed her face, her pinkish eyes. She'd put
on makeup in the morning, I guess for an imaginary camera or
the eyes of God or maybe for me. It was smeared everywhere now.
"Let's get married," she said once more.

She was mostly done with her slice of pie. I'd only eaten about
half of mine, but I slid the plate across the table to her. Harry took
it delicately, without touching my hand.

Outside the window, the trees bent in a high wind, right
down to the ground.

Acknowledgments

I want to thank Meredith Kaffel Simonoff, for her expertise, encouragement, and kindness, and for always helping me find the joy in this process. Jill Bialosky, for taking on this book and making it better, and Drew Weitman for her aid and patience. Dave Cole for his meticulous editing, Sarahmay Wilkinson for her beautiful cover design, Jess Murphy and Julia Druskin for helping my manuscript become a book, and Erin Lovett and Michelle Waters for helping that book find readers.

I'm incredibly grateful to the Program in Creative Writing at UW-Madison and my classmates there, for giving me time to write this book and supporting me while I did. Thank you especially to Jesse Lee Kercheval for her mentorship and for being always ready to help, from the first page to the last, to Jaquira Díaz for being more confident in me than I was in myself, to Beth Nguyen for her gentle guidance, and to Sean Bishop for helping me keep my priorities straight. I also must thank the staff and students of the Alpha Writers Workshop, especially AJ, Lara, Cassie, Julie, Rachel, Patrick, and Seth, each of whom offered advice I desperately needed. I am grateful to every teacher who instructed and encouraged me as I took my first shaky steps into writing, and exceptionally grateful to Dr. Marilyn Elkins, Wendy Oleson, Greg Brown, and Jan Edick.

This book could not have happened without the friends and family who gave it—and me—so much of their time, attention, and love. My thanks and my love to Kit, so indispensable they must be thanked twice. To Danie, who read every page of this book three times over and who loved it when I couldn't. To Alana, who was making worlds with me from the beginning. And to Jesse, George, Emilia, Mica, Maddy, and Katie for their friendship, feedback, and cheerleading. And, always, thank you to my family, Beverly and John Harlan and Mike Layfield, and especially my parents, Christopher Harlan and Karen Layfield, who brought me into this world and so are ultimately to blame for all of this.

Finally, this book owes a debt of gratitude to the works of Shirley Jackson, who showed me what magic looks like on the page. And to the music of the Mountain Goats, by which every one of these stories was written. I'd also like to thank the magazines that have previously published my stories and generously allowed them to be reprinted here, listed below.

Strange Horizons—"Hunting the Viper-King"
The Gettysburg Review—"Take Only What Belongs to You"
The Michigan Quarterly Review—"Algal Bloom"
The Colorado Review —"Endangered Animals"